DEVIL'S PIT

Apollo proceeded warily through corridors and maze-like areas. Up ahead he saw movement, a person or creature edging along a wall. Whatever it was, it scampered away as soon as it saw Apollo.

"Devil's pit, huh?" he muttered. "They named it right, anyway."

A few more steps and something made Apollo glance upward abruptly. He was certain he saw more than one pair of eyes gaping down at him from the metal rafters . . .

Berkley Battlestar Galactica Books

BATTLESTAR GALACTICA
by Glen A. Larson and Robert Thurston

BATTLESTAR GALACTICA 2: THE CYLON DEATH MACHINE
by Glen A. Larson and Robert Thurston

BATTLESTAR GALACTICA 3: THE TOMBS OF KOBOL
by Glen A. Larson and Robert Thurston

BATTLESTAR GALACTICA 4: THE YOUNG WARRIORS
by Glen A. Larson and Robert Thurston

BATTLESTAR GALACTICA 5: GALACTICA DISCOVERS EARTH
by Glen A. Larson and Michael Resnick

BATTLESTAR GALACTICA 6: THE LIVING LEGEND
by Glen A. Larson and Nicholas Yermakov

BATTLESTAR GALACTICA 7: WAR OF THE GODS
by Glen A. Larson and Nicholas Yermakov

BATTLESTAR GALACTICA 8: GREETINGS FROM EARTH
by Glen A. Larson and Ron Goulart

BATTLESTAR GALACTICA 9: EXPERIMENT IN TERRA
by Glen A. Larson and Ron Goulart

BATTLESTAR GALACTICA 10: THE LONG PATROL
by Glen A. Larson and Ron Goulart

BATTLESTAR GALACTICA 11: THE NIGHTMARE MACHINE
by Glen A. Larson and Robert Thurston

BattlestaR
GALACTICA 11
THE NIGHTMARE
MACHINE

Novel by Glen A. Larson and Robert Thurston
Based on the Universal Television Series
"BATTLESTAR GALACTICA"
Created by Glen A. Larson

BERKLEY BOOKS, NEW YORK

BATTLESTAR GALACTICA 11:
THE NIGHTMARE MACHINE

A Berkley Book/published by arrangement with
MCA PUBLISHING RIGHTS, a Division of MCA, Inc.

PRINTING HISTORY
Berkley edition/December 1985

ISBN: 0-425-08618-6

A BERKLEY BOOK ® TM 757,375
Berkley Books are published by The Berkley Publishing Group,
200 Madison Avenue, New York, N.Y. 10016.
The name "Berkley" and the stylized "B" with design
are trademarks belonging to Berkley Publishing Corporation.
PRINTED IN THE UNITED STATES OF AMERICA

To Jason

And to Davy Fraser and the
Baldwinsville Squadron

CHAPTER ONE

I've been in Cylon traps before, Starbuck thought, *but this one takes the felgercarb*.

A Cylon fighter, narrowly avoiding the sweeping fusillades from the pursuing craft of Greenbean and Jolly, now headed right for Starbuck's viper. Slamming the joystick of his viper to the left, he swerved violently to avoid the pulsing bursts of fire from the Cylon ship's laser cannons. If laser fire had had odor, and if there had been air outside Starbuck's fighter for him to fling open his cockpit and smell, he might have been overwhelmed by the fumes.

Instead of pursuing Starbuck, the Cylon ship veered off and made for Boomer, attacking his blind spot from highside.

"On your tail, Boom-boom," Starbuck yelled into his commline mike.

"Watch it!"

Boomer's voice roared in Starbuck's ears:

"Got it, bucko. Thanks."

Boomer executed a precise reverse loop, followed by a rollover, and came down at the Cylon, with all artillery blazing. The Cylon ship, hit dead center, exploded suddenly, in one of those almost-beautiful displays that transformed a well-tooled piece of machinery and technology, plus its trio of alien inhabitants, into space debris in no time at all.

As he dipped his viper away from a portside attack, Starbuck got a quick glimpse of the barren planet beneath them, in whose skies the battle was taking place. Red Squadron had been on a routine probe from the *Galactica,* locating and mapping star systems and planets, looking for colonies and places where the exhausted population of *Galactica* and its ragtag fleet could find a few moments of rest, when this Cylon phalanx had appeared, as if out of nowhere, to attack them. He suspected they flew out of camouflaged pods on the planet's surface. Many ships rose toward them from the barren plains below. No matter how many of the Cylon ships they put out of commission, others seemed to materialize in new attack waves. Already three vipers had been destroyed. If Starbuck was right about their pilots, a trio of young cadets had been blown up with their ships in the first ambushing volley. Even in the midst of his anger, tears of mourning flowed out of his eyes.

"Attaboy, Boomer," came Jolly's voice over the commline after his well-executed victory.

"Right on target," shouted Ensign Greenbean.

"I try, fellas," Boomer answered, more than a touch of relief at surviving probable death mixed with the pride in his voice.

"Don't pat yourself on the back yet, Boomer," Starbuck cried. "Another one coming at you starboard!"

Boomer yelped with both fear and joy as the laser fire from the attacking Cylon raider came so close he was afraid it nearly singed his hair. Zeroing in on the Cylon ship, he split it wide open stem to stern before it exploded. He whooped again with the victory.

Greenbean, zooming up behind him as backup, laughed. "I don't believe it," he said. Greenbean had never quite gotten rid of the naive country boy sound that made his voice go high when he was excited. "Good shooting, Boomer. Fellas, an ace has been hiding secretly in our midst. Son of a—"

He hadn't seen the Cylon ship that, with the sudden acceleration so characteristic of these powerfully built enemy craft, had grown from a distant pinpoint to a gigantic marauder in an instant. Jolly saw it first.

"Greenbean!" he shouted. "Hit the deck!"

Frightened, Greenbean responded quickly, plunging his joystick forward and accelerating his viper in order to avoid the shots of a ship he hadn't yet seen. Arcing around to face the Cylon raider, he hit his firing button with a ferocity uncharacteristic of the soft-spoken shy young pilot. His shot was on the mark, adding another destroyed Cylon spacecraft to Red Squadron's growing and impressive kill-score.

Greenbean, who hadn't breathed since Jolly's abrupt warning, inhaled deeply and muttered to himself: "That was close." As it often happened when a Galactican pilot narrowly missed death, Greenbean mentally reviewed, in a fast sequence of battle memories, all the times that his life had been on the line, and he wondered what kind of blessed luck had been flying with him. Starbuck was, after all, the warrior with the legend of luck attached to his records. Greenbean had hardly been aware of his own luck until this moment. How long could he survive? How long could any of them survive, fleeing to God knew where with a ragtag fleet to protect, and seemingly endless hordes of Cylon ships pursuing them?

Boomer's soft voice coming over commcircuit seemed to whisper in his ear:

"Nice move, Greenbean."

The praise was like credit from one's father, and Greenbean was pleased by it.

"Good reaction time, buddy," Jolly said.

Although they could not see it from the dark, polarized cockpits of their own ships, their comments made the shy ensign blush. A deep red blush that made the near-white blondness of his hair seem all the paler.

Another wave of Cylon raiders was headed their way.

"Would you guys stow the postbattle analysis while the battle's still on?" Starbuck shouted as he accelerated his viper to meet the new marauders.

If there had been an observer on the surface of the planet below, he would have watched a frantic and confused melee in the skies above him—beautiful sleek ships interweaving and almost touching, seemingly joined in an intricate and lovely laser fire netting; sudden fiery explosions and pieces of metal drifting slowly away from the area of battle, descending eventually to the barren planet, maybe to be later discovered as mysterious and anachronistic archeological artifacts; awesome maneuverings, quick and impressive, in which Galactican pilots saved themselves and their fellow warriors from destruction. The whole array of human battle skills was brought to bear against the dazzling numbers of well-equipped Cylon fighters. The fight raged for only a short while, the humans holding their own against their opponents. Then abruptly the surviving Cylon contingent broke away from the battle and disappeared in the distance as suddenly as it had originally appeared.

Starbuck breathed a sigh of relief that all the other pilots heard loud and clear on their helmet receivers.

"I think we discouraged them, fellas," Starbuck announced.

"They probably got a whiff of your cigar," Jolly said.

"Your folly, Jolly. I've given 'em up. Told you that."

"Believe it when I see it, bucko."

"And since when did I ever smoke in a cockpit? Why, the smoke'd—"

"We of the lower echelons are convinced you can do anything you want to, Starbuck."

"Aw, shucks, Jolly, I don't know what to say."

"Another peculiar phenomenon, Starbuck speechless."

Starbuck was disturbed by the strangeness of their enemy's sudden retreat but, for the moment, he didn't want to upset his men, so he kept mum on the subject.

"Starbuck?"

"Yeah, Boomer."

"You think they got a fix on us? They can't trace us back to the fleet, can they?"

The cautious Boomer was famous for his ways of worrying a subject. However, he had saved Starbuck's butt so many times with that exact same caution that Starbuck always gave it prime consideration.

"Well, Boomer, I really doubt it. We're pretty far off course. We'll fly back with our jammers tuned high, for safety's sake. But we shouldn't take chances. Just be careful, guys. We don't need any of those creepos tracking us. Everybody all right? Boomer, you and your ship shipshape?"

"Yo!"

"Jolly?"

"Aye, aye, cap'n."

Starbuck laughed and reminded Jolly he was still just a lieutenant.

"Don't pull rank, sir," Jolly said. "Even a lower one."

"Dump it in the head, Jolly. Greenbean?"

There was no reply. Starbuck twisted around in his seat, tried to get a visual on Greenbean's viper.

"Greenbean? GREENBEAN?!"

All of the pilots started circling around, passing each other, creating a balletic air show without an audience to see it, looking beyond the farthest ship for a magical sighting of Greenbean, swooping close to the planet's surface to try to see the signs of a crash. Finally, Jolly's voice, trembling with emotion:

"He's gone, Starbuck. He's not anywhere."

"Jolly's right," Boomer said. "Maybe one of those louses got him."

"Maybe," Starbuck said, "but I don't think so. There was something . . ."

"What, Starbuck?"

"He was flying right beside me. Right before the creeps took their powder. I don't think they got him. I'm sure they didn't. They captured his ship, took him prisoner, I'm—"

"Easy, Starbuck, easy," Boomer said.

"It's possible, Boomer. They do take pris—"

"I know. And that's what we always hope—that our

buddy's not dead, that we'll see him. It's natural."

"But, Boomer—"

"We got to assume he's dead. None of us saw it, but we were all pretty busy at the time, right?"

Boomer was always adept at getting Starbuck back on track when he seemed about to be overcome by emotion. Starbuck was such a tough hot-tempered leader that he even hated to admit the loss of a pilot under his command. Boomer was used to the response, and knew how to minister to it.

"You're right, Boomer," Starbuck said. "Greenbean's gone."

"No, he's all right!" Jolly screamed. The fact that his best buddy was lost was just now settling into his mind. He and Greenbean had been wingmates for so long that Jolly could not perceive the future with someone else flying beside him in formations. "He's got to be all right, he—"

"Steady, Jolly," Starbuck said, realizing he was now doing for Jolly what Boomer had just done for him. In the unwritten logbook of colonial warrior camaraderie, the soothing of panic was an essential ability. "You know Greenbean. If he's gone, he wouldn't want us to panic about it. And, if they got him, he'll find a way out."

"I sure hope so," Jolly said, his voice only a shade calmer.

Me too, Starbuck thought as he checked with the rest of the squadron to see who'd survived the furious and intense battle. In addition to Greenbean, four other pilots could now be listed among the missing. However, in each of these other cases the Cylon kill had been observed by a fellow pilot. No one had seen Greenbean's viper go up. *A pity,* Starbuck thought, *there should always be a friend or ally around to see your death.* Himself, he was terrified of dying alone. Telling himself to get the morbid thoughts out of his head, he ordered the squadron back into formation for the long journey home to the *Galactica*.

Close up, in the middle of the monitor's screen, Greenbean's sleeping face could be seen beneath the pale brown visor of his flight helmet. He looked peaceful, as if he were just taking a quick nap for which he'd forgotten to remove his headgear. A pressing of the camera's remote-control button, and the picture enlarged to show, through a transparent canopy, that he was still in the cockpit of his viper. Another push of the button, and the camera pulled back to show on the screen a view of the entire captured viper, where it was tied down in the landing area of the Cylon base-star. Cylon centurions clumsily approached the vehicle and, roughly pulling at the rim of the cockpit canopy, flipped it open. Two of them lifted the unconscious pilot out of the cockpit and began to carry him away.

Using the ham of his hand, Baltar punched the monitor's shut-off button and the picture faded. He laughed softly to himself. Lucifer recognized that laugh. It meant that Baltar was definitely up to something. Lucifer had to be on his guard whenever his commander chortled like that in order to help rectify any blunders the reckless Baltar might cause.

"I think we can break the spirit of this one," Baltar said. "He's so young—why, the polish of youth still shines luminously on his face. He's clearly impressionable. Don't you think so, Lucifer?"

"I am unable to read the human face," Lucifer said. *Except for yours*, Lucifer thought. Baltar had a soft-looking face whose skin lacked any tinge of health. He never suspected how emotions displayed themselves in that tarnished face.

Baltar looked at his assistant as if he were seeing him for the first time. For the first time viewing this Cylon construct, this rude robot, with his transparent bubblelike head and its slanted asynchronously moving red eyes. Lucifer, tall as he was, looked down on Baltar whenever the commander condescended to come down to floor level from his ridiculously high command pedestal. With his ostentatious clothing and prim gestures, Lucifer's stance suggested superior attitudes that could not have been originally programmed into him. As Lucifer might have said, association with Baltar brought out the superiority naturally.

"Well, take my word for it, Lucifer, this one's an easy target for us. Initiate the usual procedures."

"The torture?"

"Of course the torture. It's going to work on this one. This lad'll lead us right to the *Galactica,* I promise."

"I wait eagerly..."

As he often did, Baltar studied Lucifer's face for signs of irony. There could be none there, of course, since the Cylon creation had no mobility in his hooded manufactured face.

For his part, Lucifer also studied physiognomy, searching Baltar's face to see if he could detect what deviousness the man was planning now. Frustrated so often in his need to finally defeat the *Galactica,* and destroy his hated enemy, the *Galactica*'s commander, Adama, Baltar had grown thinner with each setback. He rarely ate anymore and his face had become gaunt and tired looking. Lucifer recalled how fat and flabby Baltar had been when he'd first rescued him and set him on the exercise and diet program that restored him to health and made him fit to command a Cylon basestar. Now it looked as if the man might collapse at any time. That was one of the troubles with humans. They broke down too easily. Lucifer did not have that problem. One of his parts could wear out, yes, but break down completely? Impossible. He was like the admirable Cylon Imperious Leader in that respect: Humans could collapse from emotion, Cylons could deteriorate, but Lucifer and Imperious Leader went on forever. Well, perhaps not Imperious Leader.

At the end of several sessions of torture, Greenbean finally did give in. His mind seemed to grow smaller and smaller, until it was only a piece of dust, a microbe, in the cavern of his head. He began to believe there was none of him left, that he had weakened to the point of physical disintegration. In his mind he saw the pieces of himself spread out on the floor like a disassembled viper in the shop for repairs. Pain was no longer any problem for him. He had experienced so much pain since his capture by the Cylons that he couldn't remember not hurting. The part he couldn't stand wasn't the physical torture, it was the way the Cylons had gone inside his head and altered his brain.

He was afraid to touch his head, because he knew that all the bone there had been turned into jelly. If he touched his head, he might prick his skin and the inside of his head would spill out. He didn't want that to happen. He would do anything asked of him to prevent that from happening. So now, whatever he was asked by his interrogator, he struggled to tell the exact truth. He spoke slowly so that he could make sure he didn't leave out anything the Cylon wanted to know.

"The *Galactica?*" he said, his voice faint. "Yeah, I know where it is. *Exactly* where it is. Its coordinates? I know them, yes. Well, I know them *almost*. Do you have something to write things down with? Good. Let's see . . . Omicron Sector . . . and the quadrant, the quadrant is . . . let me think a minute."

They let him think. It took a long time for him to recall the quadrant but finally the information did come to him, swam to his awareness through the jelly of his brain.

Baltar struggled to stay awake. When he'd been young, out wheeling and dealing to add to his considerable fortune, he'd always been able to stay awake as long as he wanted to. Many a deal had been set because of his ability to keep his wits while all around him his competitors were losing out because of tiredness or flat-out unconsciousness. There had been no stopping Baltar at his peak. He was the acknowledged young tycoon of his generation. For years he had kept the edge, even after he'd become middle-aged and somewhat obese. Even then, he could stay awake several nights running if there was a solid amount of profit to be made.

But those days were past. Now he dropped off to sleep at inconvenient times, nodded off when he should have been thinking a matter through. There were times, even when he was awake, that he had trouble focusing on whatever matter was at hand.

Now he desperately needed to stay awake, to work out his plan, his scheme to finally get Adama where he wanted him—in a trap and begging for mercy. For once Baltar knew where the *Battlestar Galactica* and its ragtag fleet were. Acting on the information supplied by Ensign Greenbean, Cylon scout ships had discovered the *Galactica* moored in space near a small planet that Star-charts said had once been the human colony of Vaile. Although Cylon information indicated that the colony had been wiped out long ago, Baltar had reason to believe that, for once, the information supplied him by the computers was wrong. The human fleet would not stop at such a place without a good reason, and that reason was no doubt the existence of an active settlement of humans there.

So the *Galactica* was there, virtually hanging in space as an easy target. All Baltar had to do was garner his forces, ready his firepower, give his troops their orders, then sit back and watch the final destruction of Adama and his misbegotten followers. If only such a strategy could be set into action, Baltar could become the biggest hero among the Cylons—a human taking his place at the forefront of Cylon history.

But he could not do it, could not mobilize his forces just now. Earlier battles had depleted his own troops and fleet, military supplies were dangerously low, and too many Cylon fighters were out of action to mount a proper assault. In addition, his own base star was crippled by mechanical difficulties. Technicians were working around the clock to make the repairs, but each report brought to Baltar complications: more parts needed, more time needed, more personnel needed. Until this work was done, and reinforcements promised by the Imperious Leader arrived, it did not seem feasible to attack the *Galactica*. There was too much risk now, Baltar felt. While there were still many Cylon ships in operation, there was not enough reserve strength to assure a victory, even with the advantage that an ambush would bring them. Baltar did not like taking risks in battle. If the attack backfired, he could himself be captured or, worse, killed. He shuddered as he thought of the possibility of his own death.

Some might have said that the caution Baltar took such pride in was really cowardice. They might have said that he had inordinate affection for his own skin. On both matters they would probably have been right.

Whatever else he did, Baltar knew it was essential that he receive the approval of Imperious Leader. The Leader had been sending regular dispatches that clearly indicated he was getting impatient for victory. If Baltar did not bring the Leader triumph soon, he might as well throw open an airlock, take a few steps into airless space and take a deep breath.

All of these matters should have kept him awake, should have given him one sleepless night after another. But he dropped off to sleep much too easily. He would be considering his dilemma, then suddenly, his body tossing and turning, his face sparkling with sweat, he'd be asleep.

And, worse, he dreamed.

In this dream he walked, staggered really, across a landscape that was thick with mists. He felt scared, especially as he passed crags that threatened to turn themselves into alien monsters, and dark shadowy caves from which emerged ugly raspy shrieks. As he staggered along, he talked to himself. He squirmed in his bed as well as in the dream.

"Why am I here? For that matter, what is this place? I don't belong here, I know it. Do you hear it, whoever you are out there, I don't belong here. I want to go back to my ship. I have so many things to do, so many plans . . . I am not to be punished. Not any more. I have served well. Ask Imperious Leader. He knows how well I have served. He knows of my service to . . ."

Springing out of nowhere, forming himself out of sprays of mist, a Cylon in gleaming uniform appeared. It waved a long sword. The sword had a shining jeweled handle and the longest sharpest blade Baltar had ever seen. He grabbed Baltar by the neck with his free hand, and roughly shoved him against a tree stump. Baltar felt pieces of jagged wood prick the back of his neck.

"Hey, what is this? I'm your commander, you can't—"

"Not . . . my . . . commander," the Cylon said, in a voice even more unearthly than their usual unpleasant squawk.

In a single swipe, the Cylon pushed clothing away from

Baltar's neck, baring it for the sword. Baltar realized the creature meant to behead him. This had all happened to him once before, after his treachery had paved the way for the Cylon ambush of the Colonial Fleet and the defeat of the twelve worlds. When he had become of no more use to the Cylons, the Imperious Leader had ordered his head to be lopped off. His head had actually been on the block. However, Lucifer had secretly arranged a rescue, literally pulled Baltar out from under the executioner's sword. Then Lucifer convinced the Leader that Baltar could still be useful to the Cylons. Now, looking up at this Cylon with the sword, Baltar realized, with perfect dream logic, that this was the same executioner.

"I must finish the job," the executioner said. "Must finish. Now. You were not to live. Leader said die, you should die. It was wrong for you to continue living. Look how wrong."

"Wrong?" Baltar said, horrified by the appalling resonance in the executioner's voice. "What do you mean, wrong? You're insane, Cylon. I am a hero. I handed my people over to you on a silver platter. I gave you their heads. I gave you the twelve worlds, the—"

Rising instantly from the misty ground, a judge's high bench materialized next to Baltar. He had to twist his head around painfully and look up from the tree stump in order to get a good look at it. Gazing down at him, that obscene self-confidence so evident in his craggy face, was Commander Adama. He looked like a giant. He *was* a giant, a dream giant. Baltar felt his body trembling violently.

"Hero, Baltar?" Adama said. "Don't you mean traitor, you oozing slab of decaying meat?"

"Adama, I don't—go away—get—"

Adama pounded his gavel. The echoes of that pounding surrounded Baltar, pressed painfully against his ears.

"Do you have anything to say for yourself?" Adama asked.

"Not to you. Never to you."

"My verdict is guilty, Citizen Baltar. You are a traitor, the worst traitor in our history, a man who would, with indifference, cause the deaths of countless millions of our people. And why, Baltar? For your greed, for power. You will die, Baltar."

Baltar cringed at the word die. He was deeply afraid of dying. He would do anything to stay alive, even beg at Adama's feet.

"Adama, I didn't mean—I wanted to *end* the war, that awful war that had gone on for too long, for a millenium. It was time for it to end, don't you see, time—"

"To end by the annihilation of your people? What kind of excuse is that, Baltar? How could you? It was your life for theirs. The life of one cowardly traitor against theirs. Their deaths are on your conscience, Baltar."

Baltar laughed, even though he knew a laugh was not the most strategic act at this time and in these circumstances.

"Not *my* conscience, Adama. I feel no remorse. I—"

"The death of millions, Baltar, all because you sold information to the Cylons, sold your people to the Cylons. Remorse or no, your life is over. You are a dead man who walks."

"NO! I am alive. I command a battlestar, just like you. I am a commander, the leader of many. I make command decisions. I pursue you and your damned *Galactica*. You're lucky to still survive. I will destroy you."

"Single-handed?"

"If need be. I will finish you off and be rid of you forever."

"Merely another murder to add to the billions that are already your responsibility."

"They are not my responsibility!"

"You are guilty of the largest mass murder in human history."

Adama pounded his gavel.

"Have it your way then, Adama. What do I care about those people? They are just numbers on a list of statistics. People are foul and deserve to be wiped out. The Cylons are right about that. Only a few should survive, and I don't mean you and your godforsaken fleet."

"You don't deserve another moment of life, Baltar."

"No, it's you whose moments are numbered, then I will return as the conquering hero to the Cylons. They've promised me a life of wealth and ease."

"They have, have they? And you believe a Cylon promise? Remember what happened the last time you trusted them. After you served them so traitorously, they were going to kill you . . ."

Suddenly, above Baltar, the executioner raised his axe. Baltar, squirming around on the stump, faced upward and watched the axe begin to fall.

He screamed.

"NO! NO! NO!"

And he woke up, sweating furiously, in his bed. For a moment he couldn't get adjusted to reality. He still saw the axe falling at his face. Then his eyes focused and he saw Lucifer standing by the bed, looking down at him.

"What in blazes are you doing here?" Baltar said. "I told you never to enter my room without permission!"

"I am here with your permission . . . in a way."

Lucifer's voice had that self-satisfied oily sound in it. He definitely had something on his mind. That sound generally foreshadowed a real hassle for Baltar.

"Don't be vague. I didn't think you were programmed for vagueness."

"I am not, but I *am* programmed for caution. Conditions suggest that I now approach you with caution since I will undoubtedly provoke your wrath."

"Damn right about that. Well, I'm already furious with you, Lucifer, so take the risk. If I didn't need you to keep this ship running, I'd have you reduced to the bag of nuts and bolts you are."

Baltar knew he hit a nerve, or whatever passed for a nerve in Lucifer's circuitry, with that insult. Lucifer was always uncomfortable with any discussion of his cybernetic existence. Since he had consciousness, he believed he had transcended his origins and was something more than a mere construct.

Lucifer, to stave off Baltar's cruel words, got down to business.

"You were having bad dreams," he said, matter of factly.

Baltar was at first surprised by Lucifer's insightful remark, then he realized that the walking machine shop had been next to the bed, where it must have been obvious from his squirming and the damp state of his bedclothes that he had been dreaming badly.

"It's true I was dreaming," he said, "but what business is that of yours? You don't number psychologist among your many programmed talents, do you? Are you going to cure me?"

"In a way, I will."

There was something spooky about Lucifer's certainty. Baltar was scared of it, although he was damned certain he wouldn't show his fear to Lucifer.

"What do you mean?" Baltar asked.

"Your dreams, whatever their images and actions might have been, were about your guilts, were they not?"

Baltar, his heart beating rapidly and new layers of sweat seeping out beneath the old perspiration, screamed at Lucifer:

"I HAVE NO GUILT! YOU'RE LYING!"

Lucifer, for the moment, regretted the immobility of his metal-based face. He would have liked to smile arrogantly at his commander.

"I was not judging you," he said. "I was merely requesting descriptive content. I think you have answered me sufficiently with the violence of your response."

To Baltar's ears, Lucifer's statements sounded curious. They had the sound about them of jotted-down notes. How Lucifer knew about the dreams, he couldn't possibly guess, but there seemed no point in trying to deceive him.

"All right, all right. Guilt was the major theme of my dream. It has been for the last few nights, the—"

"For the last *four* nights, to be exact."

Baltar, angry, strongly desired to smash Lucifer in the jaw, but no doubt he would only have broken his hand on Lucifer's metallic chin.

"How in blazes—have you developed some device to

spy on me, to spy on my DREAMS! I swear, Lucifer, if you've—"

Lucifer's soft, smooth voice came in under Baltar's squawks like a laser-saw cutting a branch off a tree.

"I have not been spying on you, Commander. But I *have* watched you sleep. A disturbed sleep, at that. And . . . I have run a few tests."

"Tests?! Lucifer, this is against express orders—"

"You do not recall the override factor?"

Lucifer was dispensing so many consecutive mysteries that Baltar had trouble keeping up with them. His mind seemed to spin.

"Lucifer, I not only don't recall the override factor, I don't know what in the cloudless Cylon skies you're talking about."

Lucifer made one of his little sounds—a rumbling that seemed to come out of his throat and sounded like the rubbing together of dry ball bearings.

"The override factor," he said, "was explained to you at the time I was first assigned to be your second in command."

That day was also the day Baltar had been saved from the executioner by Lucifer. Since the human didn't enjoy being indebted to the robot, he was irritated even by Lucifer's reference to it.

"A day I don't remember with pleasure, I assure you," Baltar said.

Again, Lucifer's statements were preceded by the bizarre throat sound.

"Imperious Leader, in his awesome wisdom, informed you that day that, in the area of weapons development, I was to be allowed all freedom to experiment and act, especially with any creation that could accelerate our victory over the human vermin. In such an instance, your authority, Baltar, would be overridden. I could, in effect, do anything required to fulfill the experimental requirements of such a project."

Baltar could not recall Imperious Leader saying any such thing. He wondered if Lucifer, for his own convenience, was making it up.

"A stupid idea, if you ask me," he muttered. Lucifer did not acknowledge the remark, which was, after all, on the Cylon borderline of treason.

"The Leader's dispensation allows me free choice in the arrangement of subjects for experimentation. In such matters, I need not, as you say, check it out with you."

Lucifer's habit of circumlocution was making Baltar even more nervous.

"And precisely," he said, "what was it you needed I couldn't know about?"

Lucifer knew he had come to the difficult moment. He could easily anticipate his commander's reaction to the information he was going to divulge.

"Well, Lucifer, what is it?"

"You, actually. As a subject. I needed to try out my device on you."

The revelation didn't disturb Baltar as much as Lucifer had feared. It was something of a relief, actually. Baltar realized that the agony he'd been going through the last few nights had been induced, not real. He felt psychologically fit again.

"And why me, may I ask?" Baltar said.

"My subject *had* to be human. Which you are."

At least marginally, Lucifer added in his mental circuits.

"Yes. But so are the several human prisoners we have down in the ship's brigs."

Baltar recalled that, on his last visit to the base-star's prison area, he had been awed by the number of prisoners there, especially the high number of captured Galactican pilots, all of them shouting the meanest possible epithets at him as he'd walked through the cell block. He had, with pleasure, reported his success at capturing humans to Imperious Leader, and had only slightly inflated the figures.

Lucifer replied to Baltar carefully, desiring to flatter the man while making his points.

"Baltar, they are merely human. Their minds were, how should I say it, inadequate for my goals. I needed someone with a more complicated mind. That person had to be you."

Lucifer decided not to tell his commander that the main

reason he had been chosen was that there was no one else available who had more reason to feel guilty about his past history.

Baltar smiled, obviously pleased with Lucifer's flattery. At the same time, he still felt angry about his guilty dreams. What right had this metal monstrosity to toy with his brain? And just what *had* he done? The two were silent for a while, then Baltar said, the sound of a mild threat in his voice:

"All right, Lucifer, tell me."

Lucifer rolled to the door of Baltar's bedchamber and emitted a soft whistling sound. A quartet of Cylons instantly wheeled a bulky piece of machinery into the room. To Baltar it looked something like a sphere on top of a pyramid that was itself on top of a cube. The sphere was translucent and flashed a bizarre mixture of purple, blue and yellow lights as it spun around. The pyramid was cluttered with dials, levers and curious little depressions on all of its surfaces. The cube had narrow vents going around it, and a number of knobs near floor level.

Baltar, flabbergasted, stared for a long while at the device before speaking again:

"What in God's twelve worlds is that junk heap?"

"I call it Lucifer's Emotional Adjustment Device—Extensive Range. The acronym for it is LEADER. Quite a clever name, don't you think?"

"I don't think. What kind of name is that? Emotional Adjustment Range whatever? Look, Lucifer, my head aches too much from your cleverness. Explain in the simplest terms your corroded memory banks can supply."

Lucifer glided to LEADER and took up a professorial stance next to it. While he talked, he pressed buttons, pulled levers, keyed symbols and checked dials.

"I have been experimenting with human brain waves. Charting them, isolating them one from the other—at least isolating what constitutes them in individual situations. The initial objective of my study was to see if human intelligence and emotions could be codified, put onto Cylonate crystals or stored on Borallian touchplates, then *reproduced* so that they could be induced into Cylons hooked up to them. Do you see, a Cylon could then think what a human thought, feel what a human felt. I thought that perhaps Imperious Leader could make effective use of such a device."

"And promote you within the hierarchy, and give you your own ship, away from my command. Yes, Lucifer, I understand. I understand well."

Baltar's sarcasm offended Lucifer. He did not like being forced to defend himself.

"You apply to me motives that are foreign to me. *Human* motives."

"Like mine."

"Yes."

Baltar's smile took on new levels of insult.

"Lucifer, you're more like me than you suspect."

"That is not possible or logical, since I am neither human nor Cylon."

Baltar laughed.

"Because you're an arrangement of junk? Even then, sometimes you think just like me. I have noticed, old friend."

Lucifer, not pleased by Baltar's amiability, turned his attention back to LEADER.

"My experiments in the recording of human emotion are still proceeding, with mixed results. I still need time to complete that phase. However, quite by accident, I discovered a function of my device that I hadn't anticipated."

"Ah, a flaw in our arrogant metallic genius. Tell me more."

Lucifer chose not to respond to Baltar's insult.

"While I was adjusting levels for human output, I came upon a feedback factor. Some of the feelings I extracted from our humans could not only be retransmitted to them, but the retransmission could be accomplished at a higher intensity and rate than that of the original feeling I was extracting from them."

"Lucifer, you're sliding into gobbledygook. I am not a computer. *Retransmit* all that in words I can deal with."

"Simply: if an emotion exists within a human, I can take it out and then put it back at double, triple, quadruple its intensity. In short, if one of them is happy, I can receive an imprint of that happiness, then direct it back into him and make him happier, ecstatic, even insanely delirious with joy. If he is sad, I can make him morose, even suicidal. And, if there is a modicum of guilt within him, I can extract that guilt and make him feel, as the human phrase goes, guilty as sin . . . and beyond. Further, I can take one human's emotion and retransmit it to an entirely different human."

Lucifer looked to Baltar for a reaction to his assertions. Baltar mulled over the information in what was for him characteristic fashion. He was attempting to think of a way he could use Lucifer's new device for his own advantage. He walked toward LEADER, saying to Lucifer in a low, sinister voice:

"And you've been using this dreadful contraption on me these last four nights."

"Well . . . yes."

"I should have you reduced to spare parts for that. Lucifer, you had no right to put me through such misery." Baltar recalled the impact of his dreams and shuddered. "I do not need to—well, never mind that. For now I'll ignore your, uh, tactical insubordination. But I want you to know that, if you ever try to use that or any other of your monstrous contraptions on me in the future, I won't be so lenient."

Lucifer knew it was time to emphasize obsequiousness with his commander. It was the best technique to adopt when Baltar's wrath was provoked.

"As you wish, commander," he said.

"Now, show me how this pile of space garbage works."

"With pleasure, Baltar."

Lucifer's tendril-like fingers pushed a button on the console of LEADER. Baltar, feeling a wave of sorrow plunge through his body, wagged a finger at Lucifer.

"No, no, no. Not on me, you fool. Demonstrate with another guinea pig."

Lucifer, a trifle disappointed, pressed the button again. The sorrow fled from Baltar immediately.

"I have just the . . . guinea pig you wish," Lucifer said. He gestured toward one of the centurions. "Guard, bring us the human called Greenbean."

• • •

Greenbean sat in the corner of his cell, trying vainly to wedge himself there so that no one would see him or his shame. He wished he were not so tall and conspicuous no matter how he arranged his body.

His cellmate, a captured shuttle pilot named Scarn, sat on his bunk and drank from a glass of obviously stagnant water as if it were ambrosia. Scarn was as thin as Greenbean, but he had once, before his long imprisonment, been a well-built and athletic young man.

"Easy, easy, fellow," Scarn said. "We've all done what you did."

Greenbean could barely hold back his tears.

"I thought I never would," he said. "How did I crack so easy?"

"Get this into your head—it's *not* easy. We all been through it. We all cracked. These tinheads got too many devices, too many—"

"That's no excuse. A colonial warrior ain't supposed to crack, not under any kind of pressure. Just give name, rank, classification numbers. Don't speak to them, even when they're friendly; always remember you're a colonial fighting man and don't—"

Scarn, furious at hearing the old regulations, yelled at Greenbean:

"Okay, hotshot, just rub it in for us, all of us. We're all cowards, all in the same boat as you, laser mouth. We all spilled the beans and only because of a massive amount of excruciating pain, all because they got machines that can pick apart our brains like picking leaves off trees, all because they can get inside our hearts and—"

"Sorry," Greenbean interrupted, "I'm sorry. I don't mean to—"

Scarn walked to Greenbean, bent down, and put a hand on his shoulder. "It's okay, buddy," he said softly, comfortingly. "No reason to keep going over it. Forget what you done. Our duty now is to find a way to escape. That's in the code, too. It's our primary, our only—"

Scarn stopped talking abruptly when he saw the Cylon

guard entering the cell. He stood up, came as close to the Cylon as he dared, and shouted:

"What in holy hell do you want, metal brains?"

The Cylon lumbered to a touchplate placed beside the cell door. He put his gloved hand against it. Circuits within the glove, imprints keyed to the touchplate, phased with it and activated tight narrow beams of fiery light that came down from the ceiling, directed right at Scarn. Scarn screamed and began to thrash around wildly. He fell to the cell floor and wept uncontrollably from the pain. Greenbean pushed himself away from his corner and ran to the still-writhing Scarn. He knelt by him and shouted over his shoulder to the Cylon:

"Turn it off, you Cylon cr—please release him, sir."

The guard removed his hand from the touchplate and the beams vanished. Scarn's body sagged. He was unconscious. Greenbean checked his pulse. It was beating a little fast, but normally. He put his arms under Scarn's body, intending to take him to his bunk, but the Cylon grabbed him and wrenched him to his feet. Greenbean could not quite get his balance, and the Cylon started dragging him toward the cell door.

"Okay, okay," Greenbean yelled. "But let me walk on my own."

The Cylon did not alter his grip.

"Please let me walk on my own, *sir*." Greenbean said, space-academy style.

The Cylon released him. Greenbean stumbled, but did not fall. The Cylon walked out of the cell and down the dank dungeon corridor. Greenbean walked sullenly behind him, his shoulders bent, wishing he could go back to cringing and crying in his cell-corner.

CHAPTER TWO

Colonel Tigh, passing by the starfield on one of his many errands carrying documents from one part of *Galactica*'s bridge to another, slowed down a moment when he saw Athena standing at the edge of the starfield lost in thought, her eyes glazed in sadness. With everyone else on the bridge scurrying about busily or staring at monitors and manipulating controls, Athena's stillness seemed both unusual and lovely. Tigh recognized her resemblance to her mother, Ila, when she was contemplative like this, just as he often noticed how much she looked like her father, Commander Adama, when she was moved to anger. He was tempted to ask her if he could help in any way, but he saw Adama approaching from the other direction. Adama caught Tigh's glance and understood it at once, in the almost telepathic manner with which the two had often communicated since their days as wingmates in the hottest fleet squadron. Tigh nodded and continued on his quest to find the proper depository for the documents in his hand.

Adama stood behind Athena for some time before speaking:

"I think you're looking for ghosts."

Even though her father's words had been spoken softly, Athena was startled.

"What?" she said. "Oh, yes, I guess ... I keep hoping to see them returning, the pilots who won't return. I mean, the ones we sent off to their—"

"Easy, dear."

He put his hands on her shoulders. She appreciated the affection. There was so little time for family affection between her, her father and her brother Apollo anymore. All their time was devoted to the *Galactica,* to its flight from the pursuing Cylons, and to the quest for Earth.

"You're not responsible for the deaths of those pilots, you know," Adama said, sympathetically.

"I know," she said, "I know that. But it's hard to get rid of the idea. I mean, I give the commands to launch them. It's ... it's as if I send them to their deaths myself."

"But you don't! You're just doing your job, working at a console, following the set drills and procedures."

"Yet, I'm the last voice aboard the *Galactica* they hear, don't you see? I speak to each and every one of them before they take off. When they're launched, it's like they're, well, leaving home. Pretty sentimental, huh? Still, they're like family to me."

"They *are* family. We're all that's left, after all. We have to regard our people, everybody on all our ships, as family."

She turned to him and smiled.

"Forgive me," Adama said, "I fall so easily into command-style homilies."

Athena wiped away some tears from her eyes, noted a tear or two welling up into her father's eyes.

Neither of them noticed Apollo standing near them. He had quietly climbed the stairs to the starfield.

"Sorry, father, I'm just in a morbid mood," Athena said. "I've felt sad ever since we lost Greenbean. He was kind of goofy, but I was very fond of him."

"We're all feeling sad, Athena," Apollo said. "I really miss old Greenbean, too."

Athena reached out her hand to her brother. He took it, and she was pleased that, for once, the three of them were in actual physical contact.

"Starbuck says he thinks the Cylons've got him and he's still alive," Athena said. "I don't even know if that's consoling. I can't bear thinking of him being tortured. He's so innocent they'll, well, they'll eat him alive."

"I know," Apollo said, "I know."

The three of them stood in silence for a while, looking out the starfield, thinking about their lost pilots. In spite of the sadness of his daughter's mood, Adama felt a moment of pleasure at the family tableau. It was rare, and the demands the *Galactica* made upon them might not allow another such moment for many, many centons.

"Back to work, the both of you," he said finally. Athena returned to her console. Obeying his father's gesture to accompany him, Apollo walked across the bridge with Adama.

"Your report?" Adama said.

When he says back to work, he really means it, Apollo thought.

"The people of Vaile have offered us their entire cooperation," he said, "any help we need."

"Even under threat of Cylon retribution if their collaboration with us is discovered?"

"Even under that. They've heard too many threats from the Cylons, they told me. They're happy to aid us."

"Well, that *is* good news, Apollo."

"They're a brave people. You'll like them."

"I'm sure I will. Any people courageous enough to agree to supply the *Galactica* and the fleet with fuel, food, and supplies are admirable to me before I ever actually see them."

Apollo smiled, enjoying Adama's irony.

"When can the loading operations begin?" Adama asked.

"Soon. Our logistics specialists are working out the details with the Vailean representatives in their capital city."

"Fine, fine." Adama stopped walking and gripped his son's arm. "I'm happy with your work on this, Apollo."

Apollo felt the usual surge of gratitude when Adama complimented him, even for a job as simple as the liaison with Vaile. The fleet was lucky that the colonies on that planet still existed, and even flourished. The leaders of Vaile had told Apollo that they had no idea why they were overlooked by Cylon assault forces. Their assumption had been that Vaile was just too much of an outpost for the Cylons to bother with. Apollo found it hard to believe that the Cylons, who hated humans so much, would leave any colony unattacked, no matter how remote.

Adama acknowledged Tigh, who had been standing nearby, waiting for permission to speak.

"Sir," Tigh said, "Sire Uri has requested an audience with you."

"Uri?" Apollo said. "I haven't heard a peep from him since the Carillon disaster."

Sire Uri had been the leader of a faction which had demanded that the citizens of the Galactican fleet throw down their arms, destroy their ships and settle on the leisure planet of Carillon. He had almost swayed a majority of people to his side when the Cylons attacked Carillon. Many had died in that debacle, and Uri had been uncharacteristically silent since.

"Commander," Apollo said, "I wanted to speak to you about Uri. He was on the commission to Vaile, as representative of the Council. He was extremely interested in the place, kept talking about what a delicious paradise it was. That's what he called it, a delicious paradise."

"Is it?" Adama asked.

"It's beautiful. Green fields, lovely aromatic flowers, clean and attractive communities. Yes, it is beautiful. A gentle, idealistic society."

"Idealistic? I never knew Uri to be attracted to anything idealistic."

"Well, I don't know about that, but it's clear to me he's attracted to any place that he can legitimately call paradise.

He got on that tack at Carillon, remember?"

"Oh, I remember. I remember only too well, Apollo. Well, I'll have to grant him an audience, I suppose. I just won't listen to anything he says."

"No doubt the best approach to the situation, sir," Tigh said, smiling.

Apollo saw nothing to smile about.

"I'm not sure about that," he said. "I'd listen to him. Not for what he says out loud but for what he's *not* saying, for what's going on in his twisted brain."

"You really don't like Uri, do you?" Adama said.

Apollo recalled the first time he had encountered Uri on the fancy starliner, *Rising Star*. With the memories of the Cylon destruction of the twelve worlds fresh in everyone's minds, and with more than half the people who had survived desperate and starving, Uri had been reveling in a private club. He'd been stuffing precious food into his flabbily handsome face and celebrating like the lord of the manor. Apollo had been especially disgusted by the way he already had a doxie in tow, when his wife had been one of the casualties of the Cylon attack.

"No, sir," Apollo said, "I don't like Uri. Worse, I don't trust him. I hear he's been stirring things up lately, holding meetings, working on the dissatisfactions of our people, planting ideas in their heads."

"That's the Uri I've always known," Adama said, almost nostalgically. He remembered first meeting Uri when he'd been part of a military mission on Uri's home planet of Leo. Uri had been a newly elected leader in those days, and he actually had noble aspirations. Adama had been too concerned with the war to pay much attention to Uri's later rise to wealth and power and had no conception of the steps of corruption that had led to the weasely but smooth crook Uri had become.

"We'll just have to pay Sire Uri more attention," Adama said, then addressed Tigh:

"Tell him I'll see him in my quarters at the beginning of second watch."

"Yes, sir."

Adama and Apollo watched Tigh walk briskly away, receiving a pile of papers from a subordinate without breaking stride. When Adama looked at his son again, he could see concern in his eyes.

"Something more, Apollo?"

"It's the people of Vaile, sir."

"What about them?"

"Many of them wish to join us, join up with the fleet and help us in our quest, fight with us. They're quite excited by the prospect of finding Earth."

"That's terribly optimistic. We may, after all, never arrive there."

"But you really believe we will, don't you?"

"Yes, I do believe that."

"And we have faith in your faith."

Apollo rarely spoke of their goals, being content to perform the day-to-day tasks skillfully, so Adama was quite touched by his son's affirmation of their quest.

"Thank you, Apollo. That means a lot to me."

"And the colonists?"

"We'll take as many as logistics, space, and supplies'll permit."

Apollo smiled. He was clearly satisfied with his father's decision.

"Thank you, sir."

He saluted, did a properly executed about-face, and left the bridge. Adama watched him go, and considered what he'd said. *We have faith in your faith.* Hearing that was gratifying to Adama, but was he, in truth, leading his people on a fruitless journey to nowhere? Was there even an Earth? Apollo had been right about Adama's faith. He had abundant faith, and yet he also had many doubts, doubts that had haunted him ever since the Cylon ambush had originally set them on this frantic journey across the universe. Sometimes he wished he could go back to that time, to the period just before the Cylon double-cross, but return with the knowledge he had now. He could have persuaded President Adar and the Council to be more vigilant. He could have warned the twelve worlds so they would have been prepared for the Cylon assault. The Cylons would have been defeated, perhaps for good, and Adama could have retired, gone back to Caprica to the arms of Ila. If things had just occurred differently, Ila and his son Zac, both casualties of the Cylon attack, would be alive now. Ah, well, you couldn't travel in time and correct the mistakes of history and fate, so it was probably no use thinking about it.

He shifted his attention to the bridge crew, who appeared calm and happy, for a change. He was proud of them, and happy they could enjoy a respite from the threat of Cylon attack, however brief that respite might be. He had advised Tigh to allow them as much liberty on Vaile as the proper functioning of the ship would allow.

He felt quite peaceful himself, and confident that there would be no danger from the Cylons for some time.

Baltar stared down at the weeping young ensign. Tears rolled out of Greenbean's eyes. Although he sat on a chair, he seemed draped on it, his body so limp it seemed just thrown there in a pile. Baltar had never seen anyone look as glum as Greenbean did now. He smiled at Lucifer, who stood next to the chair. Although no emotion could, as usual, be detected on Lucifer's face, Baltar thought he could see some pride in his demeanor, even in the nonhuman way this cybernetic creation stood.

"I do think it's working, Lucifer. How's it done? I don't see any wires."

As if to prove the magic of the device for himself, Baltar walked all the way around the chair, casting his arms out to try to find invisible wires. Lucifer's reply to the question sounded quite smug to Baltar.

"There are no wires, nothing between the device and this pathetic creature. The machine transmits duplicated brain waves in the form of intensified high-density rays, which are absorbed in the victim through the skin and then travel to the brain through the medium of the bloodstream. At least, that's how it works on humans."

"And it's set on guilt, as I commanded."

"On guilt, Baltar. In heavier doses even than I used on you. Look at this man."

"I know. He looks like he's going to fold up." Baltar's voice was at the soprano level, which meant he was excited. "Are you sure the settings aren't too high?"

"He's a very resistant specimen."

"I want further demonstration. Use different settings."

"I'm not sure if his physical—"

"That's not important. Something happens to him, we'll bring in one of the other prisoners, keep the machine going."

"He might die."

"That's all right. He's outlived his usefulness to us. I don't think there's much more to be obtained from him. Go ahead, Lucifer, do it!"

"By your command, Count Baltar."

Lucifer manipulated a series of controls with a dexterity that only a mechanical being could achieve. Not that Lucifer ever thought of himself as a mere mechanical being. He had a soul, housed in his left shoulder. He had created the soul himself.

Greenbean now laughed hysterically, even though his previous sorrowful tears were still rolling down his cheeks. Baltar, happy with the sudden change in the pilot's mood, yelped with delight.

"More, Lucifer, more!"

Baltar's urgings made Greenbean laugh even harder. He slapped his knee over and over again.

"You're a card, Baltar," Greenbean said, "a real card. Tell me another one. Go on."

Baltar was at first taken aback by the pilot's response, then he realized that his words had been taken as a joke by the manipulated man.

"Look at that, will you," Baltar shouted, amazed.

Greenbean laughed and slapped his knees again. The pilot's pleasure was disconcerting for Baltar, and a little disturbing. It was so bizarre to be giving someone mirth. Baltar wasn't accustomed to it. He didn't like it.

Lucifer worked more of the controls. Greenbean's laughter stopped abruptly. The lines of his smile plunged downward. His youthful eyes narrowed. He was, under LEADER's guidance, clearly worried.

"What's the matter, soldier?" Baltar said, making his voice soft and friendly. It was his prisoner interrogation voice.

"I'm worried."

"What about?"

Greenbean looked up at Baltar with doleful eyes. Baltar nearly startled backwards at the yearning appeal in the man's eyes.

"There isn't any sense to the universe. Why is there war? It's so senseless. Why are the Cylons so mad? Why does God—"

These were not subjects Baltar wanted to hear about.

"Shut him up, Lucifer!" he screamed.

Lucifer again touched a few protuberances on the face of LEADER's control panel, and Greenbean started to cry.

"Back to guilt, again?" Baltar asked.

"No," Lucifer said, "this is remorse."

"All those people dead," Greenbean moaned. "My family, my section officer, those cadets, all those warriors I served with. Serina. Do you know, I loved Serina secretly? Oh, she was Apollo's wife, his fiance before that, and I was glad for both of them, but she was the loveliest woman I ever saw. I guess it was all right for me to adore her. From afar, I mean. I miss her so. God, I miss—"

"Lucifer," Baltar yelled, "stop this drivel!"

"As you wish."

Lucifer shut off LEADER. Greenbean relaxed in his chair, unconscious. Baltar ordered the Cylon prison guards to take the pilot away. When they had dragged Greenbean out of the room, Baltar turned to Lucifer, smiled in that insidious way that Lucifer immediately distrusted, and said:

"I'm pleased, Lucifer. Very pleased."

Lucifer was shocked by the compliment. He was also pleased, although there was no way he could show it, nor would he have wanted Baltar to see it.

"Does Imperious Leader know of this machine yet?" Baltar asked.

"That would violate command procedure. I am ordered by my programming to report to you, Count Baltar. You have the responsibility of informing Imperious—"

"Yes, yes, of course." Baltar started to pace. Lucifer had noticed that, whenever Baltar needed to think something out, he usually paced. It was as if he could not get his mind to function unless his legs were mobile. "Yes, we will tell Imperious Leader. But not just yet, not just yet. I want to consider all this for a while. Leave me now."

An order which Lucifer did not at all mind. He responded immediately, but before he got out the door Baltar summoned him back, asking:

"Lucifer, this pilot, this Greenbean, can you mind-wipe him, make him forget all he's seen on this ship?"

"That would be simple, yes. But to what purpose?"

"I'll let you know that later."

"As you prefer."

After Lucifer had left the command room, Baltar began to walk slowly, then a little faster, then quite fast. From time to time, as he devised a new facet to his plan, he burst out laughing quite excitedly.

Adama enjoyed the portion of each watch when he could lounge in his quarters and dictate his log for the day. It was especially comforting when everything was going well, as it was now. His voice became lighter and more relaxed. Nestling the flat microphone in the palm of his hand, he held it close to his mouth as he spoke:

"Trade with the Vaileans has been successfully initiated. Our supply shuttles are presently loading down on the planet's surface for the first of what shall be several trips back and forth exchanging goods. The Vailean people are, Apollo tells me, cooperating in every respect, making personal sacrifices to fulfill our requests, and procuring us even out-of-the-way items. Apollo is handling the logistics of the operation and doing a fine job, I might add. He's ably assisted by Sheba, who is continuing to prove she has command potential—inherited, no doubt, from her father, one of the greatest leaders and fighters in our history. If only she doesn't inherit his brashness and recklessness."

Adama paused the mike for a moment as memories of Sheba's father came back to him. Commander Cain had been quite a martinet, and he sometimes made dreadful tactical mistakes, but he could whip up a battalion of troops to fighting readiness faster than a battlestar could work up to light speed.

"I expect," Adama resumed his log, "that we can complete the operation with all due efficiency and expediency, and then be off again on our journey, removing the Vaileans from the danger we pose to them."

The knock on the door that he was dreading came in a steady rhythm. Adama shut off the mike and replaced it in its slot on the log console.

"Come in, Uri," he said.

Uri entered the room with the youth and grace that was surprising in a man of his age, height, and bulk. Adama noted that, no matter how much good living Uri stole surreptitiously from the fleet, his handsome face never displayed the proper signs of decadence.

"You knew it was me?" Uri asked.

"It's time for our appointment, is it not? Beginning of the watch?"

"Of course. I am, uh, merely echoing the feelings of so many others. All the people who seem to feel that you have, uh, supernatural powers."

Adama was puzzled both by Uri's remarks and his uncharacteristic attempt to flatter.

"Your, uh, feats in rescuing us time and again, your continued success in fleeing our pursuers, the miracles you achieve as part of your daily routine—these all have, uh, impressed everyone. Some of us regard you as a god. Therefore, it would not be surprising if you could see through doors."

Uri gestured toward the thick metal portal of Adama's quarters. Adama felt unsettled, thrown off by Uri's new clearly strategic approach. Still, even with the flattery, Uri sounded as unctuous as ever. Adama felt certain the man was plotting something.

"What is your business, Sire Uri?"

"Ah, so efficient. Your trademark. Well, I'll not waste your time, old friend."

Adama winced at the words, old friend, but Uri did not, or pretended not, to notice.

"Vaile is a marvelous place," Uri said. His voice had an oozing sound in it. "The most beautiful planet I've seen—except, of course, for the twelve worlds themselves."

Uri's invoking of the twelve worlds was a clever ploy. Adama frequently regretted that he could never return there. He recalled his last time on Caprica, when he had assured himself of Ila's death and then conceived his plan to search for Earth. That memory recurred often. He had to force himself to concentrate in order to attend to Uri's next words.

"I don't know how, uh, to say this, Commander Adama. We admire you so much for your leadership, your courage, your intelligence."

Adama struggled not to show his repulsion at Uri's condescension.

"And," Uri continued, "in the time of our ordeal, you have earned the respect of one and all. At this moment you may be the single most respected man in our entire history."

Adama remembered the time when he wasn't so respected, when his leadership had been questioned by the Council of the Twelve. And Uri, of course, had led that sortie against him.

"You're buttering me up, Uri. I appreciate your compliments, but get to the point."

Adama's brusqueness momentarily flustered Uri, and he had to compose himself before going on:

"While we all admire your quest, your grand dream to rediscover Earth, your hope to end once and for all the war with the Cylons, not all of us share in your, uh, faith, Commander."

"You keep saying we, Uri. We, us. Are you speaking merely for yourself, or are you a spokesman for others?"

"Others. Uh, a few . . . some of the people in the fleet who are tired of the tedium of the journey, fearful of the Cylon pursuit. Some who are not, uh, in complete agreement that there is an Earth or *any* point to your quest, Commander Adama."

Staring Uri in the eyes, Adama resolved to hold in his angry reactions to Uri's unctuous words. Uri, sensing the commander's wrath, squirmed in his seat.

"Let me be more personal," Uri said. "As you know, I've not always been in complete agreement with your policies. In none of them do I disagree with you more than in this fruitless seeking of Earth. I am not impressed by myth, however powerfully conceived and held. After all, we don't know whether Earth exists, do we, Adama?"

"Not empirically perhaps, but the evidence in the records of the Lords of Kobol—"

"Mythology, all of it. Stories made up to explain the unexplainable. Imaginative—"

"Uri, let's not get into the ancient arguments. We both know them by rote, both sides. So there's no point to the two of us hashing them out here and now. You didn't come here for that particular ritual. Get to the point."

Uri was obviously miffed, but his voice was smooth as he continued:

"Adama, there is no chance of your giving up this ridic—this quest, is there?"

"You already know there isn't."

"Yes, I expected it. What I ask—and I am asking on behalf of the citizens of the fleet (the majority of them noncombatants, I may say)—is that you allow us to remain on Vaile while you persevere in your expedition to Earth. With, incidentally, our blessings."

Their blessings! How could Uri dare? Adama could contain his anger no longer.

"With your blessings?! And who are you to present your blessing, Sire Uri? What have you done for humanity, except to push your selfish fat self into—"

"Adama, Adama, please! I'm aware of your dislike for me. I have publicly apologized for my part in the Carillon

disaster. There's no need for you to vilify me now. I have
... shortcomings, I admit, and sometimes I—well, never
mind about that. What I meant just now was that we respect
your idealism but, Commander, we have been journeying
for a long while now. We have been uprooted from our
homes, subjected to—"

"All right, Uri. I understand. And I'm sorry for blowing
up there. Wrong of me. We were friends once."

"And we could be again."

Adama resisted saying that he found that prospect extremely doubtful.

"Yes, who knows?" he said. "It may surprise you, Uri,
to find out that I do sympathize with your argument. We've
all been under terrific strain, and there's really nothing wrong
with wanting to escape from it. I wish I could shuttle down
to Vaile, find myself a shady tree to sprawl out under, and
take a good long rest, but—"

"Then why don't you? Why don't we *all* settle there?
We could, you know. The people of Vaile would welcome
us."

"Yes, and then we could sit in comfort, our minds eased
into a false contentment, just waiting for the Cylons to find
us and wipe us out for good."

"No, no. That's where your military mind is so short-
sighted. You've lived so long for battle that you forget there
are alternatives that have nothing to do with war."

Adama sighed. He could anticipate Uri's next arguments,
but he had to allow them.

"All right, Uri. Explain."

Uri grinned, clearly warming up to his task.

"We can transfer all the *Galactica*'s technology, all the
supplies, all the personnel, all the firepower down to Vaile.
Once everything valuable is taken off the ships, we can
destroy them. With them gone, we've left no evidence the
Cylons can trace us with. We can—"

"Enough, Uri. You're just revising the arguments you
tried to use back at Carillon. They won't wash now either."

"Adama, you're killing us all!"

"What—?"

"You're taking us across the endless tracks of space, keeping us going until the Cylons finally catch up with us. *That's* when the Cylons will ruthlessly annihilate us. Not on Vaile, but out in some backwater of space. We'll be hanging there as sitting ducks. Then all your reputation, all your honors, won't mean a damn thing, Commander. You're leading us to catastrophe, and you have no right to!"

Uri, as usual, had taken his one step too far.

"Uri, you're out of line. You are dismissed."

"You forget, Adama, I don't belong to the military. I'm not one of your cowering underlings and I won't be treated like one."

"There is no point in continuing this discussion, no—"

"No point because you're too pigheaded to—"

"Uri—"

The threatening tone of Adama's voice seemed to frighten Uri.

"As you wish," he said. "Then you won't allow those of us who don't wish to continue the voyage to remain on Vaile?"

"I promise to take your request under consideration. Look, Uri, every ship in the fleet is understaffed. We need more personnel rather than less. There are too many important jobs to be done, we can't afford—"

"Jobs to be done? Adama, my important duty in the last week was cleaning out sanitation units!"

That's perhaps the only job you're suited for, Adama thought but did not say.

"That is ... unfortunate," he said. "But everyone has to draw that kind of duty from time to time. If you wish special considerations for health reasons, I'll—"

"No ... no special considerations. You can save all of them for your son and his—"

Ever since Apollo and Uri had first clashed, Uri had been publicly charging nepotism, especially since Athena also held a command position. Adama decided not to pursue the subject with him.

"Uri," he said, "I must ask you—"

"I'll talk with you again, Adama. Next time you'll know

just how many people support my views."

"I welcome that, Sire Uri."

Uri strutted out of Adama's quarters without leaving any formal farewell behind him. It was just as well, Adama thought, there was no point in the two of them being polite to each other.

Tigh, who'd obviously been lurking outside Adama's cabin in case he was needed, came into the room.

"Sounded like a rough session to me," he commented.

"Well, Tigh, you know Uri."

"Only too well. A topflight troublemaker. You better watch him."

"Oh, I'm doing that all right. What's the state of the Vaile operation?"

"Everything proceeding smoothly."

"And elsewhere?"

"Good news, mostly. We just received information from the foundry ship *Hephaestus* that production of new vipers is now approaching optimum manufacturing rate. A number of the new models have already been transferred to the *Galactica*."

"I'm impressed. That should bring us close to full strength again."

"Correct."

"Good. That is good news, Tigh. Carry on."

After Tigh had left, Adama leaned back in his chair and reviewed his conversation with Uri. He could sense that the man was ready to provoke trouble again. He might even attempt another coup. But you couldn't lock a man away just for having the wrong notions. Still, he would bear watching. Close watching.

Starbuck's smile was as smooth as a viper launching. Cassiopeia almost couldn't resist it. But this time she was determined. Pushing at his shoulders, she tried to get out of the corner he'd angled her into. He backed away gracefully, still pressing his case.

"How about it, Cassie?"

"Don't call me Cassie, I told you."

"Cass? Cass's okay?"

"I can live with it."

"Well then, Cass, what do you say? You'll be off-duty soon. I've got a jugful of ambrosa, latest vintage. I cleaned and polished the old secret hideaway. We can simulate a—"

"Your line's wearing thin, Starbuck. I've heard this routine before."

"This's the first time you've complained."

He looked hurt. His pain was so boyish and appealing, she nearly gave in and said she'd go to the hideaway with him.

"Yeah, well," she said, "I've thought about it enough. Buy a new approach, Starbuck."

"C'mon, darling, I know you've been overworked and—"

"What? You call triple shifts in Life Center *overwork?* Seeing pain and blood and—you call *that* overwork? You call shipping corpses out a chute overwork? Starbuck, you—"

"Easy, easy."

He put his arms around her. His touch was so gentle that she wondered how she could turn him down. But, ever since her childhood when she'd vowed to be a socialator when she grew up, she always had been a demon when it came to resolutions, so she said:

"Sorry, sky pilot. I'm bushed. I'm just bushed. Hit me some other time, okay?"

"Bushed? I can revive those weary bones, Cass."

His cloying and patronizing confidence made her really angry.

"Starbuck, you louse, sometimes I could just—"

She whirled around and began to walk down the corridor away from him. He chased after her, pleading in a coaxing voice:

"Please, Cass, who knows what might happen my next patrol? I could get—"

That did it. She turned and glared at him, saying:

"Starbuck, don't you ever feel guilty, the way you treat women?"

"Who, me?"

His face displayed an innocence that anyone who didn't know him would have believed.

"I thought so, you slug."

She threw up her arms in despair and marched off. Starbuck stared after her, incredulous. He wasn't used to being turned down by any woman.

"What did I do now?" he muttered.

Cassiopeia's words stuck with him as he roamed the *Galactica*'s corridors, looking for something to do. Had she been right about his treatment of women, about his "line," as she'd called it? Was he too cavalier, too inconsiderate? He did have his tricks, his ploys, his way with persuasive words, all of which he'd used on women in the past, with more success than not. At times he neglected to think of their feelings, of their needs. Maybe he should, as she suggested, feel guilty. He made a conscious effort to feel guilty, but the feeling would not come. He walked on.

Once he muttered aloud, "Me, guilty?"

Baltar sat on his command pedestal and surveyed the activity beneath him. Cylons scurried about. *Well,* he thought, *they didn't exactly scurry, but they were lumbering along at a good clip.* He had really whipped his crew into shape. They now followed his orders adeptly and with speed. His communication with them was nearly as efficient as the telepathic manner in which Imperious Leader sent messages to his officers. The next time he inspected Baltar's basestar, Imperious Leader was certain to be impressed.

Lucifer glided into the command room and approached the pedestal.

"Lucifer!" Baltar shouted happily.

"By your command."

"Is the viper of Ensign Greenbean now ready?"

"Affirmative, commander."

"And the mind-wipe?"

"It has been performed successfully. Once the ensign has traveled far enough, he will suddenly awaken in deep space and have no memories of ever having been captured. He will think he has strayed from his squadron. He will return to the *Galactica,* unaware of what we've done. There will be no clues to his imprisonment. Even the marks of torture have been removed from his body."

"And what exactly have we done, Lucifer? How does your device work from a distance?"

"Similarly to the computer network to which I am connected. I have planted several relays on the ensign's clothing. Some are in the form of buttons; others are so miniscule they are concealed in the threads of his garments. These relays will be activated by remote control. I will do the honors. When they are operative, the waves from the central unit, as programmed by me, will be transmitted outward through the button relays and will permeate every level of the *Galactica.*"

Baltar grinned widely, considering the sweet revenge Lucifer's device would bring him. He could almost see Adama nailed to the wall.

"But won't Greenbean change his uniform once he gets aboard? What happens when he's not wearing it?"

"It is of no consequence. The relays will function effectively no matter where the clothing is put. They are composed of powerful but tiny Cylonate circuits that are virtually undetectable and indestructible. The Cylonate power will be tremendous, no need to worry yourself about that."

Lucifer's explanation elated Baltar.

"Splendid, splendid," he said joyfully. "Good work, Lucifer. I mean it. *Really* good work."

Lucifer was not immune to a compliment, even if it came from Baltar. The lights that gleamed from inside his bulb-shaped head glowed noticeably brighter.

"Well," Baltar said, "what are we waiting for? Let's launch that viper!"

Lucifer turned to the centurion in charge of the base-star's launch bay and ordered:

"Strange as it seems to say it, launch the human's spacecraft."

The centurion began the elaborate Cylon countdown. As it progressed, Baltar whirled around on his pedestal chair, chuckling with satisfaction.

"It'll only be a matter of time now, Adama," he whispered. "This time it will be your head on the block, your head staring up at the falling axe."

Lucifer, his sensitive hearing circuits picking up his commander's whisper, studied Baltar for signs of madness. As Baltar cheered the launching of Greenbean's viper, it occurred to Lucifer that it was possible that Baltar's desire for revenge severely impaired his judgement.

CHAPTER THREE

Athena stared at her monitor screen absentmindedly, barely noticing the few blips and circles that represented the routine alignment of the fleet. Her thoughts were again on the lost pilots. They drifted ghostlike across her screen in a steady line. Her brother Zac led the march. Poor buoyant lovable Zac, his life cut off too soon. A little farther down the line were some of the cadets who'd barely learned to fly a viper before the ships became their coffins. She remembered particularly one cadet named Shields who was prone to practical jokes. His viper was turned into a fireball by a blast from the Ravashol cannon on the ice planet Tairac. Then there was "Killer" Killian, a happy-go-lucky adventurer, shot down while defending the *Galactica* shuttle from Cylon attack. Lining up with the rest of her taller fellow pilots was poor little Gemi, pressed into service as a viper pilot when so many of the other warriors had been felled by that strange disease. She had been killed during the battle in the skies above Kobol. Only Athena and a few others had ever known of the crush that quiet Gemi had had for Starbuck. *What a waste*, Athena thought. Gemi was one of the few pretty young women around whom Starbuck had never hit on. Now she was dead.

As the line of dead pilots passed, Athena was astonished at how many of them had been friends and acquaintances. This was one of the by-products of war, she supposed, to have quick friendships that always could be ended abruptly by a stray Cylon laser beam. She hated living with the threat of unexpected death for all whom she knew, even for those she had never met. It had to end, she felt, but how? When?

Bringing up the rear of her imaginary march of deceased warriors was Greenbean. She didn't know why his passing had so affected her. She'd always liked him, yes, but she'd never spent much time with him. Most of their encounters occurred when he was in the company of other hotshot pilots, when Greenbean was usually hanging back and listening with amusement to their banter. Nevertheless, he'd become a symbol for her of all the dead pilots.

A flashing blip suddenly appeared at the right side of her screen. A blip where no blip should be.

"What—? Colonel Tigh, an anomaly in Sigma Sector."

Tigh was standing behind her an instant later, staring at the screen. Whatever kind of object the blip represented, it was heading toward the *Galactica* at high speed.

"Any I. D.?" Tigh calmly requested. Tigh was never calmer than when there was a possible threat to his ship.

"Too far away to tell," Athena said. "One thing sure, it's a lone spacecraft. No one else anywhere near it."

Tigh swung around and started barking orders.

"Rigel, scan for identification profile."

"Aye, aye, sir."

"Sound yellow alert."

"Yes, sir."

"Ready emergency patrol for launch!"

Starbuck and Boomer rushed into launch bay together. "What's up, Boom-boom?"

"Got me, brother. I was asleep when this roust came."

"This is lucky."

"Lucky?"

"Boomer, I was on the worst run of pyramid draws since I was at the academy and playing the cadet sergeant-major for removal of demerits."

Catching the helmet tossed at him by his ground crew C. W. O., Jenny, Starbuck bounced onto the wing of his viper and performed his famous into-the-saddle leap into the cockpit.

Tigh raced around the control room, shouting orders as he went.

"Instruct the pilots to launch when ready."

"Transfering launch control to viper pilots."

Starbuck's voice could be heard on the open comm-circuit.

"Ready, Boomer?"

"Roger."

"Launching!"

The bridge crew watched their monitors as the two vipers plunged down the launch tubes and out of the *Galactica*. They joined each other close by the ship and headed toward Sigma Sector.

"Anything on the anomaly, Rigel?" Tigh shouted.

"Aye, aye, sir," she answered. "It looks like a viper."

"A viper? But we don't have any patrols out now, do we?"

"Affirmative. Last patrol returned and logged."

"Then who is it? Alert the patrol. It might be another Cylon trap."

"Or one of our pilots, Colonel Tigh," Athena said, "one of our own pilots."

Tigh scowled at Athena.

"What?" he said. "Returned from the dead? There are no—"

"Let's wait and see, sir. I really think we've got one back, I really do."

Athena spoke with the kind of certainty characteristic of her father, and Tigh chose not to attempt to contradict it further.

"The unknown craft seems to be on a steady course for the *Galactica*," Rigel reported. "Red squadron vipers intercepting momentarily."

"It's not trying to avoid our vipers," Athena said. "It's coming right at 'em."

"Colonel?" Rigel said.

"Yes?"

"I have a visual on the intruder. Proceeding now with a scan of its markings."

"Keep at it, Rigel. Has the commander been informed?"

"Affirmative."

"He's here, Colonel," Adama said quietly. He was standing right behind Tigh and his voice, though soft, startled the colonel.

"Adama!" Tigh said. "How long—"

"I arrived only a moment ago. Carry on."

"Colonel!" Rigel shouted.

"What is it, Rigel?"

"We have a positive identification on the intruder. It *is* one of ours apparently. A Colonial Viper, Q series, full batteries, signed out to . . . let's see . . . signed out to Ensign Greenbean!"

"Greenbean!" Athena yelled. She whooped with delight. She recalled that just moments ago she'd been thinking about Greenbean. Had her will somehow brought him back?

"Take it easy, Athena," Adama said. "We only know that it's his viper. It might not be him inside it. Wait and see."

"It's him," Athena said. "I *know* it's Greenbean. I prayed for this."

"Cut the patrol vipers' commcircuit back in, Rigel," Tigh ordered.

"Cutting in . . ."

Starbuck's shout, amplified to such a degree it echoed around the control room, reverberated with joy.

"GREENBEAN! I don't believe—it's really you?"

Greenbean's voice was gentler than the brash lieutenant's.

"Why, sure. Who'd you think it was?"

"A ghost," Boomer said, "that's what I thought."

"Oh, I ain't no ghost. It's just me. I got lost, is all."

"Lost?" Starbuck said. "Do you have any idea how long you've been missing?"

"Well, no. Not long I guess. I just got lost during the battle. Don't know just how 'zackly. Blacked out all of a sudden. I came to, not far from here, just now."

"That doesn't make sense," Boomer said. "You know how long ago that little scrape was?"

"Well, no, guess I don't."

"We'll straighten it all out back on board the *Galactica*," Starbuck said. "C'mon, fellas, let's fly triad formation back. Impress the VIP's with our precision-flying skills, what say?"

"You got it, bucko," Boomer said.

"I'm with ya both," Greenbean said.

"Well, then, let's touch wing tips and give 'em a show."

They did not of course touch wing tips. The phrase was hotshot lingo from the academy. What they did, and everybody aboard the *Galactica* watched the maneuver on monitors, was dip their wing tips toward each other in an elaborate parody of flight etiquette. Then they glided into a triangular formation.

Athena turned away from her console and gloated. She made especially sure her father saw her satisfaction.

"See?" she said.

"Yes, I see," Adama answered, smiling. "Well, ladies and gentlemen, we got one back!"

The crew laughed and cheered. There was a great sense of relief and happiness in the room. The members of the crew couldn't stop glancing at each other and smiling. For a short while dereliction of duty was a virtue aboard the *Galactica*.

Adama approached Tigh and asked:

"Your evaluation?"

Tigh appeared doubtful for a moment, then he said:

"Sir, I'm happy about Greenbean, but—"

"Out with it, Colonel."

"He said he blacked out. That's a long time to be drifting around deep space, unconscious in a viper."

"My sentiments exactly. What do you advise?"

Tigh's voice dropped. Except for Athena, no one but Adama could now hear him.

"For starters, a thorough search of pilot and vehicle. Get a reading of the air inside the cockpit before the ground crew have pried it open. It should show normal signs of content deterioration after so many recyclings. Have Doctor Salik give Greenbean an intense physical. Everything. Especially scan the contents of his stomach to see when nutrition was last ingested. If he's consumed anything other than the normal survival input from viper energy-tubes, it should show up. Interview the pilot extensively, monitor his reactions, use truth-scansion devices."

Adama nodded at each of Tigh's suggestions. He stared at the colonel beneath the frowning aspect of his thick dark eyebrows.

"Tigh, consider those advisements as orders, to be supplemented immediately—as soon as Greenbean's viper slides into launch bay. Don't allow the other pilots or crew anywhere near him until all the initial checks are accomplished."

"It's done, Adama."

Tigh strode off, giving orders as he went.

"What was that all about?" Athena asked. Adama detected the trace of annoyance in her voice.

"Normal cautionary procedures, Athena."

"Normal procedures? You're treating Greenbean like he's a spy. He's the least likely spy in the whole damn crew. Excuse me, father, but—"

"Athena . . ."

Adama spoke her name warningly, to remind her that she was not to invoke their father-daughter relationship while on duty. She caught the message but, angry as she was, would not allow herself to apologize.

"I just think it's important to trust—" she said.

Her persistence angered Adama.

"I trust Greenbean!" he shouted, then noticed the crew watching them. His voice became softer. "That's not the point. There's something . . . something odd about the way he's materialized so suddenly. I've learned never to trust what seems real until I've made every test of its reality."

"I know, I know. If it looks like a daggit, and seems like a daggit, and smells like a daggit, and walks—"

"It's not necessarily a daggit until you've made all the proper tests. I'm sorry, Athena. I *am* overcautious, no doubt about it. Just consider such precautions as part and parcel of the burdens of command. Learn from it. It may not, after all, be long before you—"

"I know, before I command a battlestar, although where you're going to manufacture this wonderful battlestar is beyond me. Apollo is destined for the *Galactica* if you indeed ever give it up. Right now, I'd consider myself lucky to be awarded the helm of the Colonial Movers Transport Ship."

"You know, I believe there may be a position opening up on that very ship."

"Please, Dad—please, commander, I was only joking."

"I'll take that factor into consideration."

The jokes had eased the tension between them. Athena knew her father respected her abilities and that he was short with her only when she failed to perceive the logic of his decisions.

"Vipers approaching launch bay," Rigel said. "Continuing in triad formation. It's quite a sight, sir."

Adama went to Rigel's monitor, watched over her shoulder at the ships gliding and sliding in flamboyant maneuvers as they zeroed in on the *Galactica*'s launch bay.

"A marvelous sight!" he said. "Truly marvelous!"

"Precision flying, huh, Commander?" Athena said, deliberately using one of her father's favorite phrases. He smiled in agreement.

Starbuck's voice again resounded across the bridge:

"Boomer! Greenbean! Let's show those louts on board the *Galactica* what a perfect pinpoint landing looks like when performed from the triad formation. All together now, academy style!"

The crew watched in admiring silence as the trio of vipers, speeding into the launch bay in close formation, performed the landing just as perfectly as Starbuck had promised.

As soon as his viper had stopped, Starbuck gave out with his famous staccato victory yell, knowing he was probably driving a good percentage of his listeners deaf. Then he bellowed:

"Kobol bless my soul, I'm going to break my arm patting my back for that landing. Boomer, Greenbean!"

"Yo!"

"Yo!"

"I want to see the both of you in an instant. We're going to appropriate a case of ambrosa and celebrate the return of our wandering warrior in style!"

"With you on that, Starbuck," Boomer said.

"Oh, I don't need any ceremony, fellas," Greenbean said. Starbuck thought he sounded like a child, almost as young as Apollo's son, Boxey.

"You may not need ceremony, ensign," Starbuck said, "but we sure as hell do."

"Always good to have a reason to celebrate," Boomer agreed happily.

"Then I guess—what the—"

"What is it, Greenbean?" Starbuck asked, alarmed by the confusion in Greenbean's voice.

"I don't know," Greenbean responded. "I just got the high sign to remain in my cockpit. Starbuck, the whole launch crew is crawling all around my viper."

"Ah, they just want to be the first to welcome you home, buddy."

"Maybe, but—well, I just don't think so, Starbuck. They got tools and stuff. What's going on?"

"Sit tight. I'll be right there."

Starbuck sprang out of his cockpit, flinging his flight helmet into Jenny's waiting arms, their traditional returning ritual. He leaped off the viper's wing onto the launch bay floor and broke into a run. Boomer joined him, halfway to Greenbean's viper. They didn't see Tigh until he stepped into their way, gesturing for them to stop. The two pilots' skidding to a stop was not as fancy as their pinpoint viper landing had been.

"Whoa, boys," Tigh said. "You can't go over there just now. Command orders."

"What is this?" Starbuck demanded.

"Greenbean's being, well, quarantined for a short while. Normal procedure for—"

"What do you mean, normal procedure?"

"Yeah," Boomer said, "we just want to welcome our buddy back, that's all."

"And you will," Tigh said. "But we have to take a few steps to protect the personnel aboard the *Galactica*."

"There's no precedent—" Boomer protested.

"There is now," Tigh said firmly, making sure his volatile pilots recognized the authority in his voice. "Remember, Lieutenant Boomer, how you came back from a routine patrol carrying that organism inside you, and then nearly killed off the entire crew with your illness? How's that for a precedent? We don't know what Greenbean may have picked up out there."

"In his cockpit?" Starbuck asked.

"We don't know for certain he was always in his cockpit," Tigh said.

"Are you saying he's lying? Greenbean wouldn't know how to lie, sir."

"I'm not suggesting he's lying. We merely have to take some precautions, and that is all. Please excuse me, lieutenants, I must see to Greenbean's reindoctrination. He will be returned to duty soon, don't worry."

Tigh joined the crew at Greenbean's viper and began to supervise operations there. Starbuck and Boomer felt both humbled and confused.

"I don't like this, Boomer."

"Nor I, pal."

"I don't like it when anyone impugns the honor of a colonial warrior, I don't care who it is, even Tigh."

"Well, we'll just have to adopt the old academy attitude: wait until they get off the pot and then fire when ready."

"Don't think I don't intend to make a few waves about this. C'mon, let's get a dose of ambrosa, wash the taste of all this out of our mouths."

As they left launch bay, Starbuck got a glimpse of Greenbean, still in the cockpit of his viper. The poor boy appeared to be bewildered, and more than a little sad. Starbuck swore to himself, invoking all seven levels of Caprican curses, and once again told himself that, if things got worse, he'd quit the service. Although he knew that, as long as there was a single Cylon in pursuit of them, he could never turn his back on the fleet, making that vow usually made him feel better. This time, however, even the vow didn't work. He continued to feel angry, and miserable.

Signing off on a clipboarded Vailean invoice, Apollo let the stevedores know they could begin unloading the cargo shuttle. Sheba and Bojay followed him out of the hold into a corridor leading to the elevators.

"That's the last shipment of braka, according to my figures," Sheba said.

"Braka?" Bojay asked. "Never heard of it. Some kind of machine oil?"

Sheba's laugh had that high delicate sound to it that made others perceive her as friendly and merry.

"No," she said. "Braka's a vegetable native to Vaile. Quite tasty and chockful of nutrition. You'll love it, big guy."

"I never met a vegetable I liked. I doubt braka'll be any different."

"You sound like Boxey," Apollo commented. "I can't get good food down his—what's that?"

Apollo pointed to a group near the bank of elevators. They were citizens of the fleet, talking eagerly among themselves. The group parted slightly, and Sire Uri could be seen in the middle of it, chattering away energetically.

"What do you mean?" Bojay asked. The group looked normal to him.

"Those people," Apollo said. "They're up to something, I know it."

"Apollo," Sheba said, "you're getting downright paranoid. They're just a bunch of civilians talking. I haven't heard about any martial law being invoked recently. They're still allowed to congregate anywhere except in the restricted areas, aren't they? Discuss anything? I hadn't noticed that freedom being taken away from us lately."

Apollo was a bit annoyed at Sheba's gentle chidings. It was difficult to get angry at her, but she could easily ruffle a fellow's feathers with a few words.

"Of course they're—it's just that, look . . . look who's in the center of it all."

"Well, I'll bite, who? I can't say as I know any of those people."

"It's Uri. Sire Uri. Remember, I told you about him. I just warned father that he was becoming dangerous again."

"Dangerous?" Bojay said. "Apollo, he's just chatting with a few people while waiting for a lift to come."

"Sire Uri never chats," Apollo said. "Not without a purpose anyway. And a devious purpose at that. He's never happy unless he's causing trouble." Apollo took another close look at the group, then announced: "I'm going to break this up."

Both Sheba and Bojay reached for Apollo's arms to try to stop him from recklessly confronting the civilian group, but Apollo was quickly out of reach. Sheba looked at her brother and shrugged, then the two of them followed after Apollo.

"Sire Uri," Apollo called as he reached the group.

Uri separated himself from the others and, with a cunning and sinister smile, greeted the young captain.

"Ah, the commander's son," he said. It seemed Uri could never resist announcing Apollo's relationship with Adama loudly and clearly. "You all know Captain Apollo, the hero of . . . well, the hero of innumerable impressive exploits."

The small crowd murmured its approval. At the same time they seemed, in unison, to shuffle backwards, as if afraid of Apollo's authority with them.

"What can I do for you, Captain Apollo?"

Apollo could barely keep his voice at a normal level.

"You're trying to soft-soap me, Uri."

Uri's eyes became unnaturally wide in exaggerated innocence.

"Never, captain, *never*. You have my genuine admiration."

"What's this all about?"

"What's what all about?"

"You and these people. What's going on?"

"Apollo—" Sheba said and touched Apollo's arm. He shook off her loose grip. She looked away, hurt by his gesture but not wanting him to see it. She didn't have to worry. All of his concentration was on Uri.

"Nothing is, as you say, going on," Uri said.

"Come off it, Uri. I heard enough as I came down the corridor. This is about Vaile, isn't it? My father's orders on the subject aren't enough for you, are they? You're trying to influence—"

"Influence? Me, influence? Captain, you insult me—as usual, I might add. You've not been off my back since that day on the *Rising Star*." He turned and addressed his next remark to the group: "It's a vendetta."

The crowd, with their mutterings and nods, appeared to agree with him. Apollo was slightly disconcerted by their antagonism toward him. He had always had difficulty with assembled groups of people. He did not know how to be affable, how to appeal to them—an ability that Uri had mastered incredibly.

Sheba made another attempt to ameliorate the situation.

"Come, Apollo," she said, "we've got work to do. Another shuttle due in a moment."

Apollo did not seem to hear her words. He kept staring at Uri.

"You know the commander's will on this subject," he said. "We cannot stay on—"

Uri's expression was so stagey, one would have thought he was playing to a massive audience, instead of this intimate little convocation in a Galactican corridor.

"The commander's will. You mean, your *father's* will, don't you?" He turned to his people. "This man is the puppet of his father. Ignore him."

"Uri—" Apollo yelled.

"Ignore him," Uri stage whispered.

The people in the group slowly and showily turned their backs on Apollo. Uri, smirking, joined them, speaking in his unctuous way:

"As I was saying . . ."

What he did say was innocuous, something about scarcity of rations. Apollo was not sure what he should do—stay where he was and stare at backs or cut his losses and walk away.

"Let's go, Apollo," Sheba said softly.

"Uri!" Apollo shouted.

Uri stuck his head out of the crowd, smiling arrogantly.

"Yes, Captain?"

"I'm reporting this."

"Please do. The commander does so like to be informed of the popular sentiments. Good day, Captain."

Following Uri's lead, the group walked away from the bank of elevators. Not a single person looked back. How does the man hold sway over others, Apollo wondered.

"C'mon, buddy," Bojay said, "I got a new joke that's too hot for Sheba's tender ears."

Sheba laughed.

"No way, Bojay," she said. "I want to hear it."

"I'm in no mood for jokes," Apollo mumbled sullenly.

"Exactly the time when you should hear one." They began walking down the corridor to the hold where the new shuttle's goods would soon be unloaded. "Now, once there was this Cylon who had a peculiar defect . . ."

Baltar would have been pleased to see how well the relay transmitters had been concealed in Greenbean's flight uniform. The clothing was scanned and studied intensively but the implantations were not discovered. Lucifer's methods of concealment, interweaving the thin microcircuits with the threads of the clothing and manufacturing the transmit-units to duplicate exactly buttons and snaps, prevented the Galactican investigators from detecting the devices. Since Greenbean had been launched on the series of interrogations and tests the investigators were subjecting him to, the uniform had been laser cleaned and pressed in the commissary laundry, and he was wearing it again. The rays that poured off the suit did not show up on any of the ship's detecting devices.

Greenbean's last ordeal was an intense physical examination. After body and brain scanning, Doctor Salik tested him with various injections and extractions. It was all very painful and annoying to a young man who just wanted to get back to his friends and party for a while. As Salik poked his stomach, Greenbean squirmed unhappily.

"Ticklish, ensign?" Salik asked.

"A little."

"The women must just love you."

Greenbean did not understand what the doctor meant, but he chose not to question the man. Salik often responded brusquely and made his patients feel foolish for asking.

"Well," Salik said, turning away from the examination table, "you check out all right, far as I can see. Get dressed, ensign."

Greenbean buttoned up his tunic, unknowingly touching at least three areas that concealed Lucifer's relay devices.

"Gosh," he said, "the way everybody's been studyin' and pokin' at me, I thought I was either the enemy or dyin' o' some rare disease."

"You're the hologram of health, ensign. Now get out of here. I got real work to do."

Salik went to his desk intercom, and spoke into it—to the commander, who'd been monitoring the dull routine of the physical exam.

"Commander?"

"Yes, doc?"

Salik didn't like being called doc, and usually discouraged people from the practice. But he had never chided Adama about it.

"Greenbean checks out A-one. You could put him on patrol right away."

"That's good news. Relay my good wishes to the ensign."

Salik turned away from the communicator as Greenbean finished dressing.

"You heard that?"

"Yes."

As Salik resumed his work, Greenbean approached him tentatively, unsure of whether to speak to the gruff doctor or not.

"Doctor?"

"Yes?"

"You think something happened to me out there? You know, something dangerous?"

"I don't diagnose the military aspect of an operation, ensign. From a medical standpoint, you appear to be the same Greenbean who left here, except for some bruises on your back, which probably came from being knocked around in battle. Brain-scan shows you definitely were out, but not why. That's about all I know."

"I realize you'd just be guessing. I just want somebody to tell me somethin'. What do you think?"

Salik fidgeted. He was always annoyed when a patient started asking questions, especially after he'd said all he could reasonably say.

"Well, ensign, you want intuition, I got that by the beakerful. Yeah, I think *something* happened to you out there, but I'm damned if I know what."

"I feel something, too."

"What?"

"I just don't know. It's like I lived through something, and then some god or other cut that part right out of my life. I thought I'd blacked out, but I don't think that's it. I didn't just black out. There was something else. What do you think, Doctor Salik?"

"I don't know either, son. Might just be something in your head, something mental—"

"You think I'm going crazy?"

"No, didn't mean that. I'm saying you might be right. Something might have happened. We'll have to wait until you remember it, that's all."

Greenbean frowned.

"Maybe. But I think I *am* crazy."

Salik often encountered cases where the patient considered himself crazy. Sometimes the feeling was just the result of battle fatigue or loneliness or too much attention focused on duty, and sometimes the patient was genuinely crazy. Greenbean was, according to his personality profile, acting strangely, but Salik doubted he was crazy.

"Get some rest or get drunk," he told Greenbean. "Have some fun with your buddies or a girl friend. Forget about all this for a while. You need anything to help you sleep?"

Greenbean smiled.

"You forget, doc, I just had the longest sleep I ever had."

"Don't call me doc."

"Aye, aye, Doctor Salik."

Greenbean slouched toward the door so pathetically that Salik could not help but speak compassionately to him:

"Don't worry, son. You know the saying: it'll all blow out the chute before the journey's finished."

"I don't understand."

"Get away from here."

Salik shook his head after the door had slid closed. The ensign was so young. He shouldn't even have to devote his life to fighting battles.

The door slid open again and Salik's assistant, Cassiopeia, came into the room.

"I have the other reports on Greenbean, as you requested," she said.

"And?"

"Everything checks out okay. Greenbean, his ship, his clothes, all okay."

"Now I'm *really* bothered."

"Why's that?"

"I don't like it when everything checks out okay. In any given situation, there has got to be something wrong. Something small, something you don't notice at first, but something."

Outside the room, Greenbean had started walking slowly down the hall. Most of the people he passed didn't pay much attention to him. For some of them, sad and regretful memories suddenly assaulted their minds.

CHAPTER FOUR

The command chamber of Baltar's base-star had not been so busy since the last massive assault wave had been sent out against the human fleet, and that had happened some time ago. Now all the complicated flight and detection machinery was activated. Lights flashed so incessantly the room seemed in the midst of an internal lightning storm. Cylon centurions, who normally moved with an almost comic awkwardness, now worked with such fury that they were momentarily graceful. Beeps, buzzes, squawks, and whistles were rapidly emitted by the overwhelming array of Cylon technology, and these sounds frequently built to such a cacophony that Baltar had to hold his hands over his ears.

The activity made Baltar nervous and he paced more frenetically than usual. Occasionally he interrupted his pacing to shout orders to Lucifer, who appeared to act on them while actually continuing to guide all operations his own way. He had become quite adept at the clandestine subversion of his superior's orders. The more Baltar paced, the surlier his frequent remarks to Lucifer became.

"Lucifer!"

"Your wish, commander?"

"The relay devices for—for your contraption—"

"LEADER, you mean?"

"Of course, LEADER! You should know what I mean even when I don't say it. That's what being second-in-command is all about, you fancy sack of scrap metal."

Lucifer disliked Baltar's hurling of insults at him, but his long tenure with the human had taught him to conceal his anger. Baltar's insults became more savage and more childish when he was in an agitated or worried state. Lucifer used such clear indicators of Baltar's temperament to manipulate the man without him being aware of it.

"Well?" Baltar asked nervously. "Well, tell me!"

"You have not completed your request, commander."

Lucifer's voice was so smoothly modulated that Baltar could not detect the sarcasm in it.

"You're supposed to read my mind and carry out orders before I articulate them. Lucifer, if you can bring yourself to concentrate, answer me this: is the LEADER relay setup in operation as yet?"

"Yes. It has been ever since the ensign returned to the *Galactica*."

"I'm happy to hear it. What's happening there?"

"Since we cannot monitor directly, I cannot accurately respond to that question. However, my ratiocinative circuits do give me the ability to surmise..."

Lucifer interrupted himself in order to give an order to a centurion who was about to make a course change mistakenly. Lucifer had to keep a continual watch on these first-brain Cylons, who tended to mix up orders if not expressed to them clearly.

"Well, Lucifer!" Baltar shouted.

Lucifer glided to Baltar.

"Yes?"

"Surmise, surmise..."

"If my calculations are correct, and they must be, the

guilt-waves that we are transmitting now should be gradually but steadily permeating through the *Galactica*. By this time, I believe, the humans there are feeling the onset of uneasiness. Creeping doubts about their present and past actions are perhaps making them irritable or sad or overemotional in their actions and reactions. They will undoubtedly also be wondering why everyone around them has become so strange. It is possible they will begin to distrust each other. Discipline will become lax. Interpersonal relationships will deteriorate severely. Life, in general, will be difficult."

As Baltar envisaged the result of LEADER's rays upon the people aboard the *Galactica*, his pleasure at the prospect of ultimate victory increased. He had an urge to pat Lucifer on the back, even though he knew it would have no effect on the creature and might, in fact, injure his hand.

"Wonderful, Lucifer, wonderful. I'll give you a medal for this."

"I would prefer not."

"You don't care for medals? Come, Lucifer, is it possible that you are humble?"

"Not humble. Medals are exterior boasts of achievement. I require no such displays, which are best for humans and the lower order of Cylons."

Baltar, irritated, resumed his pacing.

"You'd take all the joy out of life, Lucifer."

"I see no utility for joy. It only—"

Lucifer was interrupted by a courier-centurion carrying a dispatch from Communication Center. After he had read the dispatch's surprising words, he approached Baltar and said:

"A message from Alliance Headquarters, Baltar. A liaison ship is on its way to us."

"Liaison ship? What in Kobol is that?"

"In this case, it is a vessel whose main passenger is a special messenger carrying a communication for us that cannot be sent through the normal channels."

"What's it for? Is it important?"

"Undoubtedly."

Baltar began lightly pounding his fist against his forehead, a gesture that Lucifer knew indicated extreme perturbation.

"Do you know what this is all about?" he asked.

"Since it has been classified secret, I cannot know."

Baltar could not think straight. What was Imperious Leader up to? Why this secret ship? Was it a threat to him?

"Lucifer, what should we do about this . . . this liaison ship?"

"Wait for it to arrive here, I expect."

"Not with this base star in the shambles it's in." Baltar paced now at a rapid rate. "Dispatch cleaning squads." His voice was high and thin, even though he was trying to shout his orders with authority. "Polish up everything, every surface, every nut and bolt. Polish up the command consoles. Polish up yourself, Lucifer!"

Lucifer could not figure why the need for shiny surfaces always seemed to emerge when Baltar felt threatened. The man seemed to equate stern discipline with high polish. Nevertheless, such mundane details would serve to occupy the commander's mind for a while and keep him from bothering Lucifer about more important matters, so Lucifer didn't mind implementing these particular orders.

"By your command," Lucifer said and rolled out of the command chamber.

With Lucifer out of the way, Baltar felt free to speak aloud. There were only the Cylon warriors to listen, and they never paid attention to anything but a direct order, anyway.

"What should I do? This messenger, he wouldn't be coming to remove me from command, would he?" He recalled the dream in which the executioner's axe had fallen and wondered if it had been an omen. "They'll have to drag me off this ship kicking and screaming." In his mind the axe fell toward his face over and over again. "No, not that again. I can't—but that *was* just a dream. Lucifer planted it in my head with his damn device. I'm in the hierarchy. They won't just—just—they couldn't! Could they? Everything's got to be just right. Centurion! Report on the status of the ship!"

"Status conditional," the navigator-centurion said in that flat scratchy voice that first-brainers seemed to share. "Engine repair crews working at all times. Progress is reported as slow. Full work report is forthcoming."

"Tell them to step on it!"

"Step on it?"

Baltar could tell that, as so often happened, his phrase was being understood literally. The Cylon was clearly wondering why Cylon feet should fall on the work report.

"No, not step on it, idiot! I mean, get it to me as fast as possible. What is our troop deployment level, centurion?"

"Reinforcements are in transit. Arrival is imminent. Troop strength will then be full."

"And the fightercraft status?"

"New ships have arrived and are being fitted. They will be in readiness imminently."

"What is all this *imminently?* Inform all crews I want all work done now. Not imminently, but now. Yesterday, if possible."

"Yesterday? But—"

"Never mind. Just do it!"

Baltar, for the first time in centons, felt confident. With troop strength up and a full wall of Cylon raiders soon to be ready, he *knew* that this time he would totally wipe out the *Galactica* and its ridiculous ragtag fleet. He would have to time the attack carefully. Allow time for LEADER to take its toll, and then strike.

Adama gripped the microphone to his journal-recorder tightly, as he always did when considering a problem. He leaned his elbows on his desk and spoke:

"Tigh informs me that all tests on Ensign Greenbean have proven out negative. There is nothing physically wrong with the young officer, except for some minor contusions. His viper also checks out fine. There seems little reason to doubt his story, strange as it does seem. Well, there have been stranger occurrences in my experience as the skipper of this battlestar."

He didn't usually refer to himself as skipper. It sounded too undignified. Yet, that had been how his father had referred to the job in the days when it was his. Even after the transfer of command had taken place, crewmen tended to call Adama's father, "the old skipper." That had been so long ago . . .

"I have devoted practically a lifetime to serving our people in the war with the Cylons, a war that seemingly will never end, which has been extended by our flight from annihilation. I will always wonder if—but never mind, scratch that, that is not even a personal entry."

He rubbed his eyes and tried to remember what it was that he had intended to record in his journal. He found it hard to focus his mind. He did not usually feel so unsettled when in the privacy of his quarters.

"Let's see. What else is there to log in? The operation on Vaile—it is proceeding superbly. Captain Apollo has everything well in hand. Shuttles are going to and fro, bringing supplies and fuel to us. On return trips we are sending our experts to help out the people of Vaile in their— their—"

He shook his head, trying to clear it.

"I can't seem to focus on what I'm saying. Perhaps this isn't the time to record this. No, it's important to keep up such a discipline. The log must be maintained."

He stared off into space, at the many stars he could see out his viewport. The stars suggested to him the magnitude of his journey and made him wonder if their goal of seeking Earth was futile. Perhaps he had misread the lights that had appeared to inform him of Earth's coordinates. Well, it was no time for such reveries.

"Maybe it's time for a personal entry. Although I don't know what I can say. It's extremely difficult to describe feelings for which there don't seem to be words. Feelings that are so vague they seem just out of reach. I've held command for so long now, have seen my fellow officers destroyed in battle, annihilated in the cowardly Cylon ambush, have seen members of my own family killed. I've done everything I could to—I could to—to do what? To perform my duty? To glorify ideals that are in some ways questionable, or at least speculative. I'm not a fanatic for war. I never have been. Yet—here I am, with a lifetime of warring behind me. Although I deeply believe in love, kindness, generosity of spirit, faith, I have to order others to perform violent acts, have to watch them kill and be killed. How long can it all go on? Does Uri have the right idea? Forget Earth, settle on Vaile. We haven't been troubled by Cylons for some time. If we hid away here, on Vaile, perhaps they never *would* find us, as Uri suggests. But could I ever be sure of that? Could I ever become as enamored of paradise as Uri has?"

The party for Greenbean was rapidly becoming one of the most raucous in the raucous history of *Galactica* celebrations. At any given time so many people were laughing that there seemed to be one continuous choral laugh that had begun shortly after the party had gotten rolling. Ambrosa flowed steadily from silver and gold pitchers, and the hardier drinkers were downing the rougher tasting grog so quickly that the crewpeople who'd been drafted as stewards were running themselves ragged trying to keep the grog bowls well filled.

Greenbean sat at a table at the center of the gathering, and was very much at the center of everyone's attention. Men and women came by in an almost steady stream congratulating him on his return. He felt proud, both for the friendly waves emanating from his friends and colleagues, and for the unusually spick-and-span way he looked in his clean well-pressed uniform. The slight epidermal tingle that he felt from the operation of Lucifer's relay units he attributed to his excitement.

Lieutenant Jolly sat beside him, chatting energetically.

"You're looking tiptop, Greeny, even to the spit and polish."

"Thanks, buddy."

"They should make you admiral."

Jolly's slightly drunken good humor made Greenbean laugh uproariously. Starbuck, sitting across from Greenbean, raised his ambrosa glass high.

"A toast to the returning hero!" he roared.

"Another one?" Boomer said.

"That makes ten, don't it?" Ensign Giles said.

"Nah," said Cadet Cree. "At least twelve."

"Frack!" Starbuck shouted. "Who cares? To Greenbean, warrior supreme."

At the end of the toast Starbuck sat back down hard, realizing that the ambrosa was rushing to his head faster than usual. He ought to go search out a bunk and lie down. He wanted to think, anyway. In spite of the general joyousness of the party, Starbuck felt low. He couldn't figure out why. It was just a mood that had flowed over him along with the flow of ambrosa.

Sipping at his drink, he glanced around the room. Cassiopeia was a few tables away, glaring at him. Her eyes were unemotional. He couldn't tell whether they were friendly or not. Breaking eye contact with her, he then saw that Athena glowered at him, too. He thought of the way he'd courted both women, sometimes simultaneously, and wondered if what Cassiopeia had said about him were true. Maybe he should feel guilty for the way he treated women. Maybe he should settle down and cease his philandering habits. Maybe he should become more like Apollo—less hotheaded, more considerate of people outside his squadron. Maybe he should stop chasing women altogether. He could, after all, be kind of a creep sometimes, expending his energy in the pursuit of his romantic goals instead of considering the needs of the women themselves.

As he continued to survey the partygoers in the room, he noticed that there was a large number of the *Galactica*'s female personnel with their eyes on him. He had made a play, at one time or another, for each and every one of them.

He gulped down the rest of his ambrosa and quickly poured more from the table's gleaming golden pitcher. He was afraid to look; he might find more women staring at him as part of the chorus of his disapproving victims.

Now he really felt lousy.

A bizarre weakness had enveloped Adama. He was no longer able to dictate his log entry and merely stared off into space. He still held the microphone.

A knock on his cabin door shook him out of his trance.

"Come in," he said.

Apollo came in the room, looking distressed. Adama wondered what had made his son so often somber. He longed for the times when they had joked together more freely, or at least had been generally more at ease when in each other's company.

"Commander—"

"Yes, son, sit down."

"Son? What happened to command discipline, the no-referring to family relationships during duty hours?"

Apollo smiled warmly as he pulled up a chair and sat in it. Adama was glad to see that smile. It reminded him, at least momentarily, of the better times.

"We're alone here. Nobody can hear, so I guess I can call you son if I want to."

"The log mike is still open, Father."

"I forgot."

Adama slid the flat microphone back into its niche and shut off the log. Swinging around on his chair to face his son, he said:

"Well, Apollo?"

For a moment Apollo appeared reluctant to speak, then he said slowly and cautiously:

"Don't bite my head off, but . . . it's about Sire Uri."

"I've talked with him."

"Well, perhaps the talk did no good. I caught him trying to stir up a fuss with some people in a corridor down on Delta Level. I don't know exactly what he was saying to them, but it looked to me like he was being his usual conniving self."

"But you don't have any clearcut evidence he was—"

"Father, we can't wait around for him to go public with his treachery, we have to—"

"Apollo, I will not have anyone convicted of a crime, or even an offense against the common good, on anyone's word. Even yours."

"My word is the *last* one you'll take."

That remark, and the bitter manner in which Apollo voiced it, brought back the old distance between father and son. Both men, although cool when quick action was required, could become inflamed with anger rapidly when one of them attacked the other. Adama vowed to stave off this conflict and, although he was furious, kept his voice steady in replying:

"I believe you, Apollo. I know you're telling me exactly what you saw. And fairly. And I have good reason to believe that Uri is trying to create a little dissidence in order to get his way."

"Then why—"

"We have to wait. If Uri doesn't coax enough people to his side, we have only a minor disturbance. If he does, well, *then* we have a problem we'll be forced to deal with."

"Deal with? Why be even polite to Uri and his gang? Father, we could leave Uri on Vaile, and it'd be good riddance for the fleet."

Adama felt a strong urge to just agree with Apollo, and then turn that agreement into an order.

"I wish we could, I really do. But Vaile has too many . . . attractions, Apollo. If we let Uri go there, others would surely follow, with or without our blessings. We can't afford to lose many more of our people."

"And we can't deprive them of your dream, can we?"

Apollo's sarcasm was broad, so that his father couldn't miss it. Adama could not keep his anger out of his voice as he responded:

"I don't know what you mean, but—"

"I mean, you believe that, because you so desire to find Earth, you have to take the rest of us with you."

"Apollo!"

"I'm sorry, father, I didn't mean to say that. I have faith

in your dream of Earth. I really believe we'll find Earth.
It's just that there's no reason to drag the whole fleet there
with you. Perhaps you *should* let some of them settle here,
let—"

"That will be enough, Apollo."

The icy coldness that the entire ship feared had come
into Adama's voice. Even Apollo knew he couldn't fight
that.

"I'm dismissed?" he said bitterly.

"You're dismissed, Captain."

After Apollo had stalked out, his anger trailing after him
like vapor from the exhaust of a vipercraft, Adama regretted
his terse withdrawal from the argument. There had been no
point to increasing the distance between him and his son.
One of them had to loosen up; they couldn't both be stiff-
backed all the time. On the one hand, he was proud of
Apollo for the Adama-like firmness and conviction of his
actions; on the other, he hated that coolness in Apollo nearly
as much as he sometimes despised it in himself.

Perhaps he should have followed Apollo's advice. Uri
was of little use to the *Galactica*. If you blew him out a
waste chute right now, you'd have a hard time telling him
from the space garbage. Yet, it was more important to keep
the fleet together than to sacrifice its unity by treating a
single person as expendable, even one as clearly expendable
as Sire Uri.

No, he had been right. Uri must stay. But he wished that
he had not alienated Apollo at the expense of command
necessity.

The party for Greenbean had become wild, outrageous,
loud, and a trifle unpleasant. Nerves were getting frayed,
tempers were rising, all emotions were becoming heightened. Joy had seemed to flee the room, replaced by a fake
heartiness that was deteriorating into sheer noise and the
frantic effort to look happy in order to hide the growing
sadness that was affecting almost every partygoer.

In the midst of all the jauntiness, many among the
Galactican personnel were already under the influence

of Lucifer's guilt machine, moaning or whining or loudly complaining.

A young ground crewman, his eyes tearing up, was saying: "I should have checked that pin. If I had, Stentron'd be alive today. All I had to do was check one little—"

Two or three tables away, a brawny engineer was protesting: "So what? I served some time in the brig. I deserved it. So, what's it to you?"

A pretty but sad-eyed woman in a corner of the room, leaned close to the face of her lover and whispered: "I'm sorry, darling, I really am. I never meant to—"

A red-haired launch-bay supervisor was crying vehemently and saying:

"Yeah, I cheated, and don't think I don't regret it. Every day of my life, I regret it."

The woman in charge of personnel duty rosters spoke flatly:

"When I was a child, I slashed my brother's face with a broad sharp knife. He was disfigured. Ragged lines across his cheek. For life. For as long as he did live, anyway. The lousy Cylons got him, they—"

A man from the logistics section held his head in his hands and said to no one in particular: "There's never enough time. I work hard, damn hard, but I got to work harder. I'll never be able to—"

Even if he could have listened to any of these people, Starbuck would have heard nothing. After downing several ambrosas in a row, he was now, uncharacteristically, nursing a drink. He felt as if all energy had been siphoned out of him. Although he actively surveyed the party with his dark blue eyes, the eyes were glassy and he saw little. He did trace some of the movements of the women he'd known.

Boomer, who was speaking jovially to Starbuck, was one of the few in the room who was quite unaffected by the relays in Greenbean's clothing. He may have been immune to the device's rays, or perhaps, in his careful intellectual way, he had defined his own guilts well and could not succumb to emotional concern over them.

"You look like the bottom of a Cylon battlesuit," Boomer said to Starbuck. "Cheer up, pal."

"Get lost, Boomer."

Boomer was shocked. He simply wasn't used to his old friend being surly, except to the occasional commanding officer. And, for all their history of friendly banter, Starbuck had never tried to dismiss him rudely before.

"Hey," Boomer said, "what's wrong, pal?"

"Nothing. Nothing's wrong."

"Here you are, acting like you've lost your last viper, and you say nothing's wrong."

"Boomer, stop being cute. I'm tired of it. Leave me alone, or your jaw's gonna wind up part of that far wall."

"Hey, you don't even have to produce logical arguments. I'm going."

When he saw how angrily Boomer was backing off, Starbuck realized what he'd done to his oldest friend.

"I'm sorry, Boomer. Boy, sometimes I really do treat you like so much melted felgercarb, don't I?"

"Ah, it's—"

"You know, I was just sitting here, taking stock of my life. God, I got a lot of markers waiting for me when I die."

"Say again? I'm not used to you attempting to be metaphysical, bucko."

"I mean, I've just been looking around here, this room. At Athena, Cassiopeia, half the other ladies here. In this room alone, Boomer, not to mention dozens of other rooms elsewhere. I really know how to treat a woman, Boomer. How to treat a woman *rotten*."

Boomer clamped a hand on the back of Starbuck's neck and said soothingly:

"That's the ambrosa talking, friend."

Starbuck's sad eyes looked down at the table.

"Is it?" he asked. "Maybe, maybe not."

On the other side of the room, Dietra and Cassiopeia sat side by side. Neither of them appeared to be particularly happy. Dietra leaned toward Cassiopeia, and muttered:

"You look as down as I feel, Cass."

"Do I? I don't know how I feel. I've been thinking about the past."

"You, too? Wow. I was just thinking about my folks, how they wanted me to be a social butterfly and here I am, a viper pilot. I never saw them again after—"

Her voice drifted off as she pondered her memories of her family.

"I was thinking of when I was a socialator," Cassiopeia said abruptly. "At the time I thought it was the greatest life possible. Now, I don't know. It doesn't seem like much. You know, so many people I've met, all the pure thinkers and tough judges, kind of blanch when I tell them what I was. What right do they have to judge me from their narrow experiences? Yet, I wonder, was I wrong?"

"God, I don't know."

Dietra's voice was bleary from drink.

"Me, either. I can't seem to shake the feeling that somehow I wasted that part of my life. And I used to be so proud . . ."

Cassiopeia picked up her beaker of ambrosa, but couldn't find the interest to drink any of it.

Apollo had intended to come to the party but, after the fight with his father and the old memories now flooding back to him, he couldn't work up any enthusiasm for celebration. In the corridor outside his father's quarters, he leaned against the wall, brushed away a few tears and shut his eyes. He opened them again at the sound of Tigh's gentle voice. Tigh had managed to come up to him silently.

"Are you sick, Apollo? I could walk with you to Life Center, have Doctor Sal—"

"What? Oh, no, I'm not sick. Just a little blue. Fight with father, I guess, did it. Ridiculous argument, really, but I couldn't control my temper."

"He'll understand."

"Will he? I'm never sure."

"Be sure."

Tigh walked on toward the door to Adama's cabin.

"Colonel?" Apollo called after him.

"I was thinking just now. About Zac. How I left him behind."

"It wasn't your fault."

"Wasn't it?"

Apollo didn't wait for a response to his question. He ambled down the corridor without looking back. Tigh, puzzled, watched him go. He wondered when Apollo would let go and forgive himself. There was really nothing to forgive. Apollo had had to warn the fleet after he and his brother had discovered the Cylon double-cross, which meant leaving Zac hobbling along in a damaged viper. Zac's ship had simply been an easy target for a bunch of Cylons. It was an act of war, and not Apollo's fault. *Apollo,* Tigh thought, *is too much like his father*. Both of them pursued responsibility as an animal to be cornered in a formal hunt.

Hardly anyone at the party was now cheerful or happy. Greenbean had reached new depths of glum misery. He was practically catatonic. Jolly struggled to draw a smile out of him. Finally, he said:

"I guess you must be worn out, huh? Why don't you go to your bunk, take a snooze?"

"Sure, Jolly, sure."

But Greenbean made no move to lift himself off his chair.

"Well?" Jolly asked.

"Well, what?"

"Take a rest. Now."

"Sure."

Greenbean wanted to go to his quarters and plop down on his bunk, but he couldn't work up the energy. His struggle with the guilt pouring out from LEADER's relays, the force of which was strongest in the area around him, provided him with a guilt he could not understand. The mind-wipe had taken away the memories that were the source of his guilty feelings. The result was that he simply could not recall just what it was that he felt himself guilty of.

Jolly tried to lift Greenbean out of his chair. Normally he could lift Greenbean's lightweight body easily but now it was too limp, too heavy. Some of the other pilots were

staring at Greenbean oddly. Jolly laughed and said, a bit
too loudly:

"He's had a bit too much ambrosa."

"I don't feel a thing," Greenbean muttered.

"That's your problem."

"Yep, that *is* my problem."

Jolly was about to say more, but his attention was distracted by a fight breaking out a few meters from him.

"It was my fault!" the first battler yelled.

"The Lord Kobol take you, you lie!" said the second
one. "It was *my* fault, and nobody else's!"

"Frack! You always have to take the credit."

"What do you mean, credit? I could lose my stripes at
my review."

"What do you mean, *your* review? *My* review. It was my
fault!"

"MINE!"

The first combatant took a wild swing at the second, and
soon they were head to head, mixing it up fiercely. Jolly,
who hated such absurd battles, especially when they broke
out at a buddy's party, tried to intervene, but one of the
fighters hooked him one in the jaw. He fell back. Ensign
Giles, his stubby little legs kicking away in front of him,
fought his way into the melee. A gaggle of Blue Squadron
pilots saw the chance for a good brawl and began fighting
among themselves. Soon the whole roomful of people were
either in the middle of the battle royal, or standing near
walls, gloomily watching the brawlers swing wildly and
rarely land effective blows. Tables were hurled and chairs
were broken, sometimes over heads. The ambrosa that en-
terprising drinkers hadn't liberated from tables was running
in many streams across the floor. Galactican security forces
had to be called in to break the fight up. When most of the
people had left, the room was in shambles, with nothing
upright, except for Starbuck.

Starbuck stood, his mood melancholy, in a corner of the
room, still pondering his notorious exploits with the opposite
sex.

Tigh entered Adama's quarters just after an aide had informed him that there were signs that the party was deteriorating. This was only moments before the fight started.

"Commander," he said, "they tell me the celebration's getting a little out of hand. I thought it might be good if you—Commander, is something wrong?"

Adama had merely turned and, his eyes glazed, ice formed over ice, stared at his aide, uncomprehendingly.

"Are you feeling all right, Adama?"

When he spoke, Adama's voice was soft and somewhat vague.

"No, I don't feel . . . too well. I think I should . . . rest."

He stood, listlessly. Tigh came to his side.

"Adama! Tell me, what's wrong?"

"There is nothing wrong with me," Adama said, his voice angry, its tone imperial. "Nothing wrong with me, Colonel Tigh, that a little catnap won't cure."

Without looking at Tigh, Adama shuffled toward his small bedroom. Observing the slump of his commander's shoulders and the disconsolate way he walked, Tigh muttered:

"I surely hope so."

CHAPTER FIVE

Tigh felt out of place, sitting in Adama's chair and dictating into his microphone, but even the commander would have demanded that the log be kept. Still, the mike felt heavy in Tigh's hand and, to him, his voice seemed to echo hollowly around Adama's quarters.

"Thanks to Apollo, Sheba, and Bojay and the rest of their crews, the Vaile operation is proceeding on schedule. It is about the only thing that is. Work aboard the *Galactica* is at a virtual standstill. Here we are, for once enjoying a rather peaceful time, attaining the maximum levels in fuel and supplies for the first time since we went to that little Cylon peace party and almost got knocked to oblivion.

"Below us is the kind of planet that men dream about. I have given notice that unlimited furloughs are available to all who qualify. Yet few of the *Galactica*'s crew or civilian personnel are taking any rest and recreation leave there. They seem to prefer to stay aboard, listlessly making a mess out of their jobs, moping around and sitting for long periods

staring off into space, retreating to their quarters where they
do little more than sit around and brood. I've caught several
people who don't usually show their emotions crying silently. Salik tells me there was an attempted suicide down
in the engine room. And engineers are usually the most life-
loving among us.

"It's like a disease, this brooding and crying, a disease
which has infected the vulnerable. Some of us are immune,
but for no rhyme or reason I can see. I simply don't understand. However, whenever I ask anyone what's bothering
them, they are either surly to the point of insubordination
or they supply me with a good chunk of their life history—
or at least that part of their life history containing all their
regrets.

"Doctor Salik says he can find nothing wrong medically
with anyone, nor can he figure why so many people would
suddenly sprout psychological problems simultaneously.
Whatever this . . . this evil is, it's affecting different people
in different ways."

Starbuck couldn't focus on his cards. The abstractions
on their pasteboard surfaces at first seemed to swim, then
form into patterns. He couldn't tell whether he should play
or discard, bet or fold.

He shut his eyes tight for a moment, felt dizzier as the
same abstractions, now white against the blackness, danced
a merry little jig. He opened his eyes and looked again at
the cards.

Instead of the abstractions, Starbuck now saw faces on
the surfaces of his cards. Faces of the women he'd known.
On the two center cards Cassiopeia and Athena glared out
at him.

"You're a louse, Starbuck," the Athena-face seemed to
say. "Look at how quick you tossed me over when a zippy
little blonde suddenly appeared on the scene."

"Don't call me zippy," the Cassiopeia-face seemed to
respond. "Besides, I don't think zippiness has anything to
do with it. Or intelligence. Or skill. If you're a female of
the human species and you're at least more attractive than

vapor trail residue, Starbuck'll make a play for you. It's a
disease with him. He's got to chase every reasonably attractive woman he sees. And without honor or ethics."

"Tell me about it," the Athena-face said. "He told me
there had never been anyone like me."

"You, too? Heck, the women of the *Galactica* could have
that particular line embroidered on samplers."

"Hey, hey, hey," Starbuck muttered.

The cardplayer across from him, a tall overly neat Libran
(as most Librans were), glanced at Starbuck quizzically.

"You all right, bucko?"

"Fine. I'm fine."

"He's always showing off his combat medals," the
Cassiopeia-face said. "If they gave medals for philandering,
Starbuck'd have more medals than he's got chest to put
them on."

"That's the key to him," the Athena-face said. "Woman
chasing is combat to him, the little—"

"I'm not that bad," Starbuck muttered, and all the card-
players looked at him strangely.

Starbuck understood that he was seeing things, and that
what he was seeing were, in a way, reflections of his own
concerns. The card faces were right, he was guilty of being
too frivolous in his stalking of women. Too often he used
lines that he'd used before. He'd always figured that, if
they were successful, they deserved recycling. Now he wondered if the mere fact that he often used rehearsed routines
meant that the words were meaningless, just instruments
used to attain his objectives, ways of making the ladies
respond to his manipulations in the same skillful way he
used the instruments aboard a viper to make it perform the
precision flying tricks he was so famous for. Juggling the
affections, say, of two or three different women was, for
him, essentially no different than a successful execution of
the triad formation. It occurred to him that, if he hadn't
made all his courtships so much of a challenge, perhaps he
would have treated the objects of his affection in better and
more fulfilling ways. Certainly, after a set of romantic experiences that had made his amatory skills already legendary

in Galactican history, he should feel much better about his amorous exploits. Also, he shouldn't be talking back to fantasy images on playing cards.

"Your play, Starbuck," the Libran said.

"I know, I know."

"Well, are you going to discard or would you rather have that hand bronzed?"

Normally Starbuck would have retorted with a flippant remark to a fellow cardplayer's rudeness, but today he just didn't feel like trying to keep up his image. Let 'em eat braka.

"Discard, I guess," he said. However, staring at the two cards he couldn't make up his mind which one to throw down. "I was going to give up this card," he said, staring at the pasteboard surface on which he had imagined Athena's face. Then he put his thumb on the card that had represented Cassiopeia, and said: "Or was it this one? I'm not sure."

The Libran flipped his entire hand of cards in the air and stood up from the table.

"I quit," he said. "I don't enjoy this game any more, anyway."

Starbuck put down his hand more delicately, as if he didn't want to harm any of them, particularly the Athena and Cassiopeia cards. Staring down at them, he said:

"Yeah, me, too. I'm sick of cards."

On the other side of the lounge, Sheba and Bojay sat at the bar, each sipping at glasses containing a newly invented cocktail that had been concocted from a mixture of ambrosa with a juice made from one of the recently shipped Vailean fruits.

"Tastes pretty good to me," Sheba remarked.

"Better 'n braka," Bojay muttered.

Sheba laughed. It was not a sincere laugh, just a reflex action to Bojay's humor. She hadn't felt much like laughing lately.

They sat for a while in contemplative silence. Sheba ran her finger around the rim of her glass. It made a faint deep whistling sound. Bojay tapped at the side of his glass.

"I wish Dad was here," Sheba said suddenly.

They both got a similar mental picture of Commander Cain, the man they'd both loved in spite of his stiff military manner.

"Yeah," Bojay said, "I'd like to see the old warhorse again."

"Like to see him stride in here, banging that baton against his thigh or pounding it into his palm."

"I really miss the old—"

"I can't help feeling I failed him in some way."

"Know 'zackly what you mean, Sheba. 'Zackly what you mean."

"You're drunk. You never get drunk."

"Nope, never."

Sheba thought of how she'd strived so hard to win her father's attention and respect, while Bojay recalled his efforts to be the top pilot of Cain's ship, the *Battlestar Pegasus,* just to impress him.

"How did we fail him, Bojay?"

Bojay gulped down the last of his ambrosa and Vailean fruit juice.

"Damn if I know," he said.

I'm going to get suicidal if I have to keep staring at all these heartbreaking faces, Boomer thought as he glanced around the table at Jolly, Greenbean and Giles. Greenbean looked like the world had just ended and he was depressed that nobody had told him. The rest looked just plain morose.

"What's the matter with you bozos?" Boomer pleaded.

"Nothing matter," Jolly muttered.

"Jolly, not only do you look like the last days of Kobol, but your syntax is shot to pieces. Do you mean nothing is the matter or nothing matters?"

"Both. Doesn't matter."

"Being around you guys is like attending a perpetual funeral, I—"

"Can it, Boomer," Giles said angrily.

"C'mon, guys, laugh a little. Smile. Try."

None of them moved a facial muscle. They seemed to

have adopted sadness as a style of life. Boomer threw up his hands in despair.

"Well," he said bitterly, "I don't intend to join the gloom and doom boom around here."

He grabbed his glass and stalked off, seeking a happy face in the room to build up his own spirits. He couldn't see a single one.

If Greenbean had known that Boomer was thinking jokingly about suicide, he would have thought his own mind was being read. For the first time in his young life, suicide appeared to be a sensible solution. Anything to rid himself of his deep depression, anything to make him forget that he might be guilty of something horrible, if he could only remember what it was.

What Lucifer had not anticipated about his guilt relay device was that, while it emitted powerful rays that reached through most of the *Galactica* to affect its inhabitants' moods, there were also massive doses of the transmitted emotion collected around the relays themselves. Greenbean was being assaulted by the guilt machine more strongly than anyone else aboard ship. It was as if he was at the epicenter of an earthquake of guilt.

Because he, unlike others, had no knowledge of the source of his guilt, Greenbean's mind was more disturbed than the rest. It was one thing to feel guilty about matters you could understand, but it was much worse to feel the guilt and have no idea of its origins.

The more he considered his guilt, the more he believed it had something to do with the time he had been lost in deep space. He lay in his bunk nights and tried to dredge up a memory from that time, struggled to revive a moment, but nothing would come. It was all blackness. One moment he was in an attacking sweep on a Cylon raider, the next he was waking up in his viper, drifting idly through empty space. The jolt of going from one to the other in his memory was frightening. The more he thought of it, the more he wished he could just obliterate himself, get rid of the guilt once and for all.

Lucifer would have been very much interested in the effects of his device upon its chief victim, if he could only have observed them. He might even have curtailed his efforts to make the device more powerful. But he could have no suspicion of its far-reaching potency and so, as a result of his constant tinkering with the device, the guilt aura around Greenbean was growing steadily and becoming more and more unbearable to the young ensign.

Brie had come to the Life Center to have one of her regular chats with Cassiopeia. Their talks tended to cheer her up. This time she found Cass sitting taciturnly with Dietra, both looking glum. They took one look at the comely blonde lady who'd briefly been still another of Starbuck's favorites, and gave her the saddest pair of dirty looks she'd ever seen.

Brie, like Boomer, was one of the rare few, unaffected by Lucifer's guilt rays. Her attitude toward life was too cheerful to allow more than momentary gloom to come into it.

She tried to tell a couple of her favorite jokes, but Cassiopeia and Dietra looked at her as if she'd just sung a dirge.

"Snap out of it, you two," Brie urged. "I never saw such a case of the blahs."

"Oh, we're okay, Brie," Deitra said. "Just a little blue. Right, Cass?"

"Right," Cassiopeia said gloomily. "I'm feeling pretty good, really. I just can't get a few memories out of my head."

"'Bout what?" Brie asked.

"About when I was a socialator. Ever since I've been working with Doctor Salik here in Life Center, using my talents for soothing the pain of sick and injured people, and sometimes saving lives, those old days seem so . . . so trivial."

"You mean," Brie said cheerfully, "besides feeling that your life was wasted, you're feeling good."

The remark at least drew a thin smile from Cassiopeia.

"Something like that," she said. "Oh, I know I performed good deeds then, too, but it's just that I was missing something."

"Something you didn't know that you were missing?" Brie asked.

"I guess."

"You two really are the daggit's dry meal. I'd go chum with somebody else, except you two seem to be about the most cheerful gals around these days. I think I'll take some R& R down in the devil's pit."

Brie touched the hands of Dietra and Cassiopeia and laughed softly. For a short while, they all managed some of the old cheerful banter, but soon that faded. Soon all three sat as silently as the two had been when Brie had entered. Even though untouched by the effectiveness of Lucifer's guilt machine, Brie could not fight against the strong gloom of her compatriots.

Uri believed in taking advantage of opportunity. With Commander Adama ill and so many others acting strangely witless, he knew this was a good time to strike. He'd been working furiously, assembling a team of coconspirators, talking to anyone who'd listen, addressing any group containing more than three people with skillful oratory, plotting, planning, urging and wheedling, enticing and inveigling. Already he had convinced a couple hundred people to join him in his crusade to settle on Vaile. He realized that one of the reasons his ranks were swelling so quickly had to do with the growing gloom aboard ship. So many people were dissatisfied that even Uri's inflated talk of a paradise below seemed feasible, even desirable. Anything to get their minds off their shame and remorse.

He had been able to progress from whispering in corridors and stairwells to addressing small groups in conference rooms, to speaking before a larger audience in one of the main halls.

He addressed now an auditorium nearly filled to capacity with many from the *Galactica*'s clerical and security personnel.

"Why shouldn't we have the right to choose where we want to live?" he asked them. "We don't have to live under Adama's tyranny! We can leave. Believe me, Vaile has everything we could ever want in a home planet. It is relatively uninhabited, beautifully suited to our needs, and the people already there would welcome us. And we don't have to be concerned about that piece of propaganda that Adama and his cohorts keep promoting, that lie about how we have a duty to the fleet, of how we are needed. There are plenty of Vaileans eager to take our places after we leave."

The audience, though unresponsive, did gawk at Uri with interest in his arguments.

"So," he finished, "what do you say, folks, are you with me?"

While the agreement of the audience was audible, it was also desultory. Why couldn't they work up a little cheer, a little "we're with you all the way, Uri," a little fervor for the cause? Well, Uri thought, he would take what he could get. What did he care about the nature of these fools' responses? As long as they signed up on his side in large numbers, he could accomplish his goal, which would, if circumstances demanded, include the overthrow of authority on the *Galactica*.

He wondered why the mood of so many was so low? Himself, he felt great. His pursuit of the Vailean objective had instilled in him more energy than he'd felt in a long, long time. Not since Carillon, when his skills at rhetoric had placed him at the leadership of an impressive number of people.

He had overheard Tigh talking with Athena. Tigh had remarked that many of the gloomy members of the *Galactica*'s crew seemed to be afflicted with some form of guilt or other. He had termed the affliction, the "guilt disease." Uri wondered if there had been some outbreak of guilt on the *Galactica*. If so, he certainly felt none of it. Well, if others chose to count their guilts just now, that was all right with him. It seemed that their guilt played right into his hands.

Lucifer might have been concerned by Uri's lack of guilt.

Certainly there was no one aboard the *Galactica* who had
more reason to feel guilty than Sire Uri. His actions back
at Carillon had caused many deaths, and would have caused
the annihilation of everyone in the fleet, including himself,
if he had been successful. More than anyone else, he should
have been overwhelmed by the forceful emissions from the
guilt relays. But, in fact, he felt none of that guilt. He never
felt guilty about anything. There was, therefore, a limit to
the effectiveness of the guilt machine. It did not easily
induce guilt in someone evil. In Baltar's case, the man's
deeds had been so awesomely evil that he couldn't ignore
his own villainy. But, for the most part, evil people had to
have at least the spark of goodness in them to make Lucifer's
device effective.

Lucifer would have found it ironic that his creation worked
best on essentially good people, people who could see the
values of relative concepts instead of absolutes. As a result,
Uri, with all his reasons for feeling guilty, was gleefully
plotting rebellion while Adama, respected for his nobility
of character, was in a comatose state, squirming in his bed
with guilty dreams. Lucifer would probably have been
amused by the irony. Amusement was part of his programming, although guilt was not.

Apollo watched Sheba and Bojay walk wearily into the
cargo hold where he was supervising the unloading of crates
from the newly arrived shuttle. Bojay looked especially the
worse for wear.

"What's wrong with Bojay?" Apollo asked Sheba.

"A touch of hangover, I expect. A few too many cocktails
before sleep period. Me, too, a little."

"But you're not drinkers, the two of you."

"Nope, not usually. Just a touch of the devil's pit doldrums, I guess."

"The devil's—the what?"

"You don't know about the devil's pit? I'm told it's a
name given the lower reaches of the ship by its engineers.
The devil's pit's an area just below the fuel storage holds
and the engines. They say our ghosts are on patrol there."

"I've heard something about that, but it's just superstition, Sheba."

"Of course it is. Like all superstition, it explains mysteries. The devil's pit doldrums are those indefinable sadnesses that come over one unexpectedly and for no apparent reason."

"I know the kind . . . kind of sadnesses you mean."

Apollo turned away from her and pretended to examine an invoice. Sheba wanted to touch him, gently massage away the kind of sadness he felt. But Apollo wouldn't have allowed that. Not good old colder-than-ice Apollo.

"I've noticed," she said, "you haven't been your usual ebullient self lately, Captain. Something bothering you, too?"

"Something."

"Serina?"

He was surprised by Sheba's insight. He had been thinking of Serina lately, in the quiet of his cabin, seeing her in fleeting moments in the shadows. Serina had been killed by the Cylons in a gunfight on Kobol. He couldn't have saved her life, but he nevertheless felt guilty for not performing some miraculously heroic act to prevent her death. It was irrational, he knew, to feel such guilt, but he'd never been able to shake the feeling that if he'd been just a little sharper, he might have seen the Cylon warrior in time to prevent him shooting and killing her. In his mind he had seen her fall to the ground over and over since that time. Why couldn't he have been just a few steps closer to her so that the shot that had killed her would have dropped him instead? It always seemed as if he was in the wrong position with his timing just slightly off. If not for such small distances, both Serina and Zac would be alive today.

"Yes," he said to Sheba, "I've been thinking about Serina some. And Zac, too. Zac was my brother, he was—"

"I know, he was killed."

"I could have saved him, Sheba. Could have stayed with him and—"

"And, from what I hear, allowed the *Galactica* to be blown up along with the rest of the fleet. Everyone believes you did the right thing, Apollo."

"Yes," Apollo said gloomily.

"Everyone but you, apparently."

She gave him a friendly tap on the shoulder, but he didn't react to it. His response brought on her own guilt in a new form. Now she felt guilty that she was not the strong person her father had intended her to be, the female copy of himself. She wanted to talk to Apollo about her father, but she sensed that now was not the time.

Even after dictating several entries, Tigh didn't feel comfortable doing log duty. He was the perfect subordinate, the ultimate in carrying out someone else's orders. In battle situations, he could take over from Adama and run the helm just as the commander wished. But he had no wishes to be the commander. He had realized long ago that, in becoming Adama's chief aide, he had reached his most efficient duty level. So, the log mike felt like dead weight in his hand as he spoke.

"I can't fathom what is driving everyone into such bleak moods. I feel nothing of it myself, and some others are apparently their usual selves. It seems ironic to me that just when we should be feeling—"

His dictation was halted by a knock on the cabin door.

"Enter, please."

Athena came in. She looked like everybody else, glum and lethargic. Although Tigh could not know it, Athena had not been particularly affected by Lucifer's insidious invention. Her emotional state derived from her worries about her father.

"Just me again, Colonel. How is he?"

"No change. I just looked in on him."

"My turn, I guess."

She went to Adama's bedside. Her father was restive. He moved from side to side nervously. It looked to her like he was in the middle of a very bad dream.

"Should I try to wake him up, you think?"

Tigh shook his head.

"Salik says just leave him be. Even if he does wake up, he won't wake up for long."

Athena remembered the few times she had seen him awake since the illness had first come upon him. He had barely recognized her each time. The last time he hadn't known who she was at all. He'd called her by her mother's name.

She felt panic inside her as she looked at her father and imagined him dead.

"Is he going to be all right, Colonel Tigh?"

"I don't know. We can't even figure what's wrong with him. Salik says—"

"Whatever's wrong with him, a lot of folks've got it."

"I've just been thinking exactly that."

Athena sat on the edge of the bed and smiled up at Tigh.

"Starbuck was just at me," she said. "He kept saying how he regretted the cheesy way he'd treated me. Well, it *was* cheesy, true, but I didn't like him apologizing for it, you know? He was so abject and melancholy. I liked him the old way. You couldn't trust him, but he didn't go all oozy over you. Why do men get these urges to dramatize their failings?"

She was about to pursue that thought when she realized she was, after all, complaining about men to a man. Tigh had always been so avuncular with her that she couldn't place him in the same category with Starbuck and some of the other hotshot pilots, even though her father had once told her that Tigh, in his youth, had had an admirable reputation as a ladykiller.

"I'm sorry, Colonel Tigh."

"No need to be."

"You know, I've been listening to a lot of people gas off. It seems there's one thread. Have you noticed?"

"Well, they're all guilty about something. Some past event, some way they treat people, some personal or professional trait. I don't know why, but it's like they all sniffed in some guilt-virus. You know, in the same way Boomer infected so many in the crew that time?"

Tigh recalled Boomer's disease and the way it had spread so quickly among the fighter pilots. Guilt had taken over the *Galactica* in much the same way that disease had.

"You may be on to something, Athena, but I'm not sure what we can do about it. Salik is definite about there being no medical causes for the current plague or whatever it is. I just don't know what we can do but wait it out."

"If we can wait it out."

There was a bitter tone in Athena's voice.

"What are you implying?" Tigh asked.

"I don't exactly know. There just seems to be such a force behind all this, as if somebody is manipulating us. A puppeteer pulling strings or a chorus master leading us in doleful song. I wish I could figure it out."

Tigh shrugged.

"We'll just have to keep working on it. I'm going to set up a team to go through the ship, inspect everything, see what they can find."

"Seems like a good idea to me. Who're you going to tap for this team?"

"Starbuck and Apollo, I think. Apollo's been in kind of a funk, too, although it hasn't impaired his efficiency as with most of the others. And Starbuck—well, I especially hate to see him so glum. I'm so used to him bouncing around here enthusiastically. Maybe giving the two of 'em this job'll perk them both up."

"Maybe. I'll keep my eye out, too."

"Good."

Adama stirred. They both looked down at him. Athena studied his face, noted how unhappy he seemed. He didn't wake up, but did mumble incoherently.

"I haven't seen him so sad since he came back from finding out Mother was dead," Athena said.

Tigh nodded agreement. Adama did look haunted.

CHAPTER SIX

Adama floated through space without a single qualm or any interest that his apparently weightless body was unaffected by the fatal dangers of outer space. The trip across galaxies was restful. Free of the agonies of command, he could enjoy the stars. Untroubled by day to day trivialities, he could see patterns in passing asteroids. His eyes no longer pained by the frequent glare of the *Galactica*'s interior lighting system, he could drift with closed eyes and feel the cool darkness on his eyelids. It was good, this trip, whatever its purpose. The load he had felt before was gone, left perhaps in his bedclothes. He didn't know whether he was dreaming or adrift in some kind of astral-body travel. But he didn't care, it was no concern of his. He would wake up or he wouldn't wake up. For now, the trip was meant to be enjoyed.

Ahead of him, a gleam of light circled a dot like a spotlight. He felt he was meant to drift in that direction. As the dot grew, he saw other dots, some of them nearly as bright. Soon they were a field of sparkling lights, all growing larger as he approached them. Their shapes took definition and he saw they were, as he had suspected, a fleet of ships. Had he floated around in space for a while and then returned to his own fleet? No, the star configurations were all wrong. This was another fleet.

In a moment he saw what fleet it was and his heart beat rapidly with excitement. It was the Colonial Fleet! The Colonial Fleet, in loose formation, proceeding at one-quarter speed ahead.

What? he thought. *The fleet? But it was destroyed. It's gone. Where am I? When am I?*

He found the *Galactica* easily. Easing along at the center of the fleet, just behind the command battlestar, the *Atlantia*, it was like an especially finely cut jewel selected as the centerpiece of a collection of bright rare and beautiful gems. The other stones were also impressive but none as sharply faceted or as radiant as the *Galactica*.

He could tell he was viewing the *Galactica* as it had been. There were scars of battle missing from its surfaces, scars he had memorized from Cylon attacks that had occurred since the *Galactica* had begun its voyage across space.

Knowing he could pass through its thick outer walls in an easy swoop, Adama directed himself toward this earlier incarnation of his ship. Inside, he floated down familiar corridors, corridors he had traveled for so large a chunk of his life, to the bridge.

He walked the bridge in his normal way, with his confident graceful stride, and he knew that nobody there saw him. No matter how corporeal he felt, he was invisible to his crew. That did not matter to him. He was calm.

Tigh was his usually busy self, going from console to console, collecting and depositing papers with an almost careless ease. Everyone appeared quite happy, doing their jobs with smiles and frequently exchanging cheerful glances.

He sensed someone coming toward him. He turned and saw a bearded man in white robes, the robes of presidential leadership. It was his old friend, Adar. Adar, alive again and looking quite impatient and angry. For a moment Adama hoped Adar was also a dream ghost so he could talk with him, two observers floating through their mutual past. But it was clear that Adar, like the others, didn't see Adama.

Adar beckoned Colonel Tigh to him.

"Colonel Tigh, has the commander been apprised of my arrival?"

"Aye, aye, sir. He sends his regrets and says he will be here imminently. There was an engine room problem that had to be seen to."

Adar dismissed Tigh. As the colonel walked away, Adar muttered to an aide:

"Like him. Adama. Always puts duty over command procedures and diplomacy. I should be insulted, but I'm not."

Adar fidgeted. Adama remembered seeing him killed, watching his friend's death on a television monitor. Adar's last words were regrets that he had been taken in by the Cylons. The memory of his friend's death made Adama look at him closely, taking in the details of a face he had known well but rarely looked at during their friendship. There was a dark, almost black, mole just under Adar's left eye. Had Adama ever noticed that mark before? He couldn't remember it.

Tigh paced cautiously behind the bank of communication consoles. He was keeping tabs on Adar while checking all entranceways for the appearance of his commander.

"Has Count Baltar been summoned?" Adar said to his aide.

"Yes, sir. His arrival is expected soon."

"Good. Now, if only my dear friend Commander Adama can pull himself away from his beloved engine room, we can expedite matters."

Adama wanted to tell him he was right there in front of him, but knew there would be no response.

"Where is he?" Adar said impatiently.

Before Adama had realized that Adar would move, Adar had walked right up to him, then through him. Adama felt a slight fluttery sensation, like an inward wind. Perhaps he *was* a ghost then. Perhaps he had died in his sleep aboard the *Galactica*. But then, why was he here? Was this the afterlife, going back to the scenes of your life? That didn't seem logical.

But he was definitely on the *Galactica*'s bridge at some time in the past, and nobody could see him, so there was no choice but to accept that. He felt quite relaxed, a relaxation that faded instantly as he turned and saw himself stride onto the bridge briskly, smiling at Adar. Both men reached out their arms and embraced each other.

"Adar, old friend," the Adama of the past said. "Please accept my apologies for not being here to greet you. A problem down—"

"Yes, yes, I know. Always a problem, Adama. Sometimes I think that, without the energy you absorb from continuous strenuous duty, you'd be an empty shell."

The past Adama smiled and said:

"Ila's always saying things like that to me. Maybe you're both right."

Adama could not adjust to watching himself, especially the younger version of himself without the deep worry lines he had acquired in the flight from the Cylons. There was also a jauntiness in his movements that he had either not been aware of before, or had lost. He hoped he hadn't lost it.

"My regards to Ila," Adar said genially. "Is she still the most beautiful wife a Colonial Fleet officer's ever had?"

"Beautiful as ever."

"I hope to see the both of you again soon, at home, as in the old days. God, I miss those visits. One of the things you lose when life raises you to leadership levels, I guess."

"What brings you here?"

Adar's voice became excited.

"News. The best of news. So valuable I didn't want to entrust it to normal communication channels."

Adar paused dramatically, looking pleased with himself.

"We are to have peace, Adama!"

The past Adama seemed genuinely surprised. Adama couldn't remember how he'd felt at this moment, even while watching himself experience it.

"Peace?" the past Adama said. "You mean, the Cylons—?"

"Yes!" Adar said happily. "The Cylons have agreed to a peace negotiations conference."

"A summit meeting? With the Cylons?! After all this time, and all the bloodshed, I find that hard to believe."

"But it's true. The war, after a millennium, is all but over. Just a few details are left to be ironed out. Count Baltar tells me—"

"Baltar! Has he got his sweaty hands somewhere on this?"

Adar frowned, not pleased by his friend's reference to the peacemaker.

"Well, yes," he said irritatedly. "He's arranged it all."

The past Adama walked away from Adar. He wrung his hands worriedly.

"A peace conference? Arranged by Baltar? And you're willing to accept it at face value?"

"Adama—"

"You can't trust Baltar."

"He's changed."

"Changed? If he's changed, it's for some devious reason."

"Adama, he's bringing us peace. You mustn't turn that down over a matter of petty jealousy."

Adama saw his past self become furious, veins standing out on his forehead, and he suddenly remembered this incident more clearly. He had been so surprised by Adar's announcement that he hadn't been able to think straight. As he watched himself now continue to protest Baltar's "deal," he wondered if there was more he could have done to prevent what he had even then suspected might happen.

I forgot, he thought, *that I'd perceived Baltar's wicked plot even at this early time. Why didn't I act successfully on my intuition? Why didn't I work harder to convince Adar that his wish for peace had blinded him to the treachery of the peace bringer?*

Adama, succumbing now more deeply to the power of Lucifer's guilt device, began to feel he had mishandled the meeting with Adar he was now observing. He began to despise his too complacent past self for trying to approach the subject rationally. He should have fought Adar and the council tooth and nail. He was skilled at oratory. Perhaps he could have at least convinced them to be more cautious about the details of the peace meeting, which Baltar deceitfully had fixed to the Cylons' advantage, knowing full well that they planned the most evil act of war in the history of warfare, and all in the name of peace.

His feelings of guilt over this incident were heightened when he watched the newly arrived Baltar come onto the bridge, looking every inch the smug evil traitor he was. Why couldn't they have seen his treason on his sneering face at that moment?

"Mister President," Baltar said. "Commander."

Adama perceived a slight difference in the way the man pronounced the two titles. "Commander" was slurred cleverly to indicate condescension. Baltar had never forgiven Adama for being more popular, talented and intelligent back at the academy. Especially since Baltar had been kicked out in an incident shrouded in scandal.

After the polite preliminaries, Adar got right to the point.

"Count Baltar, the commander doesn't feel that the Cylon's peace offering is sincere."

Baltar's stage grimace was so exaggerated that Adama recoiled, recognizing now the lie in the man's face. Even his blotchy skin seemed to gleam more in the perspiration of deceit.

It became a struggle to stand helplessly by and watch his other self deal with Baltar in the formal diplomatic manner such a consultation generally demanded.

"Oh, they are sincere all right," Baltar said, full of pleasure with himself. "I, uh, explained the concept of peace to them."

The past Adama smiled sarcastically.

"I didn't know they misunderstood the 'concept of peace.' It was always my impression that it meant nothing to them, that the only peace they understood was one in which they held absolute power over every other race in the universe."

Baltar, untouched by the sarcasm, smiled with even more self-satisfaction.

"The old rhetoric, eh, Adama? The kind of inflammatory words that have helped you and your kind to keep this war going on for so—"

The past Adama took two steps toward Baltar, his fists clenched, his angry face looking like he had every intention of using them. Adama was quite willing to join his past self in the battering of Baltar.

"My kind!!" the past Adama screamed. "*We* didn't start the war; the Cylons did with their cowardly sneak attacks, their pusillanimous efforts to conquer weaker civilizations. *We* didn't continue the war; if you had any sense of history, Count Baltar, you'd know that we were the ones who sought peace over and over, the ones who sent peace legations that were barbarously slaughtered, who kept—"

"Adama, Adama," Baltar interrupted, his voice insidiously soft, "that was all generations ago. Generations of Cylons as well. The Cylons have new leaders, too, and they don't hold the warlike attitudes of their predecessors. They have assured me—"

"Oh, you have their assurance, do you?" Adama whispered sardonically. "Well then, we have *nothing* to worry about, nothing—"

"Adama, with your militaristic attitudes you can destroy any chance we have with—"

"Gentlemen, gentlemen," Adar said, his voice insufferably kind, "these altercations will get us nowhere. I am the president of the Quorum, am I not?"

The past Adama and Baltar muttered agreement together, each with their own private reasons for resenting Adar's conciliatory interruption.

"And I believe in the present Cylons' sincerity," Adar said. "I have seen the documents that Baltar has brought back from them, and I believe they genuinely want peace. The Quorum agrees with me, unanimously. So there it is, you two. Make peace."

The past Adama and Baltar completed a desultory hand-shake. Adama hated his past self for doing it at all. He should have stood his ground. There must have been something more he could have done! He was sure of it.

At any rate, he should have made clandestine preparations to be ready for ambush. He might have thwarted the sneak attack on the peace fleet and gone on to save the twelve worlds. Was he, in effect, guilty of the destruction of the twelve worlds, the annihilation of his people? Not directly, of course, but indirectly? Was he, by this kind of reasoning, guilty of the acts he so condemned?

As he considered these possibilities, he felt energy drain out of him, felt himself become woozy, sick with life.

Apollo and Boomer kept passing each other as they paced the conference room. Starbuck sat sprawled in an easy chair, watching them lazily. He was bored. He had been bored since this meeting had started. He had not even participated in the shuffling of papers as Boomer and Apollo searched through several reports, logs, daily summaries.

Starbuck noticed idly that Boomer's pacing was more energetic than Apollo's. He did not, of course, realize that the difference in physical energy was due to the fact that, of the three, Boomer was the only one unaffected by the waves of guilt flowing out strongly throughout the ship from the implantations in Greenbean's clothing.

Boomer stopped pacing, glared down at the papers, and said:

"Well, fellas, where do we start?"

"I'm not sure," Apollo said wearily. "Colonel Tigh said we have a free hand. He suggested we check anything that seems relevant. Look for any correspondences that don't jibe, any clues that appear suspicious. He isn't even sure we actually have a problem."

Boomer shrugged.

"Well, that gives us a lot of leeway all right. You think there's an answer in any of these documents?"

"Maybe. They at least tell us of everything that's gone on aboard the ship ever since we all started feeling so low."

"I can't get any ideas from all this paper stuff. How about either of you? Starbuck?"

Starbuck, his eyes dazed, barely nodded in acknowledgement of the question.

"Well," Apollo said, "I first tried to tie things up with the fact that the situation corresponds to our docking here over Vaile."

"Hey," Boomer said, with sudden enthusiasm, "that might be it. What do you think?"

"Not sure. I considered the bad feelings might be due to something in the food we've brought up from there. After all, it's been incorporated into several mess hall menus."

"Yeah, that fish that cooks up all orange and purple is real tasty. Think it might be the fish? It's been popular."

"I checked on all kinds of food, not just the fish. I ran menu checks through the computer, suggested all kinds of correlations, came up with zip. Nothing matched. And, to make everything more complicated, the same food items have been introduced on other ships of the fleet, and they haven't had any subsequent difficulties. Everybody on all the other ships are happy as daggits. Only the personnel aboard the *Galactica* have come down with this . . . this illness, if that's what it is."

"I don't know what it is," Boomer commented. "I don't seem to have it. Though, after watching you guys for a while, I just might come down with it."

"And that's another factor. We've all pretty much been following the same dietary regimen, performing the same routines, been breathing the same air, yet not everyone has been showing the emotional symptoms."

"Some kind of immunity in some of us, you think?"

"Possible, but my hunch is that food and air aren't part of the problem."

Boomer sighed.

"Then we're back to square one."

"Feels like square minus-one."

Again, Boomer turned to Starbuck, this time staring right at him and leaning a bit in his direction.

"What do you think, Starbuck?"

"What?" Starbuck muttered. "Me?"

"Any other fool here named Starbuck?"

"Don't ride me."

"If I can't ride you, I'll kick you. C'mon, bucko, what do you think?"

"Simple. I don't know. I don't even think we got a problem. I don't care."

"Don't care?!" Boomer exploded. "You gotta care! Something's *wrong* and we got to do something about it."

"You guys take care of it. I'll follow along. But don't expect any swift detective work from me. I just don't feel like it."

Boomer threw up his hands in despair. He was used to Starbuck being reluctant to accept a mission, but in those instances his refusal was a jaunty act, and he never meant it anyway. Now he was truly lethargic, truly uncaring. It annoyed Boomer to see his buddy so transformed in attitudes, appearance, and mood.

However, both he and Apollo decided silently to leave Starbuck alone until he was his former self again. They started going through the papers again, searching for nonexistent clues.

Starbuck lost interest in their activity and returned to considering the folly of his philandering lady-killing ways. He remembered what Cassiopeia had said to him about the selfish and devious ways he treated women. He was beginning to think she was right. And he felt terribly guilty.

Adama had followed his other self on a shuttle to the *Atlantia* for the Quorum meeting to ratify the Cylon peace offers. He had floated along beside the shuttle, glancing from time to time at his other self piloting the shuttle.

He had observed the conference itself, watched Baltar sneakily stand in for the absent Cylons and smoothly explain away their absence. He told the Quorum that they would now travel to the place where the treaty would be signed by the Cylon representatives themselves. Of course, Adama knew there were no Cylon representatives waiting at the coordinates Baltar announced. But the Quorum had been pleased and displayed a collective relief at the expectation of peace at last.

After the meeting the members of the Quorum celebrated joyfully. The past Adama separated himself from the celebration and strolled to a starfield where, Adama recalled, he contemplated the events and his distrust of the peace. Adama stood next to his other self and studied his own face. They were probably both thinking the same thing, that Adar had once relied on Adama's advice, but now he was seduced by the fancy lying words of Baltar. Looking over his shoulder, Adama saw, as his memory had led him to expect, Adar come over to his past self to try to smooth things out between them. Adama listened to a conversation whose words he recalled so well he could have mouthed them along with his past self and Adar if he had chosen to.

"Well," Adar said, "I see the party isn't a huge success with *all* my children."

Adama felt pain in his chest from the longing to appear now to Adar and speak sense to him. What kind of ghost would he have seemed to be? A twin, appearing from the ether.

"It's what awaits us out there that troubles me," his past self said glumly.

"Surely you don't cling to your suspicions about the Cylons. They asked for this armistice. They want peace. For myself I look forward to our coming rendezvous with the Cylon representatives."

Adama wanted to wipe his friend's smug confidence right off his face. Why hadn't he been more firm with him at the time? Why had he been hamstrung by a useless respect for the office? Old friend or not, Adar had been, with his shrewd political skills and need to be approved by others, a poor choice for the presidency of the Quorum. But had he really believed that at the time, or was he now only making the judgement out of hindsight?

"Forgive me, Mr. President," the past Adama said, "but—but the Cylons hate humans deeply, with every fiber of their existence. In our love of freedom, of independence, our need to feel, to question, to affirm, to rebel against oppression—in all these ways we are different from them. To them *we* are the aliens and they'll never accept our ways, our ideas, our—"

"But they have *accepted*. Through Baltar, they have sued for peace."

Suddenly Adama had to speak. He knew he could not be heard but he had to speak, if only for the chance that somehow his words would pass through the barrier of future and past, and change this moment.

"Don't capitulate," he yelled at his former self. "Tell him, tell Adar. Baltar can't be trusted. You know that. You can change things, you fool! Say something!"

But, as he knew already, history could not be changed and so the past Adama would say nothing but:

"Yes, of course you're right."

Adama felt such shame at his capitulation. He turned away from his past self and Adar, and walked away, furious.

"No, no, no!" he muttered. "That wasn't like me. Why did I say it? Could I have changed things if I'd pressed harder? Could I have altered Adar and the Quorum? Maybe I could have. Why didn't I?"

Of course he could not answer his own questions. There were no answers. There were only the building guilts that, back on the *Galactica,* back in the present, Lucifer's device was implanting into his sick, writhing body.

Apollo and Boomer gave up the documents simultaneously. Some time had passed and they both were weary of the task. Next to them, Starbuck listlessly turned pages. He had been doing that ever since Boomer had insisted he do *something*. However, Boomer had been forced to surreptitiously take such documents and check them out for himself when Starbuck was through with them.

"Nothing," Apollo said, throwing his last sheaf of papers into a far corner. "No correspondences, no clues."

"Maybe there's something we haven't seen," Boomer suggested.

"Boomer, we've looked at all these printouts and records at least twice apiece. We haven't missed anything. The

Galactica has been functioning normally. A bit sluggish in some respects, but normally."

"Maybe that's the abnormality. How often are we functioning normally? Maybe the whole gloomy gus routine is brought on by normality."

"I don't follow," Apollo said.

"I don't care," Starbuck interjected.

"Shut up, Starbuck," Boomer said. "Listen. What if we're so used to being under the tensions of Cylon pursuit and the everyday crises of running this ship that, when we finally go get everything going right for us for a change, we don't trust it and begin to feel down because of this uncertainty. Maybe it's simply happiness that's making us gloomy."

"Ah, Boomer—" Starbuck said, disgustedly.

"No, Starbuck," Apollo said, "he might have something. But I don't know how we could prove something like that, except to let everything run its course. And I don't think Tigh would buy that as our final report. Even if it *is* so, we have to keep looking."

"Well, frack, it sounded good there for a micron. Perked *me* up, anyway."

Starbuck yawned theatrically.

"Can I go to my bunk?" he asked. "I'd like to grab some shut-eye."

"You been sleeping like it's your hobby lately," Boomer said, sarcastically.

"Get off my back!" Starbuck shouted, with a disgusted anger. "I'm just not . . . not up to par, that's all."

"Starbuck—" Boomer began, but Apollo interrupted:

"Wait! Maybe we've been tackling this problem from the wrong direction. Of the three of us, who's the worst hit?"

Apollo and Boomer scrutinized the yawning Starbuck simultaneously. His yawn stopped at half-mast when he realized what they were thinking.

"Fellas," he said, "I have no intention of being a guinea pig."

"It's an order, lieutenant," Apollo said firmly. "As my father is so fond of saying, you have no other choice."

"Yes, I have. I can go to sleep."

"Starbuck!"

"Okay, okay. But I'll remember how you pulled rank on me, *Captain.*"

"So what? Now look, I want you to think about when you started feeling this way."

"Feeling what way?"

"Morose, gloomy, guilty . . ."

"Oh, *that* way."

Starbuck scowled as he sincerely considered the question.

Baltar agitatedly paced along his usual route, a wide circle around an open area of the command chamber. He was worried about many things. About the success or failure of Lucifer's guilt device, about his plan to attack and destroy the *Galactica,* and especially about the coming of the Imperious Leader's liaison ship with its messenger and who knew who else?

Lucifer rolled into the room. Baltar, seeing him, stopped his pacing and asked anxiously:

"Has the delegation arrived?"

"No delegation. Just one representative."

"Just *one?* Only *one?*"

This news depressed Baltar even more. Perhaps he was being slighted by the Leader, or even removed from duty. He wasn't sure which would be worse.

"One," Lucifer said, "but not the one I would have chosen."

If Lucifer hadn't deliberately programmed certain inflections out of his voice when he'd become Baltar's second-in-command, this remark would have been heavy with sarcasm.

"What do you mean?" Baltar asked, confused.

"You will see. Now, in fact."

Baltar's attention was directed toward the command chamber entranceway, a wide arched portal. Standing at the center, beneath the arch's zenith, was another ambulatory cybernetic sentience, looking something like Lucifer but recognizably from a different series. Whoever it was, there was something vaguely familiar about him. Baltar felt he had met this one before. But when?

Lucifer could not look toward the portal. He felt such revulsion for the social-climbing, rank-pulling, hoarding, degenerate figure standing there that he hoped it would go away. It was not normal for Lucifer to feel disgust, but it was an ancillary part of his emotional programming.

The newcomer slid into the room with the same kind of smooth motion that propelled Lucifer, although it was not quite as graceful and made an irritating squeaky noise on the floor of the chamber.

"Count Baltar," the newcomer said, "I have been looking forward to meeting you for ever so long."

Baltar, unaccustomed to hearing one of these creations speak with warmth, was nevertheless bemused by the newcomer's familiarity. The figure stopped, his blue robe continuing to whirl around him for a moment, and said gently:

"I was commander on the planet Antila. We communicated regularly when I captured the Galactican pilot Starbuck..."

The memory of that incident returned to Baltar, as did the realization of the newcomer's identity. And this was Imperious Leader's representative? Baltar now felt he had nothing to worry about.

"Ah, yes," he said, "Spectre, isn't it?"

Spectre, pleased at Baltar's recognition, continued his path toward the commander.

"Yes," he said, "Spectre, at your service."

Lucifer thought he'd rather short-circuit than stay in the room and watch these two oil each other. Yet, he observed, there was something fitting in this meeting, something perhaps even destined.

"Good to see you," Baltar said gleefully and threw his arm around Spectre's shoulders. Lucifer realized Baltar had never touched him that way. He didn't know whether he was glad or sorry. Still, the easy familiarity of the gesture worried him.

"I was impressed," Baltar said to Spectre, as they began to walk together, "by the way you handled yourself during that Antila operation, even in a losing cause."

"Yes, it was unfortunate that the pilot escaped. I was so close to breaking him."

Spectre easily readopted the line he had promoted at the time of the adventure. In reality, he had never seen the pilot, who had been in custody for no more than a few microns.

"We all have to endure failure from time to time, Spectre."

If Lucifer had had blood, his face would have been drained of it with that remark. Baltar had quite a history of failure, especially in his several failed schemes to capture or destroy the human fleet.

Lucifer was appalled at the mutual admiration society that continued in front of his glowing red eyes. He was certain Spectre was a fraud who had covered up his own failures on Antila. And he knew how fraudulent Baltar was. They deserved each other, he concluded.

Watching Spectre flatter and cajole Baltar, Lucifer wondered how this transparently false creation could have risen so skillfully in the Cylon hierarchy so that he was now a special messenger and personal representative from Imperious Leader. How could an ambulatory cybernetic sentience *in his own series* become a slick scheming bureaucrat? What kind of expediencies had formed Spectre's personality since he came out of the factory? And why should such a fraud rise in Imperious Leader's regard, while Lucifer, obviously of a superior series, and certainly a more evolved intelligence, was trapped on this base-star with an incompetent like Baltar. It irked Lucifer that an inferior being should have the Leader's ear, while Baltar would rarely listen to *him*.

"And what is your business with us, Spectre?"

Baltar's voice was so affable and sly, you could have knit spider webs with it.

"Imperious Leader has sent me to prepare the way for him," Spectre announced. "He is coming to your base-star on a visit."

"Oh, is he?"

Baltar's voice, not so delighted now, dropped half an octave. Was this a visit, he wondered, or an inspection, perhaps an inspection leading to his removal. If it was merely a visit, a royal one at that, it was the perfect opportunity to aggrandize himself in the Leader's eyes. If he played his cards right, he could take credit for Lucifer's guilt device, and then top that with the final defeat of the *Galactica*. There were many dangers, many risks in the scheme, but he thought he could pull it off. And then he would be in the catbird seat within the Cylon hierarchy.

On the other hand, the Leader might be coming to put him on the spot. He might intend to dress him down, or even make another attempt to lop off his head. Well, he had to take that chance. Anything went wrong, and he could go around smiling from the neck. But, with Lucifer's machine and the *Galactica*'s shipment to the scrap heap, the Leader wouldn't dare do anything to him. He would be a hero, even in the Leader's many eyes.

It was a delicate situation. But Baltar felt he could handle it.

"What is to be the purpose of the Leader's visit?" Lucifer asked Spectre.

Spectre whirled smoothly around and faced his fellow being, knowing Lucifer was the one individual in the command chamber to be wary of.

"He wishes to buoy up the spirits of his troops and of the command leadership," Spectre managed to bow his head obsequiously to both Baltar and Lucifer, "with his approving presence, and to encourage you all in your present worthy endeavors in the pursuit of the *Galactica* and the loathsome human fleet."

"He's coming all the way here for that?" Lucifer asked, incredulous.

"As I said, honored Lucifer."

"Interesting."

"Why do you say interesting, Lucifer?" Baltar asked, wondering just what Lucifer was up to.

"Oh, nothing," Lucifer said. "My interest is just . . . piqued, that's all."

Baltar smiled sneeringly.

"Come on, Lucifer," he said. "Out with it. You know I demand openness in my command chamber."

Lucifer nearly exposed this patent lie, but decided to let Baltar let out his own string until somebody scissored it.

"I am merely puzzled," Lucifer said.

"Puzzled at what," said Baltar.

"Imperious Leaders do not conduct routine inspection tours. They are assigned to lower echelon personnel. Imperious Leaders do not sent cybernetic advisers as advance personnel for their visits. Imperious Leaders do not—"

"Perhaps this one does," Baltar commented.

"I assure you—" Spectre began.

"I am properly corrected, Baltar," Lucifer said. "Indeed, perhaps this one does."

Baltar knew there was sarcasm somewhere in Lucifer's statement. Perhaps Spectre could perceive it. He didn't want that, so he said to Lucifer:

"Leave us. I wish to consult with our Leader's *personal representative* in private."

Lucifer hesitated.

"About Imperious Leader's coming visit, of course."

Lucifer, not at all certain that all Baltar planned was a routine discussion with his visitor, glided out of the command chamber, knowing he would have to watch the both of them, Baltar and Spectre, from now on.

Baltar did not say a word until he was certain Lucifer was out of hearing distance. He was uneasy about the implications Lucifer had suggested. Was there something more to this visit of Spectre's, and did Lucifer see what it was? Baltar knew he must be cautious, wary.

The best way to start, he thought, was to butter up his visitor.

"Spectre!" he bellowed heartily. The bellow was quite unnecessary, since Spectre was practically next to him.

"By your command, Count Baltar, liege."

Damn, but he liked this Spectre's style, especially the liege addendum.

"I'm delighted to see you again," Baltar said, "this time in the . . . in the . . . in the—"

"You may say flesh," Spectre said. "I appreciate human metaphor. And irony. I adore irony."

Baltar, impressed, smiled broadly.

"You're quite impressive, Spectre. I wonder . . . do you think someone like you is wasted in rear echelon duty? I mean, even with the Leader? I mean, wouldn't you like to see some real frontline action, use your considerable talents for the excitement and stimulation of real battles?"

"Are you saying I could be useful on your staff here, Count Baltar, sir?"

"I'm saying exactly that."

Spectre paused for a scant moment, a fraction of a micron. He was employing his own logic circuits to see the possibilities of Baltar's offer.

"It is definitely worth considering," he announced.

Baltar was delighted by Spectre's response. It had been worded with the kind of care that Baltar liked to employ.

"You could be just the ticket for me, Spectre. I'm sure I could create an opening for you."

Both of them looked toward the portal through which Lucifer had just exited. A link that both felt seemed to be forging itself between them.

CHAPTER SEVEN

"I think he's nearly in coma now," Salik said, "and getting closer all the time."

Tigh's blood seemed to stop in his veins and freeze as he listened to the doctor's pronouncement. For a moment he had to look away from Adama, who was tossing and turning, getting the bedclothes in a tight mummylike wrap around his body.

"Can you do anything?" Tigh asked the doctor.

"Just what you're doing. Watch. Pray. Any levels hit critical points, we ship him to Life Center and I do what I can. How long since he was last awake?"

"Just before you came in. It was odd. He sat up suddenly and stared at me as if he knew me. Then he said, 'That was my son, Mister President.'"

"That mean anything to you?" the doctor asked, puzzled.

"Unfortunately, yes. That's what he said just after his son was killed. He was speaking to Adar, the last president of the Quorum. It was right before the Cylons attacked."

Salik shook his head and shrugged.

"Kobol only knows I'm not a specialist in things of the mind, but it sounds to me like the commander's mind has gone out the launch tube."

As he often did, Tigh felt distaste for the doctor's brusque, sometimes inconsiderate way of expressing himself. But the man was doing his best for the commander, so Tigh kept his criticism to himself. He was too distressed to care about Salik's thoughtless way with words.

Salik put away his instruments and went to the door, saying:

"Let me know immediately if there's any change."

"Right, doc."

Salik left and, shortly thereafter, Athena entered the bed-chamber.

"Any change?" she asked Tigh.

"Nothing good. How are you?"

"Hanging in there. I'm—"

Adama twisted around and half-leaned off his bed. As Athena rushed to help him, he said softly:

"Prepare my shuttlecraft. I'm going down to the surface of Caprica, Tigh."

Athena righted her father, and he settled his head back onto his pillow. Athena questioned Tigh with her eyes. He shrugged.

"He's been saying things like that."

"It's what he said to you just before he went down and . . . and found mother had been killed in the invasion."

"I remember. Perhaps he'd be less restive if we left him alone for a while."

They left the bedroom. Tigh suggested Athena sit down, but she said she was too nervous to sit. After walking to her father's desk and toying with a Caprican bluestone paperweight (a long-ago birthday present from Ila to Adama), Athena turned to Tigh and said:

"Somehow he's reliving in his mind the time of the Cylon ambush."

"Yes," Tigh said and ambled toward the viewport. He looked out at the vast starscape and did not speak for a while. When he did, it was in a quiet voice. "He seems to have the guilt disease—that's what I've come to call it. But he has it the worst of anybody. God knows, there're always reasons for all of us to feel twinges of guilt or get mired in long moody periods of remorse, but I can't figure why it should hit the commander worse than others. Of all of us, he's the most courageous, the most noble, the most—"

"Well, that's just it, don't you see?" Athena took a position just behind Tigh and said sadly: "A noble individual is more liable to feel the consequences of his acts, to worry at length about the rights and wrongs. You've seen father do that thousands of times. And you don't see Sire Uri steeped in the depths of gloom, do you?"

"Hardly. I hear he's stirring up a whirlpool of trouble out there. Latest report I have speculates that he's going to make his move soon—a public demand that he and his followers be allowed to remain on Vaile. If Adama's not better by then, they just might get their wish. I don't want to even deal with them. I'd rather travel on understaffed than be continually besieged by weasels like Uri and his—"

Athena put her hands on Tigh's shoulders.

"Easy," she said. "Easy, Colonel, easy."

Tigh turned away from the window and smiled wanly at her.

"Sorry," he said. "This is all off the point, isn't it?"

Athena took Tigh's arm and walked him across the room slowly.

"You know," she said, "maybe it *is* logical that Father should have more difficulty with guilty feelings than most people. He has the most responsibility. Responsibility and guilt go together. Look what he's apparently dreaming about. The Cylon ambush. Not his fault, but he often talks about it as if he were somehow responsible. The ambush, the destruction of our home worlds, this journey, the quest for Earth, that's a lot of weight on a single pair of shoulders."

"Too much, perhaps," Tigh said, disengaging from her and leaning against Adama's desk. He didn't want to express to her his fear that the commander had already cracked, that his condition was not connected with the guilt-disease sweeping through the ship. It may have been the natural result of all he had been through.

"How's the investigation going?" Athena asked after they had been silent for a while.

"Apollo hasn't reported in yet."

"On my way here, I saw the three of them. They were just sort of drifting along a corridor, arguing a little. Well, Starbuck was just drifting, but Apollo and Boomer were arguing. They seemed confused. I don't think they've found anything."

Tigh sighed.

"There may not be anything to find, Athena."

Athena stood at her father's bedroom doorway and looked in. Adama was resting quietly now. She felt a moment of panic when she thought he might have stopped breathing. But she saw him take a shallow breath and felt better. But she couldn't get the fear out of her mind that he might be dying.

Adama stood on a patch of dark Caprican soil and watched his past self disembark from Apollo's viper. Apollo had taken him down in his viper, contending that the shuttlecraft would have been too easy a target.

Even though he was some type of ethereal being or was trapped in a dream, Adama felt exhausted. He had been through the ambush, seen the battle again, watched the *Atlantia* destroyed anew. He stood on the bridge and studied the past Adama closely as he ordered the *Galactica* away from the battle because he knew that the larger part of the Cylon forces would be attacking the twelve worlds. That act had been described by some as cowardly, but he had done all he could for the fleet and there were the twelve worlds to be protected. Of course he had been too late to stop the destruction of the home planets. He watched himself see their destruction on the *Galactica*'s monitors.

As Adama observed all the destruction, he felt guiltier than ever. There had been so many points where he could have acted differently.

He followed the past Adama down the scarred path to

the cottage where he and his wife had lived for so many yahrens. It was now, as he'd remembered, in ruins, only a part of it still standing.

As he watched the past Adama enter the cottage, there was a flash of light and the sky went from night to day. Adama blinked from the pain of the sudden luminosity.

He looked again at his old home and was astonished. It was whole again. Its destroyed walls had magically rebuilt themselves. The battle scars on the house and the country-side had disappeared. As he tried to cope with the new developments, the door of the cottage opened and his wife came out.

"Ila!" he called.

She came toward him, muttering something about some shopping she had to do. He reached for her, and she walked right through him. He felt the same chilly sensation he'd felt when Adar had passed through his body. He turned to look at her. She had stopped in the middle of the path and peered up at the bright sky.

"I swear, Adama," she said, "you don't come back from that war soon and I'm off. I'll go, I really will. I'll go to Piscera, Virgo, anywhere, even Scorpia. I will, I swear it."

When she spoke his name, he thought she must see him. Then he realized that her statement, while addressed to him, was intended to be directed past the skies and to his other self in the *Galactica,* however far away the ship might be. He was astonished. She had never shown him signs of her longings. He had never known she was fed up with her life here on Caprica, as she seemed to say. Perhaps she had always been subservient to him too easily, he thought, and perhaps he'd never seen it because he was so used to being surrounded by subordinates. He regretted any heartache, no matter how tiny it might have been, that he could have caused her.

He wondered what time period he was viewing now. Ila didn't look any younger than he'd last remembered. It must not be too long before the invasion. Perhaps his past self had already seen her for the last time, a thought that sad-dened him immeasurably.

Ila foraged in her handbag, muttering:

"Where did I put my list? I swear, I'm forgetting everything nowadays."

She continued her walk up the path. Adama called after her:

"Wait, Ila, wait."

He was tempted to follow her all the way to whatever store was her destination, but something kept him rooted to the spot. His emotional reaction to seeing Ila again was so mixed up. At once he felt happy, sad, and shocked. For so long he'd been remembering her as she'd been younger, and not the slightly overweight and puffy-faced woman she'd become. Her skin was sallow and her eyes tired. She walked with her shoulders bent; it was the walk of old women whose bones had softened. Had she become old? Was he guilty of aging her too soon, with his frequent absences? He had spent more time on the *Galactica* than in this pretty little cottage.

The light shifted again, and there were now clouds in the sky. He glanced toward the cottage and saw a child playing in its side yard. It was Apollo, furiously in the midst of a game of outdoor triad with a few of his friends. Apollo had been a happy child, Adama recalled. Now his son had become so austere, especially with him. Was he guilty, too, of the change in his son's demeanor, or was that merely the function of time passing?

Ila came out of the door of the cottage again and Adama was momentarily confused. But, he realized quickly, this wasn't the same Ila who'd walked so busily away from him, up the path. She was younger now, the way he tended to remember her. She was beautiful, her darkly auburn hair framing a petite lovely face. At this past time she looked quite like Athena did now.

A young man followed her out of the cottage. At first Adama didn't recognize him. It wasn't himself, he saw first, then he saw the smile lines beside the hazel eyes and he knew it was Adar.

"That was some superior meal, Ila," Adar said pleasantly.

Ila laughed. Adama was delighted to hear that hearty trilling laugh again.

"I told you, Adar, that I saw through your flattery," she said.

"And I told you it wasn't flattery. It was truth."

Adar stopped smiling and stared almost grimly at Ila.

"I adore you, Ila," he said.

Ila poked her finger vigorously at Adar's chest.

"Adar, you're not to bring up that subject again."

Adar backed away from her threatening finger and said:

"I can't help it. I prefer your rejection to my remaining silent. And who knows? Someday you may—"

"Don't even say it. I may die someday, I may get rich someday, I may turn to a life of crime, but—dear Adar— I will not fall in love with you someday."

Adar looked so disconsolate that Adama couldn't even be mad at him for making a play for his wife.

"Ila—" Adar said, then grabbed her roughly and kissed her. Although she allowed him to kiss her, it was clear that she was not participating in the act. When Adar tried to prolong the kiss, she pulled away from him quickly.

"How stupid of you," she said softly. "With Apollo nearby and Adama due back any moment."

"A risk worth taking."

"Oh, yes? That's just some new version of your flattery, isn't it?"

As the light changed again and the figures disappeared, Adama wondered what he would have felt about the incident at the time if he'd observed it. He probably would have challenged Adar to a fight and been more than a little jealous of Ila. Now, with so much time gone, with both Ila and Adar dead, there was no anger in Adama. All he could feel were twinges of guilt, a wondering if he had treated Ila in a way worthy of her love and loyalty, especially when he considered all the time he had spent away from her.

Baltar stood over him and gleefully gawked at the torture Greenbean was undergoing. As the fire-whip came down

and seemed to cut and singe his skin simultaneously, Greenbean woke up. He couldn't orient himself to his quarters.
They didn't look right, they looked like his cell on Baltar's
base-star. He shook his head, trying to figure out whether
he'd dreamed of fantasy or reality. Had he actually been on
a base-star and been tortured by Baltar? Or was the scene
just a manifestation of his gloom? What, after all, would
he know of Baltar's ship? Yet, earlier in the dream, he had
seen it in precise detail. He remembered a strange personage
with a head that lighted up and red eyes that moved oddly.
Why had that creature seemed familiar?

Jolly stepped out of the shadows.

"You all right, buddy?" he asked.

"What—?! Oh, Jolly. You been there long?"

"A while. I returned from patrol and found you sacked
out. Whatever you were dreaming, it seemed painful, at
least judging by the misery in your face. I decided to stick
around, wake you up if you started screaming."

"Thanks, Jolly. It was a real sweat maker, whatever I
was dreaming."

He held up his sheets to show their damp spots.

"See?" he said.

"What were you dreaming?"

"I forget," Greenbean lied. "Somethin' pretty stupid, I
expect."

Jolly nodded, then sat on the edge of the bed. It dipped
quite a bit under his considerable weight. Jolly had been
on a diet recently but apparently it wasn't doing him much
good.

"How about a game of pyramid?" Jolly asked.

"I don't think so," Greenbean answered, lethargically.

"Something to drink? Eat?"

"No."

"Some triad down in the gym?"

"Nope."

Jolly's pleadings became desperate.

"Greeny, you got to pull yourself together. You can't—"

"I'm all right. Just let me sit here a bit."

"That's what's wrong. All you've done since you returned is—"

"Jolly, leave me alone!"

The vehemence of Greenbean's plea silenced Jolly. They sat quietly for a few microns, then Jolly, maintaining the silence, stalked out.

Greenbean tried to think about his dream but soon he had dozed off again. In this dream Baltar again stood over him, but he was being friendly. Baltar talked but Greenbean couldn't discern what the evil-looking man was saying. Frequently Baltar addressed something to the strange red-eyed creature in the velvet robes. Greenbean felt that it was important to hear what was being said. If he could hear it, he would know what was wrong with him. He leaned toward Baltar, struggled to hear what the man was saying. And he woke up, again dripping with perspiration.

He sat up, trying to figure out the significance of the dream. Why had it seemed so real, like something that had actually happened?

In some way he was doing something to the Galactica, he thought. He didn't know why he was so sure of that, or what to do about it. If he went to the commander or one of the other officers, they'd either laugh at him or suggest a few sessions of therapy. But he didn't need therapy or lectures from superiors. All he knew was that he was a walking bomb. If he couldn't turn himself in, what could he do? He could kill himself; that might be the only way to defuse the bomb. If only he understood what it was all about . . .

He decided to take a walk, see if he could clear his head. He put on his newly pressed jumpsuit, the one with the guilt-relay devices planted all over it, and started wandering the corridors of the *Galactica*.

Baltar really enjoyed himself as he enthusiastically described for Spectre the strategy he planned to use against the *Galactica*. He spread printouts all over the command chamber floor to show Spectre the planned movements of the Cylon forces. In the center of the floor, as the *Galactica* itself would be the center of the attack, was a paper with a diagram of that battlestar upon it.

"With the forces aboard the *Galactica* so emotionally depleted, we should be able to surround the ship and destroy it," Baltar summarized.

"Or force it to surrender," Spectre suggested diplomatically.

"Well, yes. But I thought Imperious Leader wanted the *Galactica* finally destroyed."

"I can't speak for the Leader. It just seems to me that, after its capture, we could revamp the *Galactica* and turn it into a powerful fighting base-star in the service of the Alliance. It seems a shame to waste such potential for a mere battle victory, albeit a spectacular one."

Baltar did not care for the idea of a salvaged *Galactica*, but he chose to flatter Spectre rather than argue with him. Baltar would demolish the *Galactica* if he damn well pleased, anyway.

"Of course, of course," Baltar said. "Good thinking, Spectre."

Spectre was impressed and gratified by Baltar's compliment. He was, after all, seriously considering joining the human's staff. And the *Galactica* was a key factor in his decision making. After the battle, if he influenced matters well, the *Galactica* could become a marvelous base of operations for Spectre.

"There is one thing I don't understand, blessed sir," Spectre said.

"Yes, my friend?"

Spectre noticed the use of the word friend, and became even more confident he could arrange matters his way in the future.

"How can we be so certain that the personnel aboard the *Galactica* will be unable to respond effectively?"

Baltar positively glowed with satisfaction as he answered:

"That's the wonder of it. I have devised a unit that is even now forcing such guilt upon the Galactican personnel that I expect the majority of them to be emotionally disabled by the time we launch our attack."

Spectre was impressed as Baltar explained LEADER to him. He had not suspected that Baltar was capable of such an intricate and brilliant device. This was, he was sure of it, a man to ally oneself with. Any genius who could devise such an invention *must* be worthy.

"... And so," Baltar finished, "when we attack, the *Galactica* will virtually kneel at our feet."

"Ah, another metaphor. Skilled of you, Baltar."

Baltar never used metaphor on purpose, but he accepted the praise gladly.

"And when will the attack take place?" Spectre asked.

"I've timed it to coincide with the visit of Imperious Leader. We will watch our mutual enemy destroyed together, much as we have begun this pursuit of the *Galactica* together."

If it had been possible for a Cylon-made creation like Spectre to be overwhelmed, Spectre would have fallen to the floor in admiration of Baltar.

"You have a spectacular sense of drama, Baltar. I congratulate you. I look forward expectantly to the event."

"And then, when we have won, I will formally request from Imperious Leader a favor—and how can he refuse a favor in those circumstances? I will ask him to transfer you to my staff, Spectre. That is, if you so desire?"

Being a cybernetic intelligence was quite an advantage at times like this. A human being, even a Cylon, would have paused while pondering the advantages and disadvantages of such an offer. But Spectre's analytic circuits allowed him to evaluate the aspects of an issue in an instant. His conclusion this time was to provide a carefully worded, but not fully committed, response that would sound to Baltar like acceptance, but would protect Spectre in case anything went wrong. Spectre said:

"I will at that time, I trust, consider it an honor."

Baltar, who didn't detect anybody's subtlety but his own, was delighted with Spectre's answer.

"Splendid, Spectre, splendid," he said eagerly.

• • •

If Lucifer could have observed the state of Starbuck's mind, he might have been disturbed. Starbuck had once been a prisoner of Baltar's, and Lucifer had liked him. The human had taught him a card game called pyramid, then beat him at it, and Lucifer had been devising systems with which he could beat the lieutenant should they ever meet again. Of all the humans, Starbuck was the one whom Lucifer would have most wished to spare suffering. Yet, in a bizarre side effect of the guilt device, Starbuck was slowly going mad. The disorientation and bad feelings that had been induced into him were gradually disintegrating his senses of self-confidence and rationality. The rays from the guilt machine were affecting the chemistry of his brain more severely than in most of the other afflicted Galacticans.

As he stood with Apollo and Boomer next to a railing that surrounded the triad court, Starbuck would in a short time become quite insane.

They had come to the court in their wanderings through the ship trying to find some clue to the mysterious shipboard gloom. Down below them some members of the crew were practicing fighting skills rather than playing triad. Apollo had resumed his interrogation of Starbuck.

"And that's all you can remember?" Apollo asked.

"Right," Starbuck said sullenly. "I just started to feel down at Greenbean's party and haven't been able to shake it since. Hey, look at those guys down there. They can do better 'n that. It's like they're fighting in heavy gravity."

"Keep your mind on the problem, Starbuck," Boomer cautioned.

"And you, Boomer," Apollo said, "you've not caught this . . . this disease?"

"Not that I'm aware of. Oh, looking at others makes me feel a bit down in the mouth, but I don't have the kind of specific gloom Starbuck was describing. 'Course, I don't have his way with the girls either, so that's a subject I can't—"

Starbuck was about ready to crack, and Boomer's remark almost did it.

"Belay that, Boomer," he said. "You know I'm damn sick of you ribbing me about my love-life. My love life and my gambling, you get on one of those topics and you're a—"

"Take it easy, you two," Apollo said. "This is no time for a fight."

"Even if we did fight," Starbuck said, returning his attention to the activity in the triad court, "I think we'd do better than those guys."

"Don't be too sure," Boomer muttered, still irked.

"Boomer—" Starbuck said threateningly. He felt as if his mind was about to explode.

"Back to the subject at hand," Apollo said. "You guys feel everybody started to go downhill at the time of the party?"

Both Starbuck and Apollo answered yes.

"Then let's concentrate on the party. I wasn't there. Was there any food everybody was consuming? Not just Vailean food, but any food?"

"Salik's already cleared the subject of food," Boomer said. "He says no ingredients there could have caused the problem."

"Right, Boomer, I was just trying to discover a common element."

Across from them, Greenbean entered the triad arena. He was about to wander around the court's running track, but he saw his three buddies on the other side, and decided he didn't want to socialize with them just now. He joined several spectators by the railing and watched the fighters below without really concentrating on them. He was too obsessed with his feelings of guilt and his suspicions that he'd been in Baltar's headquarters where he had, in some way, betrayed the fleet. The memories he did have of that time were vague and unreal.

"And most everybody drank ambrosa or grog?" Apollo was asking Boomer.

"Right. But that's not a common element either. A few didn't drink. And I had about as much ambrosa as the next pilot without ill effects."

"And there were people at the party who didn't come down with—"

"Greenbean!" Starbuck yelled.

"What?" Apollo said, confused. Then he saw Greenbean across from them. "Oh, yes, I see him over there. Let's concentrate on the matter at—"

"No, Apollo, that's not it. I mean Greenbean *is* the common element you're looking for. He was there. It was his party. Remember? Nobody felt bad before he came back from the dead."

Apollo noted the abnormal bitterness in Starbuck's edgy voice. There was an offbeat sound to it, a kind of lunacy. On the other hand, the thought of Greenbean had definitely lifted Starbuck out of his lethargy.

"What are you saying, Starbuck?" Boomer said.

"Greenbean. Look how long he was gone! Then he suddenly materializes out of nowhere. And he *claims* not to remember where he was. Who's to say he's not a traitor? He could be a plant, a tool of the Cylons. It might not even be Greenbean! Tear him open, you might see circuits. All this, it's his fault, the son of a—"

Starbuck started to spring away from them, but Apollo gripped his arm and said:

"Wait! Let's get a hold on this. Greenbean was cleared. He was examined, tested, inspected, you name it. He wasn't carrying any disease viruses or organisms or—"

"But that's it, don't you see? Maybe he *is* the disease!"

"Weigh anchor, Starbuck. Are you suggesting Greenbean's presence at the party was in some way—"

"I'm not suggesting anything. Greenbean hasn't been the same since he got back. It's like he's not even the same Greenbean. I started to feel bad when I was at that table right by him. Apollo, it makes sense, it—"

"What sense? Starbuck, it's not even logical, it's—"

Starbuck couldn't bear Apollo's irritating rational admonitions. In the feverish insanity taking over his brain, he *knew* Greenbean was evil and the source of his own misery. He pulled away from Apollo's grasp and leaned against the triad court railing. He screamed across the court, the fierceness of his anger making even the fighters below stop their lethargic combat.

"GREENBEAN! LOOK AT ME, YOU PIECE OF DAG-GIT MEAT!"

Greenbean, who had been absorbed in his own thoughts of bemused guilt, was startled by Starbuck's voice. He looked up, frightened. Starbuck *knew*, he thought. Starbuck knew about his betrayal. Even as he thought it, more details of his capture rushed into his mind. He saw himself in his cell, in Baltar's command chamber, writhing with pain under Cylon torture. He saw himself confessing, giving the *Galactica*'s coordinates. Shame overwhelmed him with the return of the memories.

Starbuck had started to race around the triad running court. He was shouting as he went:

"It's you, isn't it, Greenbean? Or whoever you are. WHATEVER you are."

Greenbean backed up, aware that everybody in the triad arena was staring at him. They knew, too. They *all* knew. They could all look into his mind and see his betrayal. Crying, he ran out of the arena.

Starbuck yelled something incoherent and followed him.

Apollo and Boomer were not far behind Starbuck, although neither had a clue to what was going on inside him. In spite of his crazed behavior, insanity was the last explanation that would have occurred to them.

Greenbean hurried down the passageway leading away from the arena. His mind was a melange of pictures from his imprisonment on Baltar's ship. He remembered the words of his confession, and the misery he had felt after saying them. He felt an identical misery now.

Starbuck planted himself in the center of the passageway and drew his laser pistol. He took steady aim down the long corridor, intending to hit Greenbean in the center of his back. However, as he pulled the trigger, Apollo's fist hit him in the arm and deflected his aim. His shot passed very close to Greenbean, who did not break stride.

"Starbuck!" Apollo hollered. "What do you think you're doing? You can't shoot him!"

"I wasn't going to kill him," Starbuck lied. "Just slow him down."

"Didn't look to me like you were aiming to miss," Apollo said.

"But that's Greenbean," Boomer yelled. "A colonial officer, a pilot, a buddy, a—"

"No buddy of mine," Starbuck cried. "It's him. He's killing us. Or setting us up. I'm sure of it."

Lucifer might have been amused by the fact that Starbuck, in his madness, had uncovered the truth of his intricate psychological sabotage. And, of course, nobody believed a mad man.

"Starbuck, you're not making sense!" Apollo said. "Even if Greenbean is somehow behind everything, you can't judge him until he's had his say."

"You're so hot on proper procedure—"

"And you're just hot in the head, buddy."

"Let me at him! Don't worry, I won't shoot him. I might rearrange his face a little, but—"

Starbuck abruptly started running down the passageway. Exchanging worried glances, Apollo and Boomer chased after him.

CHAPTER EIGHT

With Baltar and Spectre spending so much time together, Lucifer was freed to attend to his own endeavors. He tinkered with the guilt machine relentlessly, finding ways to refine it, to strengthen the power of the deadly rays being transmitted to the *Galactica*, to control them more adroitly from afar.

He sensed Baltar and Spectre, arm in arm, coming toward him. He resented their smug alliance and wondered what abnormal features in their personalities nurtured it. It was clear enough what Spectre wanted from Baltar. His transparent need to use others in order to obtain power for himself was obvious. But what did Baltar want? And how could he not see what a fraud Spectre was? Perhaps he did, and liked Spectre all the better for it.

While Lucifer should have been angry at Spectre for trying to usurp his position on this ship, Lucifer did not, in truth, mind the prospect of being transferred away. He preferred frontline duty but, if placed elsewhere, he could function quite well.

"Burning a little midnight oil, Lucifer?" Baltar asked.

"I don't burn oil. My oil is only for lubrication of—"

"Please, please. I know. Just a figure of speech. Place it in your memory. It means working hard and long."

"No work is hard for me, nor do I perceive the time of my labor as long."

Lucifer tried to ignore Spectre's annoyingly steady gaze. Spectre, however, rolled forward to talk.

"Count Baltar is fortunate indeed to have one so loyal as you in his employ, Lucifer."

"Yes, fortunate," Lucifer said. *More than he realizes*.

Baltar was fascinated by the eerie light show that was on display when Spectre and Lucifer communicated with each other. Their eyes lit up more, and so did the strange lights which seemed to illuminate their facial surfaces from within.

"Ambulatory cybernetic sentiences such as we have no purpose except to please our masters," Spectre commented. *Please*, Lucifer thought. He wondered how a creature like Spectre could exist in the same series as himself. Spectre was, to be sure, an earlier model, so perhaps it was only proof of what Lucifer had always suspected, that earlier models were definitely quite inferior.

"Has all been made ready for Imperious Leader's visit?" Baltar asked Lucifer.

"Everything has been done."

"Has the diversionary force been briefed on its mission?"

"Yes."

Spectre, intrigued by Baltar's words, asked:

"Diversionary force?"

"Although we undoubtedly have superior forces to send against the *Galactica*, I've planned a small diversionary action on the planet Vaile. It will serve to confuse the *Galactica*'s warriors and punish the Vaileans for aiding the fleet. We will draw the *Galactica*'s vipers away from the fleet and occupy them in a skirmish above Vaile, while two walls of Cylon raiders zero in on the *Galactica* itself."

A Cylon squadron was often termed a wall because of the tight way its raidercraft flew together, looking at times like a solid wall.

"Not only will we be able to destroy several of their vipercraft at a time when they cannot afford to lose any more—but, should they choose to abandon the fight at Vaile and return to attempt to defend the fleet, it will be too late. Our fighters will mow them down like balloon targets, thus forcing the surrender of the *Galactica*."

"A master plan, I think, honored sir," Spectre remarked.

Lucifer noted that Baltar seemed to glow with Spectre's flattery.

As Baltar and Spectre left command chamber, Spectre glanced back at Lucifer, who had resumed his tinkering on the guilt machine, and said:

"You are lucky, Count Baltar, in having such a one as Lucifer to expend so much effort in refining your invention."

The last statement made Lucifer cease his labor. *Your* invention. Did Spectre mean, as it sounded, that he believed that Baltar was the originator of the guilt device? Or did he merely mean Baltar had titular possession as the commander of the base-star? It would not be beyond belief for Baltar to undercut Lucifer and take credit for the device. Baltar would bear watching.

He returned to his work. Careful examination revealed that certain relays within the machine were being bypassed, a state he had not expected. Yet the change was, he was sure, for the better. The power going out now was much stronger and undoubtedly more effective. *The Galactica may be destroyed from within,* he thought, *before Baltar's wall of ships can even get there*.

Things were going well. Lucifer might even be able to obtain a promotion as well as a transfer from the base-star.

Uri sat, bathed in the glow of the only light in the small meeting room. He spoke to his chief aides, the ones to whom he had delegated limited authority. His voice was low.

In the strange light he looked like a supernatural apparition, a demon.

"Now's the time to strike, I'm sure," he said. "Adama can't fight us; he can't even get out of bed to face us. His comatose state is a condition we can use to our advantage. Ship efficiency is as low as the spirits of its people. Tigh is a fine leader, but he can't put down a resistance now, without Adama to back up his play. Send the word out to our lieutenants. Garner our forces for the march through the ship. We will make a public display, that way they can't ignore us. At the end of the march, on the bridge, we'll present our demands. If they stubbornly persist in not acceding to them, we'll take over the *Galactica* by force. We have the numbers to do so, I'm certain. Once that is accomplished, *everyone* can go down to Vaile."

After his aides had left to spread the word, Uri switched off the light and sat in the dark. In his mind he saw the *Galactica* burning, a new star in the Vailean skies. It was an image he relished, although he wouldn't dare reveal it to his followers.

He was confident his conspiracy would succeed. He was tired of being a nobody aboard the *Galactica* and wanted once and for all to settle someplace where he could attain power.

Greenbean ran frantically, looking for a place to hide and catch his breath. He needed to think. He had to arrange correctly the images in his head. Baltar, Cylons, the torture, the strange red-eyed creature, the odd emotional manipulation, the cell, Scarn. It was all cluttered and confused in his mind. Just as he was about to slow down and crouch in a dark alcove, he heard the running steps behind him, and Starbuck's voice:

"Greenbean! Stop! No point in running!"

He heard the lie in Starbuck's voice and his fear multiplied. He managed to increase his speed. Rounding a corner he slammed into a strolling group of people, knocking a couple of them down.

Apollo trailed right behind Starbuck. He struggled to make sense out of what Starbuck had said. Could he possibly be right about Greenbean? The guilt disease was unknown before Greenbean's return from the dead. Still, that could easily be a coincidence.

One thing he knew for sure, he didn't want to be chasing the man through the countless corridors of the *Galactica*. The best course would be to go to Colonel Tigh in order to discuss the matter. But he couldn't do that—he *had* to follow the hotheaded Starbuck, prevent him from trying anything rash. All they really had to do was corner Greenbean and calmly escort him to someplace where they could talk to him.

As they ran, other Galacticans joined them. They looked fierce. *God,* Apollo thought, *all we need now is a rampaging mob.*

Apollo caught up with Starbuck.

"He went through that door," Starbuck yelled. "He's going down."

"Down to the next level?"

"What it looks like."

"Starbuck, maybe we should let him go for the time being, take—"

"Are you kidding? Didn't you see how guilty he looked?"

"We can't go off half-cocked."

Starbuck glanced sideways at Apollo. It was a distracted look Apollo found difficult to interpret.

When they got near the door through which Greenbean had disappeared, Starbuck sprinted ahead. Apollo accelerated, knowing he had to stay close to Starbuck, who couldn't be trusted if it came to a showdown with Greenbean. Worse than that, what about the mob that Starbuck was firing up as he went?

• • •

Cassiopeia and Dietra left the supply room and headed down the corridor in the direction of Life Center. They carried cartons of medical instruments that Salik had requisitioned.

"You know what Starbuck's gone and done?" Cassiopeia asked.

"No, what?" Dietra replied.

"He sent me flowers with a little note inside saying he was sorry about how he'd treated me and he wanted to make up for it. I mean, I know I was a little hard on him the other day, but I can't figure this."

"Maybe he's reformed."

"Yes, and the universe is contained in the shell of a pea. No, I think it's some new line, some new ploy. He wants to draw out my—"

Greenbean emerged from a stairwell doorway and rushed by the two women, his flailing arm hitting Cassiopeia and knocking her off her feet. Her cartons of medical supplies flew all around the corridor. Greenbean, who hadn't seemed to notice what he'd done, just ran on.

"Hey, you louse," Cassiopeia hollered after him. "Don't you see where you're—"

"Wasn't that Greenbean?" Dietra asked.

"I don't know," Cassiopeia said as Dietra helped her up. "He hit me too fast for me to check his identity. It could've—"

The first wave of the pursuing mob spilled out of the doorway, led by Starbuck, and bumped into Cassiopeia and Dietra, sending both of them to the floor this time. They just missed being trampled.

Boomer stopped long enough to help the two of them up.

"What's going on, Boomer?" Cassiopeia asked.

"Can't stop now," he said, breathlessly. "Got to keep this mob from lynching Greenbean."

"Lynch—?"

But Boomer had run off. Cassiopeia and Dietra exchanged puzzled looks.

"What should we do?" Dietra asked.

"You chase after them," Cassiopeia said. "Do anything you can to help Greenbean. I'm going on to Life Center, tell Doctor Salik. He and Tigh are the only ones who can do something about this."

Dietra hurried after the mob. Cassiopeia took one look at the cartons of supplies spilled all over the corridor, some of them obviously stepped on, and decided not to waste time trying to pick them up.

Greenbean finally found a hiding place, a janitorial closet. He crouched among buckets and cleaning materials, and listened to the loud footsteps of the mob passing by outside.

When all was silent, he tried to make his mind function logically. Some of the images that had been whirling around in his brain came into better focus, particularly the moment when he finally gave in to the torture and spilled his guts. He felt intense shame about this memory, and he sobbed quietly.

Then he recalled being in Baltar's command chamber, remembered the machine that had manipulated his emotions. He could not remember what Baltar and his mechanical aide had said, but he knew it was about the machine, and that the machine was somehow responsible for his present misery. He did not at that moment understand how his experience then was connected to the events now, but he knew that it was an important aspect of his betrayal.

God, he thought, *I shouldn't live. I don't want to live.*

He tried to think of where to go, a place where he could quietly end his life. *What about the devil's pit?* he thought. He had never been to that mysterious area at the bottom of the ship. He only knew that people held many suspicions about it. It seemed like a logical place to go to end a worthless life.

In the Life Center Salik listened patiently to Cassiopeia's tale, and didn't speak until she'd finished.

"Damn," he growled, "I don't know what's gotten into

everybody. Has the whole ship gone crazy? Tigh's got to know about this."

He went to his intercom, called Tigh, and explained the situation.

"I'll cut it off. I'll be on the unicom immediately," Tigh said.

"I agree," Salik said.

"Keep me posted."

"Right, sir."

Salik turned to Cassiopeia who was fidgeting at the Life Center entrance.

"He's going to sound the general alarm."

Cassiopeia, nodding, opened the door.

"Where are you going?" Salik said.

"I've got to go back out there, look for Greenbean. Anything happens, there may be something I can do."

"I may need you here, Cass."

"By the time you need me, it'll be too late. I've got to see what I can do."

He considered protesting further, but saw it would be of no use.

"Okay, go," he said, trying to sound as rude as he could—his trademark. "Get away from here!"

She left. He wondered why he felt so proud of her.

Tigh's voice resounded through the *Galactica*. People on every level, every room, every corner, stopped what they were doing and looked toward the unicom speakers. Even the mob that was pursuing Greenbean.

"*Galactica* personnel, attention! I say, attention! I have been informed that a mob is presently chasing one of our junior officers in some part of the ship. I am not clear on the purpose of this pursuit but that doesn't matter, mob law is not respected in any quarter of the *Galactica*, and it must cease immediately. I say, this needless pursuit must cease immediately. Return to your posts or your quarters or proceed immediately to off-duty areas."

Tigh's words defused the fury of most of the mob, and they settled down to hear the rest of his message.

"We will not condone mob violence or the prejudgement it implies. All offenders will be prosecuted to the maximum of the law. I say, the maximum. I speak for the commander as well as myself. This incident will be investigated thoroughly. I order anyone with knowledge of how this mob originated to proceed on the double to the nearest security post or the commander's quarters, so that we may iron out this problem, whatever it is, immediately."

He paused and the people listened intently to the crackle in the speakers.

"Ensign Greenbean is also ordered to the commander's quarters on the double. All directly concerned with the instigation of this incident, I expect to see you immediately. I say, immediately. *Galactica* personnel, attention!"

Tigh repeated the message as the mob slowly broke up and headed toward their proper areas.

Boomer grabbed Starbuck's sleeve and said:

"You hear, bucko? Colonel wants to see—"

"Did I hear what? Sorry, fellas, I just came down with a bad case of felgercarb in my ears. Can't hear a darned thing."

"Starbuck, calm down!" Apollo said. "We're going to quietly proceed to—"

"Greenbean's around here somewhere. C'mon, boys and girls, we'll find him."

Starbuck gestured to the stragglers from the mob and tried to lead them down the corridor. Some appeared ready to follow but, thinking of Tigh's warnings, couldn't work up the nerve. Starbuck, running off, seemed not to care whether anyone came after him or not.

"What do we do now?" Boomer said.

"We're the only ones with a chance to defuse this," Apollo said.

"But the colonel'll ream us."

"We'll have to take that chance. We have to keep after him. C'mon."

Greenbean heard Tigh's message, but it had scant effect on him. He just kept walking on, searching for an elevator.

Turning a corner, he nearly ran into Cassiopeia again. She held up her hand to stop him.

"Greenbean, didn't you hear? Colonel wants you. Back that way, ensign."

"Ain't goin' there. Leave me alone."

Cassiopeia took Greenbean's soft innocent face between her hands and said gently:

"What's wrong, Greeny?"

He wanted to tell her. She was so lovely, so kind. But the desire was fleeting. Dominated by the guilt-aura that surrounded him, he couldn't even find a useful way to communicate. He tried to push past her, saying:

"Just leave me alone."

"Look," Cassiopeia called after him, "you want to sit someplace and talk? The Life Center. Your quarters. Somewhere."

"No! I don't want anything. I want—"

"Yes?"

"I WANT TO DIE!"

He broke away from her. She ran after him.

Uri stood with some of his followers in the civilian lounge when Tigh's message came. When it was done, Uri smiled broadly, then laughed. He had a strong premonition of imminent triumph.

"I couldn't be more pleased!" he said to his followers. "This is it! Notify our people. We can't wait any longer. We're going to strike now! We'll start the line of march from the Beta Level auditorium. Go!"

His followers ran off in all directions, eager to spread the word. Watching them scamper off, Uri gloated. He felt power surging through his body. He managed a kind of clumsy run himself, eager to get to the auditorium so that he could lead the march of the dissidents.

Sheba and Bojay stood at the elevator bank, awaiting the next available car. They had both been working with the clerical staff, sorting Vailean invoices, and were tired out.

Also, affected in their own ways by the guilt-rays, they were somewhat sad.

"I keep thinking of Dad," Sheba said, "how he looked when he really took charge of a situation."

"Yeah, that was really something, wasn't it?"

"Wish I could do that, I really do."

"You can, Sheba, I know it."

"Nope, I don't have the guts to go ahead like he did, without thinking things all the way through."

"Secret of his success."

"Yep. Well, here's the elevator. Good, I can't wait to get down to the lounge and put a couple of those new ambrosa cocktails away."

The flashing light above the elevator doors turned off, and the doors began to open. Behind them, Bojay and Sheba heard the scuffle of running feet. Bojay grabbed the leading edge of the elevator door to hold it open for the latecomer.

Greenbean dived into the elevator car, after pushing Bojay off the door and back into the waiting area. As Greenbean fell to the floor, the doors closed. Sheba and Bojay looked on, incredulous. Cassiopeia came running up to them.

"We've got to stop him!" she shouted. "He says he's going to kill himself!"

"But why?" Sheba said.

"No time to explain. We've got to go after him."

Starbuck caught sight of Greenbean just before he dived into the elevator. He ran forward and stood behind Sheba, Bojay and Cassiopeia as they all watched the descending numbers above the elevator doors.

"He's gone below engine room level," Starbuck said.

"What's down there?" asked Boomer, who had, with Apollo, finally caught up to Starbuck.

"The engines take up several levels, then there's the fuel storage areas, the devil's pit, the—"

Cassiopeia recalled Brie's earlier mention of the devil's pit.

"Nobody ever goes down there, do they?" Bojay said.

"Some say it's haunted," said Sheba.

"Well," Starbuck said, "he's going there all right."

Another elevator light started to flash. It was an elevator at the right end of the bank. They all rushed to it as the light stopped flashing and the door opened. The group began filing into it. Apollo, holding the door, held Starbuck back.

"Uh-uh, good buddy," he said. "You go report to Colonel Tigh. Tell him what we're doing. I don't want you down there."

Starbuck tried to push past Apollo, but Apollo shoved him roughly backward.

"Apollo," Starbuck protested, "you can't—"

"I said, stay here!" Apollo bellowed.

Starbuck made another attempt to gain entrance to the elevator car, but the door closed right in front of his face. He cursed. Then he looked upward and said:

"Lord, I need a miracle now."

Almost in answer, the light to the adjacent elevator began to flash.

"Lord," Starbuck said, "thanks for the quick response."

The elevator doors opened. Inside, the car was loaded with personnel. There was no room for Starbuck to even squeeze in. Before the door could close, he grabbed its edge, shouting with authority:

"Everybody off. Core Command order! This lift is dangerous."

At first the passengers didn't move. However, because Starbuck was well-known to them as a command officer, his words had effect.

"C'mon, c'mon," Starbuck said impatiently, "I'm taking this car out of service."

The passengers filed out quickly and obediently. Starbuck jumped into the car. Its doors closed, leaving him with a last sight of bewildered and angry passengers, and he pushed the button for the devil's pit level. The button was shinier than the hundred or so others on the panel. It was clear that people rarely went there.

As the elevator sped downward, Starbuck muttered:

"I see I haven't lost the old resourcefulness." He pulled out his pistol and began to run his fingers along its barrel. "Ensign Greenbean, you and I have a date."

Lucifer might have been impressed by the power his device had over its victims. He would not have liked to see Starbuck go off the deep end, but he would certainly have been intrigued by it.

Greenbean stepped out of the elevator and felt nearly stifled by the heavy dank odors of the devil's pit level. The air was close and cold. His eyes, used to the intense light inside the elevator, could not see anything around him.

He brushed away the remaining tears that had flowed during his ride down. He couldn't cry any more. He had realized the full extent of his betrayal, and he felt he didn't even deserve the tears.

"Somewhere around here," he muttered, "around here someplace . . . somewhere, there's gotta be a good place to die."

"You've come to the right place, ensign," said a gravelly voice right behind him. "The right place."

CHAPTER NINE

Adama felt weary, as light and drained as a ghost, as the ghost he probably was. He had been watching Ila since her return from her shopping trip, her frail arms loaded down with heavy overfilled sacks. He had stood near her while she unpacked her purchases and put them away, then followed her around the house as she did a series of light chores. Her efficiency and ease of movement impressed him. She took care of the cottage with the same skill with which her husband helmed the *Galactica*. She was a definite marvel, and in so many ways that he'd never realized because he'd been away at the war. She'd learned, apparently, to live alone for these long periods and busy herself with the cottage, her reading, and the music which she hummed, and sometimes sang aloud, in perfect pitch. The beauty of her singing was a minor miracle, since she was, he knew, half-deaf. Apparently what she heard inside her head was as lovely as what she sang. He wondered if she would have been embarrassed to know that she was not really alone, that her husband was seeing her private habits and idiosyncrasies.

He longed to talk with her and was sad that it wasn't possible. How did a ghost manage to materialize when he wanted to? When he wanted to so very much. Well, no matter—it was so good to see her again that he accepted the situation's limitations.

Suddenly Ila yawned and stretched her arms. She went to the television set embedded in the parlor wall and switched it on. Without waiting for the screen to show a picture, she went to a couch and lay down on it. She yawned again and looked toward the screen.

He followed her gaze and got a new shock.

There, in the center of the screen, holding a microphone just below chin level and smiling charmingly at the camera, was Serina. Serina, the lovely woman who'd become his son's wife just before her tragic death on Kobol. For a moment, he was bewildered. What was Serina doing on the TV screen here in his and Ila's cottage? Then he recalled that she had been a newswoman.

"Serina here," Serina was saying, employing her trademark introduction, "at the Caprica Presidium, where preparations continue as they have continued through the night for the ceremonies that will commence when the long-awaited announcement is beamed here for the peace conference. Even though it's early dawn here, large crowds of people have gathered around the Presidium complex. Anticipation is growing as Capricans ready themselves to usher in a new era of peace."

Adama was frightened by the unexpected sight and sound of Serina. There was something odd about it, something ominous...

"That sounds so familiar, Ila," he said, not worrying that she couldn't hear him. "The words, I mean. They—"

Then he recalled where he had seen this scene before. *Of course! This was the first time I ever saw Serina. She was broadcasting just before—just before—Oh my God!* He now remembered the frantic trip toward Caprica. When they had come within range of the twelve worlds, they had picked up TV news broadcasts. He had seen Serina there, in the same setting and saying the same words as he was watching now. That was the time when the people aboard the *Galactica* had helplessly viewed the Cylon sneak attack and the beginning of the twelve worlds' destruction.

Ila yawned and stretched again. Her eyes closed. Panicked, Adama rushed to her side, knelt by the couch, tried to find some way to arouse her.

"Ila! Ila! Don't go to sleep! They're going to attack. You've got to get out of here. Now!"

But she was settling gently into sleep, her face peaceful and composed. He realized this face would be her death mask if she didn't leave this part of the cottage, the section that was destined to be reduced to rubble by the Cylon attackers. He reached toward her, hoping to shake her awake, but of course his arms just went through her body. He nearly screamed from frustration.

"Ila! It can't have been like this. Did you just go to sleep and never wake up? No! I won't have it. You can't die. You must escape."

He looked back at the TV screen. Serina was frightened. She blinked at sudden distant noises.

"Two explosions," she reported. "You saw them on camera. People are beginning to run in all directions. This is terrible, horrible."

Adama heard faint whistling sounds. At first he thought they came from the TV, then he realized they were outside the cottage. Why were the sounds so familiar? Then he knew why. They were the reverberations of Cylon raiders streaking toward them. Adama concentrated on trying to make Ila hear him.

"Ila! They're coming now. Wake up!"

But she remained asleep as the sound of the approaching Cylon raiders grew from a distant whistle to a house-shaking shriek. He sat back on his heels, wondering what to do. At the same time he realized there was absolutely nothing he could do. This was history. It had happened. He had been transported through time back here for some reason, some purpose—but, whatever it was, he could not change history, he could only observe it. That was the hell of it—he couldn't change a thing.

"It's hopeless," the Serina-image on screen said, as if speaking directly to the ghost-Adama. "People are dying all around me. I don't even know if we're still on the air."

Adama took another look at Serina, knowing he would see the same scenes he'd viewed aboard the *Galactica*. It was hopeless, as she'd said. He studied her pretty, frightened face and thought of how radiant she had been when she'd performed the sealing ceremony with Apollo.

Outside, there was a series of explosions, each burst sounding closer to the cottage. It was as if the blasts were approaching the cottage slowly and politely.

"Ila!" Adama whispered sadly. "Oh, Ila, Ila."

As if in response to his pleas, Ila's eyes came open. She stared past him, jumped at the next explosion. It was the explosions that had awakened her then, not his voice. They were so loud their sound even penetrated her impaired hearing.

Ila looked toward the TV screen but it had gone dead. A Cylon raider, flying low, screamed by overhead. A bomb exploded not far away, and she flinched. Getting up, she went to the door of the cottage and looked out. Adama wanted to shout at her to run, get as far away from their home as possible. She did take a few steps out of the cottage.

Adama saw the swooping Cylon raider before Ila did. He ran toward her. The raider dipped down toward the ground and fired. Its shots killed her instantly. She fell onto the path. Adama, crying, knelt beside her.

Tigh sat by Adama's bed, studied the anguish in his face. Athena came into the room and stood behind him.

"No more word on the mob," she said, "but it seems it has mostly dispersed."

"None of them have shown up here yet," he said.

"I hope Greenbean is all right."

She saw the pain in her father's face and felt helpless. While he was suffering, she was just being a messenger.

"There's something else," she said to Tigh.

"Just what I need," he said, resignedly. "What is it, Athena?"

"Uri. He seems to have stirred up some trouble. There's a crowd of people assembling in Beta Level Auditorium. A new mob, maybe, with new purposes. They're going to march, rumor is."

Tigh shrugged.

"Let 'em march," he said.

"Colonel Tigh, do you mean that?"

Tigh pounded his right fist into the palm of his left hand and erupted with anger:

"Of course I mean it! Why should we even have to deal with Sire Uri and his rabble? Let 'em leave. Tell 'em to line up at the nearest space-waste chute and step out."

Athena was both scared and amused by Tigh's outburst. She liked the idea of dispatching Uri out a chute, but she was worried by the state of Tigh's nerves. Normally cool during stressful events, it was not like him to succumb to the strains of command so angrily. She decided to ignore the outburst.

"He seems peaceful," she said, looking down at her father. It was true. The pain that had been on his face had vanished.

"I wish he'd come out of it," Tigh said, sadly. "We need him now, with Greenbean running amuck through the ship, with Uri playing small-fry demagogue."

Adama stirred in his sleep. His face became frightened. He began to breathe hard, with difficulty.

"Don't go to sleep!" he hollered. "They're going to attack!"

"What—?" Athena said.

"I better summon Salik," Tigh said.

He called the doctor from Adama's intercom. Athena continued to stare down at her father, who now appeared to be squirming in pain.

She leaned down near him, whispered in his ear:

"Father. Dad, it's me, Athena."

Suddenly Adama sat up. He appeared to be awake.

"Ila!" he shouted. "Oh, Ila, Ila!"

Athena put her arms around him. She hugged him tightly

and rocked him back and forth. He was not conscious of her actions. His body went limp in her arms.

"Colonel Tigh!" Athena screamed.

Adama stood in the ruins of the cottage. The attack was over. He had watched the bombs destroy the half of the cottage where Ila had lain watching Serina on the TV screen. He had watched survivors remove Ila's body for burial. He had not wanted to follow them. It was likely they buried Ila in some type of mass grave and he didn't want to see that.

He also realized, in the back of his mind, that he had to stay by the cottage to play out the drama of the predestined past. When it was time, he walked up the path away from his home and stared at the skies. Eventually, as he expected, he saw Apollo's viper fly down to Caprica's surface and land in an open nearby field. His mind almost a blank, his emotions wracked by what he'd experienced, he watched his past self walk across the field, with Apollo following closely. Apollo's cautious stride showed he was obviously concerned for his father's welfare.

Adama stayed at the side of his past self on the path to the cottage. It felt strange, taking step for step with his centons-younger twin. Inside the cottage, he studied the past Adama's dolorous face as he examined several old family photographs. He saw the family memories reflected in the past Adama's eyes. The past Adama stared finally at pictures of Ila, then started to sob.

"I'm sorry, Ila," the past Adama said. "I was never there when it mattered. Never there when—"

The mournfulness passed from his past self to his present self, and they both cried quietly. Even as he did so, Adama wondered why he was feeling so drained, so weak.

Apollo came to the doorway and regarded his father silently and compassionately. The past Adama noticed his son, and brushed away some of his remaining tears with his fingertips. Adama could hear his other self struggle to control the emotion in his voice.

"I didn't," he said, "didn't hear you come in."

"Forgive me, Father. I should have gone away, left you . . ."

"No, no, that's all right. I was . . . was just gathering a few remembrances. You want this likeness of you and Zac?"

"No!" Apollo's response was vehement. "Look, there are crowds coming. They probably saw our ship land."

"I'm not worried about them. I'll be a few more minutes here . . ."

Apollo nodded stiffly and started to leave. Then he came back to the doorway and said:

"Maybe she wasn't here, maybe—"

"She was here," the past Adama said. "She was here."

"Yes, she was here," echoed Adama bitterly.

"Yes, of course," Apollo said.

Adama listlessly watched his other self shuffle around the cottage, clearly collecting memories instead of physical souvenirs. Then his past self left. Adama was sure he would never see him again. He didn't wish to see what happened next, the beginning of the quest, the assembling of survivors. Lucifer, if he could have read Adama's mind at that moment, would have realized that the beginning of the *Galactica*'s journey would have held no interest for Adama because there had been no guilt connected with those hopeful events.

Adama sat on the remains of his favorite chair and stared at the ruins that surrounded him. As he sat, he could feel himself grow weaker. He didn't mind growing weaker. It seemed fitting. He felt old, with nothing to live for, not even the quest for Earth. He felt like sleeping, realizing vaguely that it would be like sleeping within sleeping, if this was a dream. A dream, and not the beginning of his death.

Athena held on to her father as tightly as she could. There was pain surging up and down her arms, and she hugged tighter, glad to increase the pain.

Salik rushed in, Tigh at his side. Athena relinquished Adama to him. Using a portable bio-scan setup, Salik tested the vital areas of Adama's body.

"He's fading," Salik said softly.

"What do you mean?" Athena said, knowing what he meant but not wanting to accept it.

"Life signs are diminishing. His bio-pulse scan is the lowest number I've seen in centons."

"No, he's all right. He's got to be."

"Athena," Tigh said, and took her into his arms compassionately.

Salik stood up.

"Time to get him to the Life Center," he said. "I'll do what I can there."

"Doctor—" Athena said.

"I think he's dying, Athena. Get that into your head now. It'll be better later, when—"

"When it happens?"

Salik nodded.

"What is it, doctor, what's killing him?"

"I wish I knew."

As Salik arranged for medics to transport Adama to Life Center, Athena said to Tigh:

"Better contact Apollo. If you can find him, Tigh. And Boxey."

"I will."

After Tigh had left the bedchamber, Athena sat by her father's bed, holding on to both his hands, waiting for the medics to arrive.

CHAPTER TEN

Baltar put the finishing touches on his dress uniform, spraying a subtly iridescent shine onto the cloth at breast level. The shine slyly duplicated the bands of honor that second- and third-brain Cylons wore on their battle outfits. He was sure the extra sartorial effort would please the Imperious Leader, who was known to favor neatness in his high-level subordinates.

He examined himself in the Gemon mirror. The mirror, manufactured from crystal originally mined on the twelve worlds' planet, Gemon, displayed Baltar from all sides simultaneously, numerous Baltars in an even row. He couldn't see a flaw in his uniform from any angle.

"Well, Spectre," he said, "how do I look?"

"Resplendent," answered Spectre, who had slid up behind him to perform the examination. There were several Spectres joining the several Baltars in the mirror's reflection. "Your clothes are the emblem of your glory, honored sir."

Baltar basked in Spectre's compliments.

"Do you think Imperious Leader will be impressed?"

Spectre knew that, aside from the neatness and correctness of clothing, the Imperious Leader had little interest in the aesthetic splendor of what an individual wore. However, it was clear to him that, in his present mood, Baltar required flattery, so he received a favorable response. At any rate, Baltar would not perceive the Leader's lack of concern with clothing.

"Yes, I believe he will be," Spectre said. "The Leader will see that you are the shining example of good taste as well as supreme leadership."

Actually, Spectre thought Baltar's uniform was rather gaudy, and Baltar's selection of colors a pain to view.

"You flatter me," Baltar said.

"And I thought I had you fooled," Spectre said. He meant that, and was surprised to discover Baltar taking it as a joke.

"You have much more wit than the usual cybernetic being, Spectre. That was a rather good comeback."

Taking advantage of a compliment he did not deserve, Spectre said:

"I suppose that's because I've been in the field with the troops. Suffering hardships, seeing the ironies of battle, doing the—"

"Yes, you had rather a hard time there on Antila, didn't you?"

"It was not what I had been programmed to expect."

A centurion entered the room and informed Baltar that the Imperious Leader's base-star had initiated docking procedures.

"Lucifer has suggested it is time for you to come to the bridge, sir."

"Tell Lucifer that I'll be there when I'm good and ready," Baltar, more than normally irked, said.

"By your command."

After the centurion had left, Baltar felt more nervous than ever. He began to pace, but the tightness of his uniform made quick walking painful.

"Your comrade Lucifer is getting a bit too big for his cognitive storage banks," he said to Spectre.

"Comrade? He is no comrade of mine, sir."

Baltar scrutinized Spectre. He was again imagining Spectre as his new assistant.

"I'm pleased to hear that, Spectre. Very pleased."

"Thank you."

If Spectre had been able to blush, he might have.

"Well," Baltar said, "time to meet the Leader. You're sure I look all right?"

"You look magnificent, your lordship."

They left the room arm in arm.

Humans, with their limited abilities to see anything worthy in Cylons, would not have been able to perceive the Cylon Imperious Leader as in any way attractive, or even acceptably plain. To them he was ugly in a bestial way, with his multiple sets of sometimes luminous eyes, his knobby head that looked like a pile of swamp-gray rocks, his uneven and out-of-balance body and his monstrous size. Cylons might have found him admirably attractive, if they had been inclined to make aesthetic judgements, which they were not. At any rate, the Leader himself had no care about what anyone of any species thought of him. His interlocking but separately functioning three brains enabled him to rise above such emotional perceptions in a godlike way. That distancing ability was one of the few ways in which Imperious Leader was godlike. His goal of achieving the destruction of all other intelligent species and his advocacy of mass murder when in the Cylon cause tended to negate any of his godlike attributes.

Now, as he left his base-star to pass through the connecting airlock into Baltar's ship, he wished he did not have to devote even a fraction of his brains to the conniving human. However, the man had been the only one of his top-echelon officers to make much headway in the seeking and fighting of the human fleet. On the other hand, he usually lost the battles in spite of elaborate plots, strategems, and sneaky tricks.

Spectre had convinced the Leader to make this inspection tour. The Leader had found Spectre to be a most useful aide, even though he saw through the creature's most obvious self-seeking ploys. Such routine trips were restful and helped the Leader to devote more time to meditation on plans to spread Cylon domination to more and more of the universe.

Lucifer glided forward to meet the Leader. After the formal exchange of Cylon ritual greetings, Lucifer led the Leader to the command chamber.

"I have good reports about you, Lucifer," the Leader said.

"You are kind to say so, Imperious Leader."

"No, not kind. Hardly kind. I am merely well-informed."

While Lucifer was pleased to receive the Leader's praise, he wondered from where the good reports could possibly have come. It was hard to believe, after all their chummy regard for each other, that Baltar or Spectre could have transmitted the reports. Perhaps the Leader had a spy network aboard the ship.

Baltar waited at the entrance to the command chamber, smiling so broadly it appeared that his face was being unnaturally stretched. He rushed forward to greet the Leader. Spectre followed Baltar closely, like a child's pulltoy.

"Your imperial greatness," Baltar said, "it is again my pleasure to welcome you to our—"

"There is no need to employ excessive formality with me, Baltar. I am not impressed by it. I am here on a routine tour that should not take up much time."

"Routine?" Baltar seemed disappointed. "Well, Imperious Leader, let me inform you of my plans for your . . . your entertainment. Then this tour will hardly seem routine."

"What do you mean, Baltar?"

"Shall I tell him now, Spectre?"

Of all Baltar's poses, Lucifer thought that his coyness was about the worst. And why was he playing up to Spectre in the Leader's presence?

"As you wish, Count Baltar," Spectre said.

"Yes," Baltar said. Strutting with authority, Baltar led Imperious Leader and his contingent into the command chamber. There, he addressed the flight officer: "Centurion!

Launch the diversionary squadron!"

The flight officer followed orders as Imperious Leader observed, some questions on his minds. He did not object to the surprise, since it was generally hard to surprise him. He admired anyone who accomplished that. Baltar might just be improving as a commander, he thought.

"Diversionary squadron?" the Leader asked. "This interests me, Baltar. What is the purpose of this diversionary group?"

Baltar explained his plan of attack against the *Galactica*. Lucifer was intrigued by the aura of politics that had entered the command chamber with the arrival of the Imperious Leader. It seemed to him that Baltar, Spectre and Imperious Leader were all maneuvering for position. Each wanted something that at least one of the others could give him.

"You know the location of the *Galactica* then?" Imperious Leader asked.

"Its exact coordinates, sir," Baltar replied proudly.

"Then why haven't you attacked before this?"

Baltar was temporarily disconcerted by the Leader's directness, but he was able to counteract the Leader's implied criticism charmingly.

"I wanted the final defeat of the *Galactica* at my hands to be your little treat, sir. So I delayed the launch of the attack until your arrival."

Imperious Leader, while able to see through the devious sycophancy of Baltar's explanation, was nevertheless pleased by it.

"An interesting diplomatic move, Baltar. I only hope it is a successful tactical one."

The Leader's comment disturbed Baltar. He had expecteds automatic praise and encouragement. After all, the Leader was rabidly devoted to the annihilation of the human race. Still, as long as Baltar had known him, the Leader had always been wary of committing himself, especially to another's strategy. He was sure that, after the success of the battle, the Leader would lavish praise upon him.

"And what are the rest of your plans, Count Baltar?" the Leader asked.

"We are assembling two walls of Cylon raiders to attack the *Galactica* and its fleet while the Vailean diversion is in full swing. I expect an easy victory."

"Why is that? You have never had an easy victory against the humans before, why expect one now?"

"That is the key to my plan, honored Imperious Leader. I have effectively reduced the *Galactica*'s fighting abilities with a little . . . a little *invention* of mine that should interest and please you, sir."

Lucifer could hardly believe his auditory circuits. Not only was Baltar taking credit for Lucifer's guilt machine, he was brashly doing it right in front of him. He longed to protest, but felt that it would not do to create a fuss during a diplomatic visit from the Imperious Leader, especially with a massive assault against the humans already underway. Baltar would pay for this dirty trick, Lucifer vowed, but he would have to bide his time until he had the opportunity to avenge himself on the cloying human.

The Leader, on his part, would not have cared who invented the device. Creators were of scant importance to him. Only their creations were. And how the Leader might use them to his advantage.

"It is a most marvelous device, my liege," Spectre commented. "Very impressive."

"May I see this . . . this device?"

"Naturally," Baltar said obsequiously. "Centurion!"

"It is a guilt machine, sir," Spectre said.

"I have named it LEADER," Baltar said. "After you, gracious sir, of course."

Lucifer wished all the maneuvering for political position among these three would cease. He stayed at the tail end of the contingent as it proceeded to LEADER. Imperious Leader took a long time inspecting the machine, while Baltar, oozing confidence, explained its functions. Lucifer shut off his auditory circuits and watched Baltar's performance as a mime show.

Sire Uri's march through the *Galactica* was gathering momentum. It had started in the Beta Level auditorium, where an impressive number of people had already congregated, awaiting his entrance. Fired up by his oratory, they had flooded out into the ship's passageways, forming large groups and heading for the command bridge, their progress accelerated by their own surly energies. The ranks of the march swelled as others rushed to join it.

While it appeared that there was a mass desire to resettle on Vaile, most of the dissidents were people whose mood had been brought low by the insidious waves from Lucifer's guilt device. The irrationality it caused had led them to forget their own beliefs and principles, so that they were swayed to a cause that they wouldn't normally have believed in, following a charismatic leader whose views seemed more logical and acceptable than they actually were.

None of that mattered to Uri, who was merely happy to be achieving his wishes. He looked back on the multitude he led and gloated. *Well, Adama,* he thought, *you didn't think I could pull this off, did you? Down on Vaile I'll allow you to have a pension and live in a cottage, a remote cottage.* Playing to the mob, he roared:

"TO THE BRIDGE! WE'LL CONFRONT THE TYRANTS THERE!"

A massive deafening cheer went up from his followers.

On the bridge, panic was setting in at the thought of the coming confrontation. Flight Officer Omega, who was officer of the watch, didn't know what to do. He wondered what the manual said about civilian mutiny? Colonel Tigh, who wanted to remain close to the unconscious Adama at Life Center, had sent a message to deal summarily with Uri and his followers. But Tigh, in his worried state, did not seem to realize the proportions of Uri's revolt. Omega wished Captain Apollo could be reached. Apollo had always handled Uri well. However, nobody knew where Apollo had disappeared to.

"Reports say that hundreds of people have joined Uri's movement and are proceeding here," Rigel announced. "It's more a mob than a formal organized protest."

"They're surly," said a crewman. "Better be careful."

"What should we do, Omega?" Rigel asked.

"Perhaps we should summon a detail of security officers as a line of defense."

"But that could be dangerous. The mob sees armed officers here and there might be unnecessary violence."

"Good point, Rigel. We'll tough it out without the help of security force then."

"Too late for that, Flight Officer Rigel," said a voice behind him. He turned and saw Tripp, the chief of security, standing stiffly, his hand on the stock of his holstered laser rifle. Dressed in stark black uniform, Tripp always was an alarming figure when you saw him unexpectedly. There was a squad of other security officers behind him, all in the same black outfit, all in some way touching their weapons.

Tripp explained that he considered it dangerous to confront Uri's mob anywhere in the crowded corridors. Stray shots could not only hurt individuals, they might start a riot that even the well-disciplined security force could not contain. Therefore, he announced, he was calling in all security personnel on duty to the bridge to make a stand there, if necessary. It would, of course, be up to Omega to soothe the situation and make that stand unnecessary.

Omega said that he'd rather face the mob without security backups, but Tripp told him quite rudely that it was his duty to protect the personnel of the ship and he intended to carry out that duty now. Lucifer would have been delighted to see how well his device had caused the discipline aboard the *Galactica* to deteriorate.

However, Lucifer was occupied with matters closer to home. He watched helplessly while Baltar took credit meticulously for Lucifer's creation. He had hoped the Leader, with his trio of capacious brains, could see through Baltar's lies, but apparently three brains perceived matters no better when they received only false data. Several times Lucifer was tempted to step forward and confront Baltar with the truth, but reticence—and the realization that it would look like he was trying to outmaneuver his own commander—held him back.

"And so," Baltar concluded his explanation of the guilt device's uses and functions, "by now the situation aboard the *Galactica* should be in such shambles that our ambush will be achieved easily."

Imperious Leader's reaction to Baltar's complex strategies was not the one Baltar had expected and hoped for. After all this time of desiring the defeat of the *Galactica* and the human fleet, Imperious Leader felt a few waves of resentment that the ultimate victory should be that of a traitorous human. He realized that such a thought was not acceptable to a third-brain Cylon, but he could not help thinking it anyway. Ever since he had achieved the third brain and inherited the leadership of the Cylon Alliance, he had devoted the major portion of his active consciousness to the war against the humans. His third-brain ability to be completely objective about himself had one drawback—he was also able to perceive the unhealthy influences his obsessive goals had had on his reasoning processes. In pursuing the elimination of the human vermin, he had been required to understand their irrational and emotional thought processes, the kinds of illogical thinking that had so frequently given them the edge in battles and other confrontations. He had had to exploit a human, Baltar, in order to make the ambush of the fleet and the twelve worlds successful. He had learned to think like a human, accepted their repellent beliefs and attitudes into his trio of brains. The assimilation of human ways had, in turn, altered his ways of perceiving everything. The humans had, in effect, contaminated his mental processes. He had tried to eliminate all the human decay that had entered his consciousness, but that had become impossible. The human influences seemed permanent.

For these reasons he still regarded Baltar as an enemy, even though he had been forced to use him as an ally. Because there were disadvantages to allowing the man too much power, Imperious Leader would have to stay remote from Baltar's coming battle. If Baltar's victory was overwhelming, the Leader would have to find a way to claim it for his own, then get Baltar out of the way.

It was not so simple for Imperious Leader to remain remote from the intriguing device that Baltar had just described. He apprehended instantly that its potential uses were multitudinous. Baltar, with his small mind, had not seen the far-reaching applications it had. It might not just alter the states of humans, it could affect any species. Imperious Leader could use it to enlarge his control over Cylons, as well as all the alien species that infected the universe.

He stopped Baltar from his incessant chatter and ordered:

"I wish a demonstration of your device."

"Now? But the attack—"

"There is no difficulty. We will supervise the attack *together*. There is time, is there not, before it must begin?"

"Well yes, but—"

"Then I require you to demonstrate LEADER for me! Now!"

When Imperious Leader's raspy voice resounded through a chamber as large as Baltar's cavernous command room, rattling even objects that were set in firm foundations, there was no arguing with him. Bemused, Baltar gave the orders for centurions to bring a contingent of human prisoners from the ship's prison level.

"If we're going to have a demonstration," he explained, "then let it be a mass demonstration. A real show, your lordship."

Spectre, impressed by Baltar's quick-thinking theatrical ingenuity, edged closer to the human, so as to be associated with him in the Imperious Leader's view.

Lucifer glided to the other side of Baltar, turned his voice to its softest coherent level, so that neither Spectre nor the Leader would hear, and said:

"Are you sure you require so many of the humans? I have enhanced the output power of the transmitter, and performed many other adjustments. Further, the machine has restructured itself in some ways that I have not yet solved. It might malfunction. And, more, to use so many prisoners will require abundant power."

"Don't worry, Lucifer. It's power that we can spare. Don't interfere."

"As you wish, commander."

Even with the controls Lucifer employed to keep his voice flat and level in tone and pitch, he still sounded bitter.

CHAPTER ELEVEN

Greenbean was terrified. Not only his heart, but the majority of his inner organs were in his throat. Where had the strange voice come from? He looked in every direction, peered down dark dismal vistas, saw nothing.

"What was that?" he finally managed to say.

"Just me," came the voice again.

Greenbean swallowed hard.

"Okay," he said. "I won't bother you. Don't mind me. I'll just catch the next elevator up."

"*All* elevators go up from here," the voice said ominously, and the speaker emerged from an alcove next to the elevator bank. "Welcome to the devil's pit, ensign."

He was an old man with a long dirty gray beard. His clothes, obviously ancient, showed a history, ancient and modern, of food spots, sooty dirt, and mold. They hung in shreds about his body. As he came closer, Greenbean was almost stifled by the stale ambrosa odor that coated the old man's breath and clothing.

"Who in Hades are you?" Greenbean asked. He found it difficult to keep his voice normal.

The old man shrugged.

"Doesn't matter," he said. "My name'd mean nothing to you. I was an engineer for this tub, the rattletrap *Galactica* as I call it, yahrens before you were born, sonny. I got tired of duty. Now I stay here, in the underbelly of the ship, sometimes sneaking abovedecks to steal a little sustenance and whatever else. I've snitched an enviable collection of booze."

"You live down here?"

"Of course. I'm not the only one. Though I may indeed be the only one you'll see, sailor. We don't . . . socialize with each other, we citizens of the devil's pit."

This second mention of *devil's pit,* plus the otherworldly way the man spoke, heightened Greenbean's fear.

"Are . . . are you a ghost?"

The man laughed. The laugh echoed through the cavernous devil's pit ethereally as if it had an existence separate from the man who'd originated it.

"I wouldn't tell you if I was."

Noises of machinery operating in the elevator shaft made both men turn their heads toward the elevator bank.

"Strange," the old man mused, "there's others comin' down here. We don't usually get two visits same day."

"It may be people, friends of mine, other pilots. They're after me, chasing me."

The old man looked quizzical.

"And they're your friends."

"Yes."

"Is this a game?"

"No game. I . . . I betrayed them. I betrayed the ship. They *should* kill me."

"But you'd rather do that job on yourself, if I heard you correct?"

"Yes."

"Maybe that can be arranged. But you don't want to be in plain sight when they arrive. Come here with me."

The old man beckoned him toward the dark alcove he'd

originally come out of. Greenbean was afraid to step into it, but the old man shoved him forward.

After they had become submerged in the dark, the elevator doors opened. Apollo and the others rushed out. They stopped quickly, overwhelmed by the darkness and the complexity of passageways in front of them.

"God," Dietra said, shivering, "this place is eerie!"

"It's worse than eerie," Cassiopeia said.

"Hey, Apollo," said Bojay, "why don't we go back up? If Greenbean's down here anywhere, he can't do anybody any harm. We don't have to—"

"No!" Cassiopeia said. "He told me he was going to kill himself. We've got to stop him."

"Okay, okay. You made your point. What's the drill?"

Apollo began to gesture to each of them in turn.

"Bojay, you and Sheba head down that way. Dietra, you and Cass go down that corridor. Boomer, you try that one. I'll take this way."

After they'd each gone a few steps, Apollo hollered after them:

"Remember now. Whatever Greenbean does, shoot only if you have to, then only to stun."

There was a murmured agreement, then they were off. Greenbean listened to their steps, unrhythmic clicks, fading out to silence.

"They're gone," the old man whispered.

They emerged from the dark alcove.

"Come with me this way," the old man said. Then the elevator noises came again. "Wait! There's another elevator. That makes three in a matter of microns. Perhaps I should start a resort."

Greenbean and the man crouched again in the hiding place.

Starbuck stepped out of the elevator. The insanity that had been taking hold of him at the instigation of Lucifer's device was now evident on his face. His dark blue eyes glowed wildly as he caressed the barrel of his laser pistol.

"GREENBEAN!" he hollered. "Greenbean! Come out, wherever you are. I just want to talk."

He ran off, disappeared quickly in the ghostly devil's pit blackness.

"I'd be careful about that one, I were you," the old man commented as they emerged from the alcove again. "He looks like a killer to me."

The old man dragged at his arm. At first Greenbean resisted.

"Where we going?" he asked.

"Where else when you come to the devil's pit? To hell, ensign, to hell."

Greenbean gave in to the man's pulling and followed him down a dark corridor no one else had taken.

Cassiopeia lost all sense of direction immediately. Feeling quite spooked by the heavy air and density of the devil's pit, she stayed close to Dietra as they went down one pitch-dark corridor after another. Their noses were assaulted by a succession of unpleasant smells. They heard sounds unlike anything they'd ever heard in any other part of the ship.

"I didn't know places like this existed shipboard," Dietra observed.

"I didn't want to know. I don't want to know."

Apollo proceeded warily through corridors and mazelike areas. Up ahead he saw movement, a person or creature edging along a wall. It came to a light and Apollo saw it was human. But it was too short, chubby, and dirty to be Greenbean. Whatever sex it was, it scampered away as soon as it saw Apollo.

A few more steps and something made Apollo glance upward abruptly. He was certain he saw more than one pair of eyes gaping down at him from metal rafters.

"Devil's pit, huh?" he muttered. "They named it right, anyway."

Sheba, trudging her way cautiously and feeling quite blind, tripped over a pile of clothing. She picked up one item from the pile, held it toward the dim light cast by her microflashlight. The odor rising from the cloth made her grimace.

"Whew!" she said. "Whoever wore this's set up house-keeping in the sewage lines."

Bojay got a whiff of it and choked.

"Put it down, Sheba," he said in a strained voice.

"You don't have to worry about that," she said, flinging the cloth away from her as hard as she could.

The old man led Greenbean down an aisle between long rows of mysterious pipes. There were noises all around them. Greenbean wondered which were the movements of his pursuers and which were the scrapings and scufflings of the shadowy denizens of the devil's pit. He wished he weren't here. He wished he'd just climbed into a space-waste chute and got himself flushed out of the ship.

"How's your balance, kiddo?" the old man said.

"Good, I guess. I don't get dizzy in a spinning viper, if that's what you mean."

"Then come with me."

The old man started climbing a ladder that Greenbean hadn't seen. It led straight up from the flooring to a walkway above them.

After going up a few steps, the old man glowered back at Greenbean and told him to climb. Greenbean started up the ladder.

"Where we going?" he asked the old man.

"That walkway. Used to be for inspection when there was anythin' down here to inspect. I go up here to contemplate the good things in life."

Cassiopeia and Dietra turned a corner and saw a dark tall figure up ahead of them. It moved gracefully, the catlike walk of a viper pilot. Had they found Greenbean so soon? Cassiopeia thought. But the man came into some light, and she saw it was only Apollo.

"How did you get here?" she asked him. "You went off in a different direction."

"I don't know. I can't get any sense of direction down here. It's a maze."

"God," Dietra said, "we might be lost here forever."

"Let's hope not," Cassiopeia said. An icicle seemed to caress her back.

"Well, you guys keep going this way," Apollo ordered. "I'm going to try that forbidding little hallway over there."

"Be careful, Apollo."

"Down here, I get more cautious with each passing micron."

Unlike the others, Starbuck strode through the devil's pit as if it were illuminated by banks of fierce light. He had no idea how he moved so well in the darkness. He had been in the devil's pit once before, visiting forgotten rooms devoted to psychological therapy, but he had little memory of the devil's pit's geography.

All he really cared about was finding Greenbean. Led by his growing madness, he had become obsessive in that quest.

He came to an area of criss-crossing pipes. Ducking under one, he came out into a passageway. Looking to his right, he saw Greenbean halfway up a ladder.

He stopped and raised his pistol to eye level.

"GREENBEAN!" he shouted. Greenbean, his face terrified, peered toward him.

Starbuck pulled the trigger. The shot, which narrowly missed Greenbean, made a resonant whistling noise that sounded like an explosion of fierce wind in the echoing vastness of the devil's pit. Greenbean scampered up the ladder and reached the walkway. Starbuck ran to the ladder.

Boomer edged his thin body through a narrow opening into a rank-smelling area that he was sure hid a few of the inhabitants of the devil's pit. Up ahead of him he saw Bojay and Sheba passing through a shaft of light. He started to call to them when he heard Starbuck shout Greenbean's name and then shoot. He started running toward the sound of the shot, which he could tell was close.

Bojay and Sheba also headed toward the area the sounds had come from.

"Isn't that Boomer up ahead?" Sheba said. "How did he get there?"

"Probably just his ghost," Bojay said. "I think the shot came from down that way."

Boomer was heading in the same direction. They followed him into a passageway bordered by thick pipes. They saw Starbuck, who was now on the ladder, waving his pistol maniacally and shouting downward:

"Don't come near me, Boomer. He's mine. I'm gonna take care of him once and for all."

"Something's wrong with you, Starbuck," Boomer yelled back.

"Wrong with all of us," Starbuck responded.

"Come down. We'll go after Greenbean."

"Don't you understand, Boomer? I'm gonna kill him!"

Starbuck resumed his upward climb. Boomer shrugged and started up the ladder himself. Bojay and Sheba ran to the foot of the ladder.

"You follow them," Sheba said. "Somebody besides Starbuck's running along up there. Hear? Probably Greenbean. Somebody else, too. I'm going to follow the sound of it from down here, see if I can find another way up, ahead of them. What are you waiting for? Go!"

Bojay began climbing the ladder. Sheba ran down the aisle, pursuing the clanking metal sounds above her.

Cassiopeia and Dietra heard the shot, but didn't have a clue to its origin. They continued in the direction they'd been heading.

They came to a hallway, with rooms on either side. Cassiopeia took one side, Dietra the other, opening doors and giving quick furtive looks inside.

Toward the end of her row, Cassiopeia opened a door

and saw a cowering group of people huddled against a wall.
They were dirty, dressed in shards of clothing, and vacant
eyed. One of them snarled at her and she slammed the door
shut quickly.

She caught up to Dietra, who was staring upward.

"I heard something," she said. "Up there."

Starbuck's voice, soft and sinister, drifted down to them.

"Stop running, Greenbean. No place you can go."

There was a crazed urgent sound to the voice.

"They're up there," Cassiopeia said.

Starbuck's voice came down again, this time louder and
shriller.

"I got you in my sights now, Greeny."

He shot twice.

"Oh, no!" Cassiopeia muttered.

"You were lucky, that one!" Starbuck yelled. "Next one's
the first nail in your coffin."

This was followed by the clattering sound of running
along the walkway. Down below Cassiopeia and Dietra kept
pace with the steps.

The shot singed the railing next to Greenbean. He and
the old man broke into a run. They were pulling away from
Starbuck because of the old man's surefooted knowledge of
the walkway, when a shot, another near-miss, made the old
man lose his balance. He fell. Greenbean stopped and, over
the old man's protests, helped him up. Starbuck, a few
meters away, halted and took aim. His shot made Greenbean
veer away and bounce off the railing. The impact sent sear-
ing pain through his hip. The old man urged him to run on.
Greenbean wondered if he should. Perhaps it'd be better to
just stand still and allow Starbuck to kill him. It'd be easier
than shooting himself.

No, he couldn't have Starbuck kill him. He wanted to
die, yes, but not with the deed performed by a friend, no
matter how loony the friend was at the moment.

Apollo, moving slowly in order to pinpoint the sounds
that were echoing all around him, was aware that they seemed

to be getting closer all the time. Footsteps ahead of him, at ground level, made him set himself, his gun ready but not pointed. Sheba rounded a corner and came toward him.

"They're up there, Apollo," she said. "Greenbean and Starbuck. I've been tracking them. Starbuck's trying to kill Greenbean. Bojay and Boomer're up there, too. I've been watching for somebody to take a ladder down."

"Maybe we should go up."

"If you say so. I just passed a ladder. Over here."

When they had climbed up to the walkway, they heard the clunking sound of steps heading their way.

Boomer caught up with Starbuck while he was stopped to take aim again at Greenbean. He leaped at Starbuck and grabbed him around the shoulders. They grappled furiously, Boomer maintaining his bear hug tightly. Then Starbuck pushed backward roughly, shoving Boomer against the railing. Boomer's grip loosened enough for Starbuck to ram his elbow into Boomer's stomach. It was not a hard blow, but its unexpectedness knocked the breath out of Boomer and broke his grip on Starbuck. Starbuck hit him hard on the side of the head with his pistol and rushed off, without looking back to check damage.

Bojay ran up to Boomer, who was swaying a bit and holding onto his head where Starbuck had clubbed him.

"You all right, buddy?" Bojay asked.

"Except for seeing triple, fine. Get him."

Bojay tore off down the walkway. Boomer, watching him go, pushed himself away from the railing and loped after him. As his head cleared, he accelerated to a fast sprint and was soon running just behind Bojay.

Greenbean couldn't run any more. He stopped and stood in the middle of the walkway, searching the darkness for his pursuers. The old man dropped back and grabbed his arm.

"Don't stop now, sonny. We got some space 'tween us and them. Look, I know a place they'll never find us. C'mon!"

"No!"

The fury of Greenbean's response made the old man release his grip on the young man's upper arm.

"No? You out of your head?"

"I'm not running away from them. I want to die. Starbuck's going to kill me. I didn't want it to be him, but so . be it. Better this way."

The misery inside him was now so overwhelming Greenbean couldn't think straight. In his mind he was getting jumbled pictures—of his betrayal, of the time since, of Baltar and Lucifer. He wanted to make them stop spinning around in his head.

There were now steps coming toward them from both sides. Greenbean turned his head in one direction and saw Apollo in the distance, with Sheba just behind him. From the other way came Starbuck, waving his pistol crazily in front of him.

"Look, old-timer, we're trapped anyway."

The old man took a couple of steps toward Apollo and hollered:

"What's this all about? You can see this kiddo wouldn't hurt a Dagon nightcrawler."

"Sir," Apollo shouted back, "I don't know who you are, but this is military business. The ensign has been summoned to the commanding officer. He has to—"

"Don't be officious with me, young man. I don't care about your *commanding officers!* I'm an engineer. We take care of ourselves and our own without the interference of commanding officers."

"He's not your own," Starbuck yelled. "He's a dirty traitor. Let me—"

The old man casually interjected his body between Greenbean and Starbuck, saying:

"You'll have to kill me first."

"I don't want to kill you, old man," Starbuck said.

"You're not going to kill anyone, Starbuck," Apollo barked.

"Crouch a little bit, son," the old man whispered to Greenbean. "You're too tall a drink o' water."

Boomer and Bojay, running up, stopped a few meters away from Starbuck.

"What's got into him?" Bojay muttered.

"I don't know," Boomer said, ruefully. "We've got to jump him before he gets another clear shot at Greenbean. I'll hit him highside, you grab him low."

"Right."

It appeared as if Starbuck hadn't been aware of their arrival. However, just before they were about to spring at him, he whirled around and held his gun on them. His eyes were deranged, and the twisted smile on his face alarmed them.

"You're not going to shoot us, Starbuck," Boomer said quietly.

"Not unless I have to."

And those eyes, and that smile, told them he just might. He turned his back on them and started walking toward Greenbean and the old man.

"What's he doing now?" Sheba asked Apollo.

"I don't know, but we better get involved in it."

"Greenbean," Starbuck shouted, "how could you turn on us all, you—"

"I—I didn't know what I was doing. Starbuck, they get into your brain and turn it into jelly. They—"

"I don't want to hear about it. I'm just going to slice your head off and toss it out the nearest chute."

"I don't care. It's all—"

"What are you guys having," the old man said, "a tea party conversation? He's trying to kill you, kiddo."

"I said, I don't care."

"Well, I do."

The old man stepped toward Starbuck.

"Get out of the way, old-timer," Starbuck warned.

"NO!"

The old man's leap at Starbuck startled everyone on the walkway, especially Starbuck. It was an amazingly agile and graceful leap, his arms outspread, the rags of his moldy garment flapping. He made contact with Starbuck savagely, managing to strike his jaw and send him reeling backward.

Starbuck fell to the floor of the walkway. Bojay stepped forward to help the old man, but Starbuck gestured him backward with his pistol. The old man jumped on top of Starbuck, but he was light and fragile, and Starbuck was able to fling him off. Starbuck sprang to his feet rapidly and pushed the old man aside. The old man made a futile attempt to leap again on Starbuck, this time attacking him from the rear. He hung on Starbuck's back weakly, and then fell. He hit his head against the railing and passed out.

Boomer went to the old man's side as Starbuck, his eyes gleaming with hatred, edged toward Greenbean. Apollo and Sheba approached the ensign from the other side.

"Greenbean," Apollo called, "come here. To us."

"No, Apollo," Starbuck said grimly, "he's mine."

"Greenbean . . ." said Apollo.

Greenbean turned toward Apollo and said in a shaky voice:

"I'm not coming, Apollo. I want to die."

"And you're going to," Starbuck said. He lifted his pistol to aim it.

"Stop him, Apollo," Sheba shouted.

"Only one thing I can do," Apollo said.

He raised his own pistol. Starbuck and he squared off, facing each other, the slumping Greenbean in between them, watching them stiffly, offhandedly.

"You do what you want, Apollo," Starbuck said softly, "I've made my choice."

Apollo noticed Boomer creeping up behind Starbuck. One of Boomer's special abilities was the ability to move soundlessly.

"Starbuck, listen to me," Apollo said, to gain time for Boomer.

"I'm done with listening," Starbuck said.

Boomer, in a lightning move, pulled himself onto the railing so that he towered above Starbuck, who still hadn't sensed his approach. As Starbuck fired at Greenbean, Boomer leaped onto his back and deflected his aim just enough so that the shot went astray. Planting his feet on the walkway,

Boomer pulled Starbuck sideways. That gave Apollo the chance he needed. Aiming quickly and carefully, he shot. Starbuck's pistol sailed out of his hand and went clattering to the walkway floor. The old man, who had come to just before, picked it up and threw it over his shoulder off the walkway.

"Apollo," Starbuck yelled.

"That's it, Starbuck," Apollo said. "Enough."

Starbuck screamed a long drawn-out no, wriggled out of Boomer's grasp, and lunged at Greenbean. Before anyone could intervene, he had pushed Greenbean against the railing. Putting his arm beneath Greenbean's legs, he tried to flip him over the railing, intending to send him to his death below, onto the floor of the devil's pit. At first Greenbean didn't resist, but then he realized he couldn't let Starbuck kill him like this. He might want to die, he thought, but not this way, not as Starbuck's revenge.

Greenbean kicked out at Starbuck, catching him a solid blow in the side. Starbuck lost his leverage, and Greenbean slid off the railing. For a moment the two wrestled ineffectively against the railing, then Starbuck got a grip on Greenbean's neck and began to squeeze hard. Greenbean nearly blacked out immediately, so fierce was his adversary's hold. Fortunately for him, Boomer dived at Starbuck and weakened his grip by pulling at his left arm, then Apollo hit his other arm with a swift downward stroke that caused Starbuck to disengage. Bojay joined them to hold the violently squirming Starbuck back.

"Okay now," Apollo said. "Let's get some of this straightened out. How about we go see Colonel Tigh, Greenbean?"

Greenbean knew the last thing he wanted right now was to stand before the stern gaze of the colonel.

"Just leave me alone, all of you," he said.

"No," said Cassiopeia, who had climbed a ladder and reached the walkway level just in time to see Apollo and Boomer stop Starbuck from murdering Greenbean. "Don't let him get away with that. He'll try to kill himself."

Greenbean turned to Cassiopeia and said angrily:

"What do you care?"

Cassiopeia took a step toward him, and, her eyes filled with fury, said:

"I care! Damn it, I care! We all do, you bloody fool! We'll risk our own lives for you."

"She's right," Boomer said. "We need you back in the squadron."

"I don't need the—" Starbuck muttered.

"Shut up, Starbuck," Boomer said. "Listen to us, Greeny."

"Right," Apollo said. "Get it through your head we're not going to let you do anything to yourself."

"Try and stop me," Greenbean said ominously, then leapt toward the railing, grabbing it with the intention of jumping over it. Sheba dived at him and, in a graceful tackle, wrapped her arms around his legs to keep him on the walkway. The others joined in and subdued Greenbean. He collapsed in their arms, bawling.

"You don't understand," he said desolately. "You don't understand. It's awful."

Apollo knelt next to him and said gently:

"What don't we understand, Greenbean?"

"What I've done. I betrayed you all. Everybody. The whole ship."

There was a moment of quiet while Greenbean's listeners exchanged glances, all except Starbuck, who stared smugly into the distance.

"See, guys?" Starbuck said. "I told you, didn't I?"

"Keep your trap shut, Starbuck," Apollo said. "I don't want to hear another word from you. Okay, Greeny, tell us."

"But it's awful, it's—"

"Let us judge that. Talk."

Greenbean couldn't say anything at first. When he did speak, it was in a quiet, shattered voice.

"The . . . memories, they come back. I didn't know. Didn't know what I'd done, not until now. But I remember . . . remember everything now . . ."

He told them about his capture and transportation to Baltar's base-star. He described in harrowing detail the tortures the Cylons had put him through. The others couldn't look Greenbean in the eye as he spoke of the pain he'd felt. He told them of how his brain had turned to jelly, how his insides had collapsed inward, how he'd tried to measure prolonged pain to get his mind off it. He told them of the psychological tortures, of how he was made to feel he had been a total flop as a pilot, warrior, friend, human being. He told them how he had been injected with drugs that distorted his reasoning, that ruined his senses of logic and morality. He told them how he tried to fight all the tortures, how he struggled in his cell to train himself to resist the next session's pain. He told them of how he no longer had been able to face another session, of how he'd finally cracked and given his Cylon interrogators all the information they wanted to know. The *Galactica*'s coordinates, details about personnel and firepower, strategies, everything he knew that he thought they would like to hear.

"Apollo," he said, "that last time, I tried not to tell them. I struggled against it. I knew others are captured and don't tell—"

"And don't usually come back either," Apollo said.

"But I couldn't . . . couldn't fight it. Suddenly I had to tell them all. Everything. I *wanted* to tell them. I felt happy for telling them, relieved. It wasn't till later, back in my cell, that it hit me what I'd done. Not till later. See, I've got to die now, got to—"

"No," Apollo said, in a kind voice. "No, Greenbean, no."

"But I—"

"You cracked. Could happen to any one of us."

"Apollo," Starbuck cried angrily, "what are you saying? What he did, it's treason!"

Apollo struggled to control his temper as he replied to Starbuck:

"You know the commander's position on information obtained by the Cylons through torture. He says the informant has already been punished enough, he wants no vengeance."

"Fancy-sounding words, Apollo. But we might be killed

because of what he told the Cylons."

"Then we'll be killed. But now we know the danger, we know what they know. That just might be to our advantage. Tell us more of what you recall, Greenbean."

"But I need to be punished. I need to die."

"Don't sweat the punishment. I'll see you're not let off easy. But we need to know more. You have to tell me all you remember."

In muddled fashion he related what he could remember of his interviews with Baltar. There was something there he should recall, he knew, but it wouldn't come back to him.

"And then they let me go. And I woke up in my viper and didn't remember a thing. They'd taken all the memories of my time on that ship out of my head."

"A mind-wipe," Apollo said.

"What?"

"Never mind. Keep talking."

"I came back here and everything started going haywire. And I know it's my fault. I shouldn't have come back. I did it. I did all of it. It's my fault."

"Did what? What is it you've done?"

"I . . . I don't remember. Something Baltar did to me. His assistant, the red-eyed one, did to me."

"What did they do?"

"I can't remember."

"TRY! Greenbean, try."

Greenbean squirmed physically as he struggled to recall the incidents on Baltar's base-star. The more he struggled, the more it became clear. Suddenly the memory of sitting in the chair and being emotionally manipulated returned to him.

"They spoke in front of me like I couldn't hear. I guess they figured the mind-wipe'd take it away anyway."

"But what was it they were saying?"

"I can never quite focus on it. I can almost hear them."

"Concentrate, Greeny," Cassiopeia said, softly and tenderly.

He shut his eyes, saw Baltar, Lucifer. Gradually, like a

commcircuit receiver being slowly tuned louder, their words became clear.

"Something about guilt. Sending me back to spread guilt through the ship. After you found me, all I had to be was on the ship and everything'd happen automatically."

"What would happen?" Apollo asked.

"I don't know. Don't understand. The stuff'd go out from me in some way."

"Stuff? What do you mean by stuff?"

"I don't—the guilt! It was the guilt. I'd spread the guilt."

"How?" Starbuck said sarcastically. "With the charm of your charmless personality?"

"Starbuck!" Apollo said, threateningly.

"I know, I know. My mouth is sewn shut."

Apollo prodded Greenbean to talk again.

"I really don't—I'd—wait, I remember, it was this stupid-looking machine. It looked like a pile of junk. They sat me by it, and I felt whatever they wanted me to feel. I was laughing. Crying. I felt afraid. Then content. Just one emotion right after the other, whatever they wanted. The red-eye'd just flip a toggle."

Apollo continued his interrogation to prod Greenbean's memory. The details came out slowly. Greenbean described the manipulations, then he remembered them referring to the pile of junk as a guilt device, then he recalled them saying they could use Greenbean to transmit the emotion back to the *Galactica*.

"Use you?" Apollo asked. "How did they do that?"

"I don't know. They . . . they put it on me some way. Planted it. Somehow."

Apollo clasped Greenbean's shoulders and said, his voice intense:

"This is important, Greenbean. They planted it on you. How? Is it on your skin or inside your body?"

"No, no, I don't think so."

"In your viper?"

"No . . . It's no use, Apollo, I can't—"

"You're doing fine. Keep trying."

Greenbean scowled, forcing the memory to come.

"They . . . they said I'd carry it to the *Galactica*. Some way. It'd be . . . it'd be . . ."

He pictured Baltar talking in that sneering self-important way. The words were faint, blocked by the prisoner Greenbean's hazy mind, but if he concentrated he could hear. He concentrated.

"My clothes," he said. "My clothes, they put something in my uniform."

"What?" Apollo asked. "Take your time, think."

"They're . . . I can't . . . they're . . . *something*. Some kind of . . . they called them relays. Red eye said relays. That's it. There are relays in my clothing. Inside buttons, woven into threads, all over it."

"But your clothes were checked when you got back."

"Not . . . well enough. The odd one, Red eye, he said he created circuitry so small it'd be virtually undetectable. Not 'less you were lookin' for it."

Greenbean sounded relieved, and his voice became more energetic.

"They're on me, Apollo. On this . . . this uniform. This was the one. They're right here."

He stared down at his clothing, then grimaced as if it was crawling with bugs.

"Oh God," he said, "get them off me."

Apollo released his hold on Greenbean and said firmly:

"We will, Greeny. Don't worry about that. We'll find them."

He leaned back, smiled at the others. They were all silent, affected deeply by Greenbean's testimony.

The voice of the old man, sounding distant, broke the silence.

"See? I knew he was all right, that kid. I could tell, right when I looked at him first time."

The words were followed by an easy, shuffling sound. Apollo looked in the darkness, tried to see the old man. But he wasn't in sight. Apollo called for him. There was no response. He was gone.

CHAPTER TWELVE

Adama was vaguely aware that the stars were blinking out, one by one. Caprica and the rest of the twelve worlds had vanished long ago. He hadn't even been aware of their going. Floating now in space, he felt like an empty shell, a balloon animal sailing aimlessly along air currents. There was little inside him, he knew. Even the guilt had dissipated.

He would soon be in complete darkness, all stars gone, and he didn't care. He wanted to blink out as the stars were doing.

In the distance, as if coming from the end of a long, long hallway, he thought he heard a voice, a familiar voice. It was saying, "He's sinking." He didn't know what that meant. He didn't care to figure it out.

In the Life Center, Adama had been placed in a life-support cylinder, a long tubular device with scores of microscopic tubes, looking like threads, running into it. His skin was white, corpselike. His breathing was labored.

Salik turned away from the cylinder and said to Athena: "He's sinking."

"No!" Athena screamed. Tigh held on to her.

Salik told his nurses to increase the heartbeat-inducer rate and maximize the controlled blood flow. They scurried to obey him.

Boxey stood against a wall and tried not to look at Adama. It reminded him too much of going to see his adopted mother, Serina, before she died.

"Will grandfather be all right?" he said to Jolly, who had volunteered to come with him to Life Center.

"Sure, scout, he'll be fine."

"I think you're lying to me," Boxey said.

Jolly didn't know what to answer to that. He smiled weakly.

"He looks bad," Boxey said.

Salik walked to Tigh and Athena.

"I'm running out of solutions," he said.

Boxey heard that, and began to bite his lower lip. Jolly scrunched down, not an easy move for a man carrying so much bulk, and put his arms around the boy.

A young cadet-trainee hesitantly entered the Life Center, looking like he'd rather not be there. Tigh acknowledged him, and the young man came forward and recited the message he'd been practicing all the way there.

"Sir, Flight Officer Omega reports that the forces of Sire Uri have arrived at bridge level, and are approaching the bridge. They are growing in number rapidly. A squad of security personnel have deployed themselves throughout the bridge, in strategic tactical spots. Their commander has ordered them to be weapons-ready. Omega told me to tell you that he doesn't know how long he can keep the lid on. He says he believes your presence might effectively ease the tension."

Tigh nodded.

"Thank you, warrior," he said. The messenger was clearly awaiting his answer. Tigh walked slowly to Adama's cylinder and gazed at him. It didn't look like he would survive

much longer. Tigh very much desired to be with his old
friend to the end. In case Adama became conscious, even
for an instant, he wanted Adama to see him there, so he
could tell his commander that he would carry on the quest
for Earth.

But he was needed on the bridge. What would Adama
have advised him to do? The question was unnecessary.
Loud and clear, Tigh could hear Adama's voice telling him
to proceed to the bridge. Tigh turned to Athena and said
sadly:

"I'm sorry, Athena. I have to go. I don't want to but—"

"I understand," Athena said. "And so would he."

Tigh nodded grimly and, with one regretful look back at
Adama, left the Life Center. Athena and Salik stood side
by side next to the cylinder. Against the wall, Boxey tried
to be a proper junior warrior and hold back his tears. He
could not.

It wasn't clear whether the devil's pit chute for space-
waste had been operative recently. There were traces of rust
around the rim of its hatchway cover. Apollo and the rest
surrounded Greenbean, except for Starbuck, who stood in
the shadows, glowering.

"Okay, Greeny," Apollo said. "Take off your clothes."

"Right here?" said Greenbean, wide eyed.

"Right here. We've got to get rid of them, incinerate 'em
and send 'em out the ship."

"But . . . but there are . . . ladies here."

Cassiopeia laughed, and said:

"Don't worry, Greenbean, we won't look."

"Not so you'd notice anyway," chimed in Sheba.

"Come on, Greenbean," urged Boomer. "You ashamed
of fleet-issue underwear or something?"

Reluctantly, Greenbean started to take off his uniform.
When his tunic was off, Apollo took it from him and said:

"Let's not take any chances. These buttons are breakable.
Let's break them up. Use anything you can."

Boomer slammed a button with the butt of his pistol.

Sheba and Bojay used flight tools. Dietra bit one to see how hard it was, then crushed it beneath the heels of her heavy stylish boots.

"Knew this overpriced footwear'd be good for something besides the pain of fashion."

Cassiopeia carefully collected the fragments and shards of the crushed buttons.

Adama looked to his left. He was right. A star *had* winked back on. And there was another one. At the same time, a wave of energy seemed to enter his floating body. Suddenly he felt like going somewhere. But where? What direction?

Then he thought he heard Athena whispering to him. He could not discern what she was saying, but he propelled his body toward the sound of her voice. He began to accelerate very quickly.

Finished with the buttons, Cassiopeia's collection of debris swept into an even pile, Sheba held up one of the buttons she'd broken.

"Look, Bojay," she said. "You can see the circuitry inside here. It's shielded, that's why nobody detected it. The person who made this must be a genius."

"A sick genius, if you ask me."

Greenbean peeled off his trousers, leaving himself in standard-issue military undergarments. His skinny legs looked more sticklike than usual coming out of the wide flaps of his undershorts. His whole body blushed. Which, Apollo noted, was at least a step up from the pallor of suicidal gloom.

"What now?" Boomer asked.

"Rip up the cloth," Apollo said. "Or cut it. Anything. We're breaking circuits here, if I understand correctly."

Except for Starbuck, they all pulled at sections of the lightweight cloth until it tore. Soon, Greenbean's uniform was in tatters.

• • •

Adama felt like a comet, his body going faster and faster in a flight across the universe. He now saw more than faraway stars. There were planetary systems, asteroids, strange undefinable globules.

Ahead of him he made out a strange faroff light. As Athena's voice grew louder, he felt himself driven toward the light.

"Please, Dad," Athena's voice was saying. "Come back, you've got to. Got to."

"Don't worry, Athena," Adama said to himself. The light ahead of him expanded rapidly.

In the Life Center, Athena turned to Salik, who was giving a nurse an order a few meters away, and cried:

"Doctor! He mumbled something. I couldn't hear what, but he said *something!*"

Salik ran to her and stared down at his patient. New color had rushed back into Adama's face.

The group stood and stared at the messy remains of Greenbean's uniform, the pile of it now transferred to the inside of the space-waste chute.

"Every speck of it in there?" Apollo asked.

"You couldn't find an atom of it out here," Boomer said.

"All right then. Gentlemen and ladies, draw your weapons."

They all pointed their pistols at the pile of clothing. They fired, the beams from their pistols forming a bright set of lines all converging on Greenbean's former uniform. The clothes exploded in flame.

As the fire burned, thin wispy pieces of blackened cloth rising momentarily above the flames, Greenbean felt his gloominess lift away from him, as if being consumed by the fire itself.

Starbuck, too, suddenly felt weightless. He shook his head, as if to force out the angry images there. He couldn't believe what he had been doing, couldn't accept that he'd actually tried to kill Greenbean.

Tentatively, he stepped toward Greenbean and, without speaking, put a hand on the young ensign's shoulder. Greenbean started at the touch, but realized it wasn't an attack. He smiled back at Starbuck's friendly smile.

Adama soared across the vastness of space, moving faster than the *Galactica*'s top speed. Worlds flew by, stars kept pace with him. He now heard Athena clearly.

"He's coming to!" she was shouting. "Look, Salik, look."

He did feel as if he were coming awake. A quick image of a room replaced the universe for a moment. Then he was back flying again. Ahead of him, there was a brilliant glowing planet. It seemed familiar to him. *It must be Earth,* he thought, *it must be Earth.* Near it, the *Galactica* hovered. He dove quickly toward his ship.

The space chute flames had died down. There was just a smoldering flat area of burned cloth and objects.

"Okay, Bojay," Apollo said, "you get the honors. Flush it out. Turn the pressure system to maximum!"

Bojay flipped the hatchway door shut and turned the valve wheel that put the chute into operation. The odd gurgling, whirring, and whooshing noises inside the chute were a pleasure to hear. There was a final explosion of strange sounds, and they knew the debris had been swept out of the chute by the equivalent of a gale-force wind.

"There she goes!" Sheba hollered and laughed.

Greenbean looked happy for the first time in centons. He laughed, too. His whole body shook.

"You chilly, Greeny?" Cassiopeia asked.

"A little."

"C'mon, guys," Starbuck said, "let's get out of here. I've had enough of the devil's pit. I want to get to someplace else. Some *sane* place."

At the elevator, Greenbean held back. It was clear to one and all that he was too embarrassed to return to the populated sectors of the ship in his underwear.

"C'mon, Greenbean," Boomer said, "we'll form a shield around you up there, get you to your quarters."

"Yeah," Starbuck joined in, "we can be a viper flying wedge for you."

Athena stood by the cylinder and smiled down at her father. Boxey, also smiling, stood next to her, holding her hand.

"What am I doing *here?*" Adama said. "Athena? Salik?"

"You were ill, sir," Salik said.

"No, not ill. Something else."

"What?"

"I don't know. I was there, Athena. Really there, on Caprica. I saw your mother again. I saw the attack. I saw—"

"Hush," Athena said. "It was just a dream."

"A dream?" He found that idea hard to accept. "It didn't feel like a dream. I was there, Athena. There, and on the *Galactica*—*before* the Cylons attacked. I saw what I'd gone through. I saw things I hadn't seen before. I—"

"Take it easy, Father."

"Yes," Boxey said. "Shut up, grandpa."

While Adama gathered strength, Athena filled him in on how the strange guilt illness had spread through the ship. He listened to her for a while, then was distracted by a memory.

"Athena," he said. "Just before I flew back into the ship—in my dream—if it was a dream—I saw Earth. I'm certain it was Earth."

"I'm beginning to believe you, Father. Maybe it was."

"Maybe. It glowed. There was a feeling of . . . of welcome for us emanating from it."

Athena smiled wistfully.

"It would be nice," she said.

"I'm *sure* it was Earth," said Adama.

For the first time, Tigh realized that Uri really did have the advantage of numbers. His followers crowded onto the bridge and jammed the corridors outside. They were a desultory crowd, and they didn't appear to be reasonable at the moment. Uri, his beady eyes making a slow scan of the bridge, smiled sneeringly and said:

"Ah, Colonel. I don't see your security forces. I heard there was security personnel awaiting us."

"There were," Tigh said. "I sent them away."

Uri's mouth opened slightly in mock astonishment.

"Ah, the stand, is it? You're taking a stand against us? We're too large for you, Tigh. You have to let us go. All you have to do is order up the shuttles to carry passengers down to Vaile. A simple solution. Everyone may come, if they wish."

The crew on the bridge gazed at Tigh expectantly. He was tempted to just throw up his hands, and throw out the crowd, let them go wherever they wanted, let them ruin the social stability of Vaile with their misguided churlish attitudes and ideas. But he could not allow that.

"No, Uri," Tigh said firmly. "There'll be no shuttles down to Vaile, except for the normal supply and trade runs."

Uri's voice was soft but resonant.

"Tigh, you can't order us around. I gave you your chance. Now it's up to us. Clear the way. We're taking over the *Galactica*."

Tigh drew his pistol, pointing it directly at Sire Uri.

"Don't even think of it, Uri," he said.

Uri hesitated. He was not one to put his own life on the line. However, he didn't mind sacrificing others. He dropped back behind the front rank and tried to look like a commander inspiring his troops while carefully keeping bodies of his followers between himself and the enemy artillery.

"Don't listen to him," Uri yelled. "They won't dare to shoot."

The front ranks surged forward, pushed by rearguard rabble rousers more interested in violence than their cause.

Tigh brandished his weapon and hollered:

"I order you—"

The rest of what he said was lost in the clamor of the crowd. Tigh raised his pistol, knowing he might have to shoot a warning shot. The front rank of the mob, growling and yelling, moved toward him. He tensed his finger on the trigger.

Then the crowd stopped, and the noise died down. The

people down front seemed to be looking past Tigh, over his shoulder. He followed their gaze and turned to see Adama standing at the other end of the bridge. Athena was beside him, and Salik a couple of steps to the rear.

"Adama!" Tigh shouted, startled at the apparition of what he knew must be a ghost.

"Don't mind me, Colonel," the ghost said. "I'm off-duty. Carry on."

The mob no longer had any urges to take over the bridge. Gradually, it dispersed. Uri was nowhere to be seen. He had slipped away as soon as he had assessed the situation. Some members of the mob couldn't figure out why they'd been there in the first place. They had no great desire to leave the ship, go to Vaile. No longer under the influence of Lucifer's guilt machine, they were back to normal, or at least their many and varied versions of normality.

The bridge crew, relieved, returned to their jobs.

"Well done, Colonel," Adama said. He looked surprisingly vigorous, especially for one who'd been unconscious in Life Center the last Tigh had seen him.

"If it weren't for you—" Tigh said.

"All I did was spook them a little," Adama said. "They think I'm a ghost, you know."

"Yes, I did, too."

"You know what, Tigh? I thought I was a ghost there for a while, too."

CHAPTER THIRTEEN

Eagerness and excitement seemed linked in a chain that ran all the way from the launch bay up to the bridge. Everybody was spoiling for the fight. While only the pilots would go out and confront the enemy directly, they knew the rest of the flight would be with them in spirit.

Now, as the flight crew awaited the signal to launch and the command officers reviewed the final aspects of strategy, there was an exaggerated mood of happiness throughout the ship. Everyone who'd been affected by the guilt transmissions felt as if burdens had been lifted from them. Even the unaffected smiled more as they saw that their comrades and friends were back to normal.

Adama showed no signs of having been brought to the edge of death by Lucifer's sabotage. He was energetic, alert and ready to fight a major battle by choice instead of as a retaliation to Cylon pursuit.

There was a good chance, he believed, that *Galactica*'s strike wings could score a major surprise victory over the

191

Cylons. If his calculations were correct, Greenbean's information, elicited in long interrogations, provided a reasonable estimate of the coordinates of Baltar's base-star. With Apollo leading the attack, the Galactican forces might just track it down and ambush the ambushers. It was better than waiting for Baltar to send out a wall of Cylon raiders against them. For once, the enemy might be the sitting duck.

"Colonel Tigh!" Adama said, after he'd examined the battle plan for the last time.

"Yes sir."

"Are all squadrons ready to launch?"

"Ready."

"Then launch."

In launch bay, the pilots, itching for action, chattered noisily on the commcircuit.

"Lieutenant Starbuck?" Apollo said.

"Captain?"

"How're you feeling, good buddy?"

Starbuck was happy to hear the affection in the tone of his old friend.

"If you mean, is my noggin back on straight, the answer's yes, I am as sane as I ever was."

"Then we're all in trouble."

"You got it. And hey, pal?"

"What?"

"Thanks."

"For what?"

"Don't be coy, hero. You know, for seeing me through, and making sure I didn't do anything stupid."

"I did that?"

"Spit marbles, skypilot."

Apollo's laughter roared over the commline.

"Glad to have you back with us, bucko."

The signal to launch came. The vipers zoomed down the launch tubes in precise order, then formed up outside the ship and headed out. Flying side by side in at least threescore ranks, the viper formation, dense and symmetrical, was a handsome, harmonious sight. Adama viewed it with admiration and a wide smile.

"Precision flying, Tigh," he said.

"Reminds me of the time we were wingmates."

"Yes, we were pretty slick, right? God, so many yahrens ago..."

They stood silently for a while, overseeing the activity of the bridge crew. The mood all around them was happy and expectant.

Adama spoke abruptly:

"What did Greenbean call that wretched invention—a guilt device?"

"Yes."

Adama shook his head. For a moment he recalled being under the influence of the device.

"I can't describe how guilty I felt when I was ... in that dream. Or whatever it was. It was overwhelming, Tigh."

"I believe it."

"But, you know, it was strange, too. For all the guilt that ate me up inside, and all the willingness I had to fade away and die, at the same time I saw myself doing the right thing time and again. Making proper decisions one after the other. Oh, there were matters I regretted, and still do, and there were events that shouldn't have happened—but, you see, I wasn't guilty, really, Tigh."

"I know it."

"I'm too used to responsibility. Sometimes I lose perspective. When I do, I feel guilty for *everything* that goes wrong. And that's what was going on in my dream. I was taking responsibility for just about everything in the universe, and feeling guilty for my failings in preventing what happened. But the truth is, my responsibilities—and sometimes actual guilts—are connected almost exclusively with the ship and my family. These I can handle, the errors of the universe are not precisely in my domain. Ila always said I worried too much and that I should be selective in what I worried about. I guess I never quite understood that."

"That must have been some dream."

"Yes, Tigh, if it was a dream."

Again they lapsed into silence. Athena broke into their reveries.

"Sir, scanners are picking up some unidentified space-craft coming into our sector. Heading toward Vaile. They must've slipped by our vipers undetected."

Adama and Tigh crouched toward Athena's monitor. There had to be at least fifty blips flashing there, all heading toward the circular light that represented Vaile.

"Warbook shows them to be Cylon ships," Rigel reported. "Raiders."

"Sightings from Vaile, sir," Omega said. "They've detected the intruders and request help from the *Galactica*."

"Should we call back our fighters, commander?" Tigh asked.

Adama wondered now whether he should have committed a full contingent to the attack on Baltar's base-star. There had seemed too much potential danger there to withhold the primary forces. He could order some of the vipers to return and defend Vaile, but that would effectively weaken the attack. No, it had to be an absolute callback, or none at all.

They would have to send the reserve squadron, the wing of pilots composed of cadets and recruits from other disciplines aboard the *Galactica*. And he had the perfect squadron leader near him on the bridge.

"We'll send down the reserves," he told Tigh. "Roll out the new vipers, the ones the *Hephaestus* just sent us."

"They haven't completed the round of test flights."

"That's all right. They'll get their test flights now. Athena!"

"Yes, sir," she said, smiling because she knew what was coming.

"Athena, you're in command. Take them down. Assemble your troops!"

Athena sprang away from her console and raced off the bridge to don her flight paraphernalia. She was in the cockpit of her viper in a matter of microns, as were the rest of her hastily assembled squadron. Except for a few test flights, it was her first time flying a viper since the battle over Kobol.

CHAPTER FOURTEEN

Baltar felt like a child at a natal celebration. In front of him the show he'd concocted was playing so spectacularly it could have been choreographed just for him. Above him, on the command pedestal, the elder whom Baltar most wanted to please, the Imperious Leader, scrutinized the show with obvious interest. And soon, like the child honored by the party, Baltar would be receiving his presents—mainly, a high position in the Cylon hierarchy and the reputation of military hero.

Baltar climbed up on the pedestal and sat on the edge of it.

"Watch this, Leader," he announced gleefully.

The humans below, who had been mooning with a feeling of sensually romantic love transmitted to them by Lucifer's guilt machine, now were, at Baltar's signal to Lucifer, struck with a large dose of sorrow. Some of them began to cry immediately. Others, slower to react, looked puzzled, then settled into a mournful trance. Another group, the hardest affected, fell to the floor, where they writhed and kicked in their formidable sadness. Arms waved hysterically, and some men hit their fists against the floor. Baltar had made sure that Lucifer was transmitting emotions at triple strength so that the reactions of the humans would be sudden and dramatic. As he sat and watched the show, Baltar sometimes laughed with delight at the more extreme displays of emotion. Frequently, he glanced at Imperious Leader who, while he showed no feelings of his own, had his full attention on the display below.

Lucifer watched Baltar's playful acts with some disdain. He found the emotional spectacle too ostentatious and ugly. It made him question the legitimacy of his own invention. He wondered if it was just a showpiece and not a genuine weapon of war. Or had Baltar's claiming of the guilt machine as his own somehow tainted it for Lucifer?

Spectre eased toward Lucifer and said:

"It is amusing, Lucifer, is it not?"

"I am not amused. Such suffering is not a source of humor for me."

Spectre gave Lucifer an odd look.

"You sound almost human, Lucifer."

"Impossible."

If he was becoming human, he could always reprogram himself to eliminate such tendencies. If he ever became as human as Baltar, then he could self-destruct.

"Now, cheerfulness, Lucifer!" Baltar hollered.

Lucifer flipped a toggle on his control panel and, following the preset program, happier waves were emitted by the guilt device. Many of the humans in the center area started smiling happily. There were a few ripples of laughter among others. They looked around the command chamber at all the Cylons watching them and began to chuckle.

"Magnificent, Lucifer," Baltar shouted.

Spectre leaned close to Lucifer's hearing circuits and spoke softly:

"It's like praise from the gods, isn't it, Lucifer?"

Lucifer nearly told Spectre that this god, instead of involving himself with the proper duties of creation, appropriated the inventions and ideas of other beings, but he refrained.

"This is wonderful!" Baltar screamed, while bouncing up and down absurdly on the edge of the pedestal. "Increase the output, Lucifer!"

"Commander, I wouldn't advise—"

"Lucifer! Turn it up!"

Lucifer obeyed. The group of humans turned even merrier. They interlocked arms and danced around to chaotic music they hummed themselves. They hugged each other. And they gaped at the Cylons and laughed at their captors mockingly.

Baltar twisted his body around so he faced Imperious Leader.

"What do you think, lordship?" he asked.

"Impressive," Imperious Leader said, "and a trifle unsettling."

"Why unsettling?"

Strange word for the Leader to use, Baltar thought.

"Look at them. Although their emotions are manipulated, it nevertheless appears as if they are laughing at us."

"If it disturbs you, I can change things in an instant. Let me show you what I have done to the *Galactica.* Lucifer, change the emotion to guilt."

Lucifer attended to the proper switch and again the human mood shifted. Physically, they stood still or sat silently, sad expressions on their faces. A couple, less affected, glanced around quizzically at their guilty-feeling comrades.

Baltar sprang down from the pedestal and started passing among his prisoners. It was an apparently brave act—although, to be sure, many weapons were being held on the prisoners. He was also protected from the guilt machine's effects by a shield skullcap Lucifer had devised and given him.

"You're cowards, liars, wretches," Baltar shrieked at the prisoners. "All of you. You ratted on your comrades, your friends, your wingmates, your officers, your bloody ship."

As he prodded them on, his words took effect. Their guilt became more obvious on their faces and in the slumps of their bodies.

"More, Lucifer, more," Baltar urged excitedly. "Turn the machine up to full power. I want to see them squirm."

"Baltar, full power's never really been tested. There have been some strange bypass phenomena—"

"Irrelevant! Turn it up!"

"But—"

"Now, Lucifer!"

Reluctantly Lucifer turned up the output of the device, halfway to full power. The change had an effect on the humans even he had not expected. They began to sway with agony, to punch their own bodies repeatedly, to scream pitifully, to tremble violently, to tear at their skin and draw blood. Lucifer noted dispassionately that, while this display resembled that of sorrow, it was also importantly different. Sorrow could be shared; the humans could touch each other, stroke each other, feel part of a sorrowful world. But guilt was an individual matter. The guilty stood alone, not wanting to share the emotion with another human being.

"More, more," Baltar screamed. "All the way to full power, Lucifer!"

Lucifer would have liked to direct full power at Baltar, but the shield he wore prevented that. Instead, he followed orders. The human response was overwhelmingly grotesque. There were piercing screams and wracking sobs, and the humans began flinging their bodies about recklessly. The sounds disturbed Lucifer's hearing circuits.

The screams and sobs were suddenly drowned out by a sudden thunderous roar from the command pedestal. The Imperious Leader had stood up, his massive bulk sending enormous shadows over the command chamber. He roared again and his body writhed. Lucifer noted that the writhing of the Leader's body very strongly resembled the writhing of the humans.

Galactica's pilots on their way to a battle always had a sense of determination prodding them onward, a grim-jawed readiness to face the laser cannons of the enemy. But this mission had produced an even greater determination on the part of the warriors. They could not wait to arrive in the area of Baltar's base-star.

Greenbean, especially, had a craving for combat. He couldn't get out of his head the images of the suffering and torture that Baltar had inflicted on him. Furthermore, he couldn't forget the suffering he had innocently carried to the ship at the renegade traitor's behest. If he could only get Baltar's repulsive face in his sights, Greenbean knew he would shoot without hesitation.

"Slow down, Greenbean," Jolly cautioned. "You keep edging ahead."

Greenbean's grim reply chilled the easygoing Jolly to the bone.

"I got reasons."

Apollo glanced down at his scanner and saw the indicators he was seeking.

"I think I've got 'em, fellas," he said. "Looks to me like one very large base-star, plus the usual support and troop craft. No, wait, there's another base-star, moored just behind it."

"I got them, too," Starbuck announced. "Maybe we'll get two of those lousy base-stars for the price of one. We're closing in."

"Everybody!" Apollo said. "Check all systems!"

When all pilots had reported in the readiness of their vipers, and tightened formation, Apollo gave the attack order.

"All right, all squadrons. We're going in! Kick in the turbos!"

Together, in an impressively simultaneous thrust, the squadrons lunged forward.

Adama, utilizing transmissions beamed up from Vaile by broadcast technicians there, together with camera equipment mounted in the cockpit of the diving vipers, watched the Vailean battle develop on monitors set in the wall of the command bridge. Several small screens surrounded a single major screen. Rigel, checking all monitors, selected the pictures to be displayed on the central screen.

The Cylons were initiating their attack on Vaile. A few explosions erupted in series across the center of a field of grain. A pair of Cylon ships flew low, strafing a road to scare any inhabitants into the adjoining ditches.

Galactica's reserve squadron was not yet within striking distance.

"We have to get there on time, Tigh. The Vaileans helped us unselfishly. It'd be a shame if we let them down."

"Agreed."

Rigel tuned up Athena's voice so that it echoed through the bridge.

"Approaching the enemy. They haven't detected us yet."

"Wait!" interrupted Dietra. "There's a couple of 'em, peeling off. They're on their way. Come to Di-di, baby."

The vipers of Athena and Dietra led the way toward the Cylon craft.

"The one on the left's mine, Dietra."

"My pleasure. The right's history."

Athena swerved her viper at the last micron, in order to draw fire. Then she did a skillful slide downwards and came at the Cylon from underneath. Her shots sketched a neat singed line across the underbelly of the raider, and it began to split just before a fuel line exploded, turning it into a mass of flame. Dietra sent the raider she attacked into a downward spiral. It crashed into the Vailean ground, its nose buried into soft Vailean farm soil.

Soon vipers and Cylon raiders were engaged in a fierce dogfight over the quiltlike pattern of Vaile's cultivated fields. The Cylon ships couldn't seem to get in a good shot. Each time a raider was blown up or sent on its final trip downward, a tentative cheer went up from the bridge crew. They didn't want to get too enthusiastic, afraid to invoke the old fleet superstition that it was wrong to cheer too loudly until the victory was assured.

"I think we've got the edge on them, sir," Tigh said.

"Precision flying. That's our edge, Tigh."

"Yes sir!"

Tigh relished hearing Adama's favorite phrase every time he said it.

Lucifer worked frantically, trying to lower the guilt device's power, but it was jammed. Baltar's demands for full power had overloaded the central core, which was now spinning out of control and sending out the guilt-waves at a rate beyond the levels that Lucifer had programmed into it. The humans were driven insane. They ran haphazardly around the command chamber, attacking the confused Cylons, who were unable to function because of the shame the device was forcing on them. Even Baltar was affected from waves that broke through the shield of his protective skullcap. He was standing in the center of the chaos and weeping uncontrollably. Well, let him weep, Lucifer thought. It was his self-seeking need to put on a show for the Imperious Leader that was the cause of this disaster.

On top of the pedestal, Imperious Leader twisted and convulsed like a mythical monster about to arise from confinement. His mind had become a turbulent languageless mixture of emotional images, images he had collected during his long involvement with the human scum. They were not pictures that pleased him. First, he was able to see himself as the humans saw him, as a hideously malformed and gnarled creature, as an ugly reptilian monster with bestial appetites and distorted ideas. Worse, for the moment, while under the besieging rays of the guilt machine, he saw the human conception of him as true. He *was* as repellent as they believed. His actions proved that. He saw another image: Of the destruction and death he had caused in the period of his leadership. He saw dead humans, their limbs intertwisted and their skulls showing through their skin, massed together on an infinite pile. They were the deaths he had caused in his fierce and monomaniacal pursuit of human annihilation. Seen as victims, it seemed to him that they were not the vermin he'd always believed. They had a sense of themselves as worthy, as beings of noble longings and compassionate intelligence who sought ideals that were counter to the wretched Cylon goals of universal conquest.

As the multitudinous images of death and destruction for which he was the sole cause merged into a heinous panorama, for the first time in his existence Imperious Leader felt guilty for his evil and insignificant deeds. His guilt was deeper and farther-ranging than anything anyone on the *Galactica* had felt, than anyone in Baltar's command chamber was presently feeling. It was like a series of massive explosions all over his body, pushing against his outer skin, squeezing all of his brains.

At the same time the rage was taking him over, he fully understood that he was being manipulated, that he was not an emotional being and that the emotions inside him were inserted there, like generative charges from the outside. He still believed in the Cylon ideals of order and control of the universe. He still knew that the Cylons must spread their power until it included all worlds, all civilizations. If there were worlds beyond the universe, the Cylons must conquer them also. Further, he knew that he, more than any previous Imperious Leader, pursued the Cylon goals with absolute dedication to them. He realized fully that his devotion to the cause had, in one important way, rendered him susceptible to the destructive power of the guilt device. In his need to destroy the human race, he had had too much involvement with humans, had absorbed too much of an understanding of how the human mind worked. Infuriating as it was, his ability to think like a human had resulted in his absorbing the full effect of the guilt machine rays, constructed as they were from Lucifer's intensive study of human brain waves.

Knowing all this, Imperious Leader could not subdue his wrath. With a stentorian roar, he leaped from the command pedestal into the center of the suffering humans. Lucifer noticed that the Leader's jump was infinitely more graceful than one would have expected.

Growling and bellowing, the Leader started picking humans up and flinging them to distant parts of the chamber. Lucifer heard bones and skulls crack when they made contact with the floor, walls, or technological items. When all the humans had been flung or had scurried for cover, the Leader attacked anything else that came to his attention. He kicked in monitor screens, sending sparks arcing across the command chamber. With forceful blows he crushed navigational consoles, scanning equipment, communication centers. He punched other Cylons, who in their loyalty had no concept of retaliation to an Imperious Leader. Soon the command chamber was lying in ruins and wreckage all around him. He had taken a blow at everything except the guilt machine.

Noticing it now, he ran at the guilt machine and rammed his powerful body against it. It slid several meters and began to make sputtering sounds. Lucifer backed into a corner, making sure he was out of the Leader's range. The Leader grabbed a rifle from a centurion and shot a large hole in the middle of the guilt machine. Flames and sparks emerged from its insides. Then the Leader reached in and started smashing circuits, ripping out and snapping apart wires, crushing shards of metal in his hands. Soon the machine, once so bizarre to look at, was a conventional pile of scrap metal, some of its components still smoldering from fire.

Then the Leader stood next to the debris and examined it. His body went limp. With the origin of his guilt now wrecked, the feeling had abruptly left him.

Lucifer, evaluating what he had witnessed, felt as close to humble as an ambulatory cybernetic intelligence could. If an Imperious Leader could be so affected by emotion, was it any wonder that Lucifer occasionally sensed in himself a series of responses that resembled emotion? And perhaps in the masterly way he had supplemented and changed his own programming, he had unknowingly given himself an emotional capability.

He was both fascinated and impressed by the fact that his invention had had such strong effect upon so unlikely a subject as the Imperious Leader. If it could do that, what were its potentialities? It struck him that they were so vast that any further work he performed in that area would have to kept from both Baltar and the Leader.

Imperious Leader stood still for a long while, realizing that his actions were mysterious to all in the room. Well, he thought, it would have to remain that way. An Imperious

Leader did not have to explain his behavior, even when it appeared to be aberrant. Still, in a sense, he had lost face in front of his troops and he would have to ensure they perceived his destruction of the command chamber as a necessity that accorded well with Cylon beliefs.

However, the problem of regaining face with the troops was minor. More severe was his need to regain face with himself. The memory of his rage, and what had been inside him during it, would always be with him, forever affecting him, his judgements, his logical thinking processes. It could even render him unfit to rule. It had been, after all, a spell of insanity. Insanity in an Imperious Leader seemed a contradiction in terms. Or, if you took the infernal human view, an agreement.

He addressed Baltar in normal command tone:

"Your device, Baltar, is dangerous."

By justifying his destruction of the guilt machine, the Leader was, in effect, taking the first step in justifying his rage.

Spectre rolled to the Leader's side and said:

"A brilliant understatement, my supreme liege."

Imperious Leader barely noticed Spectre's comment, but to Baltar it was clear that Spectre had made his decision. After this incident, Spectre could not join Baltar. The self-seeking cybernetic intelligence had gone with power. Power was still Imperious Leader.

"Something," Baltar said, "something . . . went wrong . . . I'm sorry, Imp—"

"You will be more than sorry when—"

Whatever the Imperious Leader had planned to say, it was interrupted by the high shattering blasts of an alert resounding throughout the base-star.

"What is that, Baltar?" the Leader demanded.

"An alert, sir. No doubt a false alarm. Perhaps caused by your—what is it, centurion?"

"Human fighter ships have been detected heading toward us, commander. Markings suggest that they are from the *Galactica*."

"*Galactica!* But that's impossible. They're disabled, emotionally disabled. I'm sure of it. They couldn't possibly launch an attack."

"Then there are evidently emotionally disabled pilots heading their vipers in our direction, commander."

The apparent insolence was only the Cylon manner of stating a fact.

"Baltar, you fool," Imperious Leader growled. "What of your brilliant plan of attack now?"

"I don't know, Imperious Leader, I—"

Baltar suddenly could not speak. He did not know how to explain away this confusing turn of events to the Leader.

"Well," the Leader said, "what are you waiting for? Don't you have any retaliatory capability?"

"Of course. Centurion! Send out the order. Raiders launch immediately."

"If not sooner," Spectre muttered.

Bays in the base-star opened abruptly and fighting ships, each controlled by a trio of Cylons, shot through the openings. After clearing the base-star, they achieved formation and proceeded in long beautiful sweeps toward the dense onslaught of *Galactica*'s vipers.

"Here comes target practice, lads!" Starbuck shouted.

"Form up for the first pass," Apollo ordered.

The advance force came together and, flying in a kind of half-circle, they met the front rank of the Cylon legion. A coordinated firing from the vipers dispatched, with a chain reaction effect, several of the enemy ships. The opening this created allowed, as planned, the leading vipers to break through the Cylon ranks and head for the base-star. Their first shots at Baltar's dreadnought scored direct hits.

The command chamber was rocked by the initial impact of the human assault. Baltar was knocked off his feet. The wreckage from the Leader's rage bounced around the room, ricocheted off centurions, and damaged control room equipment further. Lucifer scurried around, finding it difficult to retain a graceful glide on the momentarily tilted flooring.

"Imperious Leader," Spectre softly suggested, "you must leave here."

"Yes, thank you, Spectre. You are right, as always." Spectre seemed to glow with the compliment. "I should not be trapped here in a ship not my own."

"That was my thought, honored sir."

Imperious Leader gathered the remnants of his dignity and began to leave the chamber. At the entrance portal, he glanced back toward Spectre.

"Well, Spectre, are you not accompanying me? I need you."

Spectre joined Imperious Leader at the entrance without a second thought or a look back. Ambulatory cybernetic intelligences never regretted lost opportunities. Baltar watched the Leader and Spectre leave, and Lucifer watched Baltar's watching.

"Commander," Lucifer said, "the vipers have clearly broken through our lines. There have already been several damaging hits on the superstructure and below."

Baltar could not concentrate on what Lucifer was saying.

"Are all our raiders in flight?" he asked distractedly.

"I am launching the remaining ships."

"Good."

Baltar examined the wreckage in the room, and it suddenly occurred to him that Lucifer was somehow directing the battle without proper equipment.

"What are you using to convey orders?"

He displayed a small keyboard that he held in one arm.

"Fortunately, I installed a backup system long ago. It is limited but now operational."

"Good, Lucifer, good. You're a genius. A . . . a credit to your series."

A centurion stumbled into the command chamber and announced:

"More vipers have broken through and are on a direct line to the ship."

"What is the status of our fighters?" Lucifer requested.

"Our initial losses are heavy."

Baltar tried to assess the situation. His command room was in ruins. His fighting forces were unprepared, and losing. This did not seem like the beginning of a wonderful heroic future.

The *Galactica* pilots fought fiercely. Even when they seemed trapped by a Cylon pinwheel formation, they managed to pull out, execute tight turns, and destroy the enemy ships before they could respond.

Greenbean, especially, added Cylon kills to his record. The victory marks on the side of his viper would double, at least. He was all over the battle, saving one pilot after another from certain death, occasionally swooping in toward the base-star and scoring an effective hit. One of these shots, slicing a long gap in the underside of the base-star, caused a large metal piece of the surface to shatter off and fall away.

"Good show, Greenbean," Jolly said vigorously.

"You see that, Apollo?" Starbuck cried.

"How could I miss it?"

Sheba and Bojay flew in tandem, wingmates. Three Cylon raiders rushed at them, laser fire streaking ineffectively by Sheba and Bojay's cockpits.

"Hey, Bojay," Sheba said, "let's try the Commander Cain strafe and pincer."

"You got it, Sheba."

"I'll take highside."

"Righto."

They maneuvered their vipers sideways, as if they intended to retreat from the trio of Cylon fighters. Then they forced their ships into an abrupt flip and turn, and made right for the Cylons. Sheba arced above them, while Bojay zoomed below. Shooting precisely, each aware of the position of the other, they managed to destroy all three vehicles in a single pass. Sheba whooped with delight and was about to tell Bojay that Cain would have been proud, but her gladness abruptly changed to fear.

"Oh my God, Bojay!"

"What is it?"

"Over there, it's Starbuck, isn't it? They got him trapped!"

Starbuck was indeed in a doomed situation. He was surrounded by Cylon ships. They were spread around him in such a way that any maneuver out seemed impossible. It was what the pilots called the "grit your teeth and fire at them until they get you" battle position.

"Apollo," Starbuck called, "tell Athena and Cassiopeia—"

Before he could finish the sentence and before the Cylons could fire the one shot that would send Starbuck to viper heaven, Greenbean whooshed in through a small gap in the Cylon formation. His guns were blazing and he turned several ships on the far side into space debris. He and Starbuck, their vipers more or less back to back, or tail to tail, revolved and with amazing accuracy blew several of the Cylon ships to smithereens. They had reason to believe that the surviving Cylons might be angry, so Greenbean said:

"Let's get out of here, Starbuck, before they get any ideas."

They flew off, their parting shots cleaving a couple of Cylon raiders down the middle. When they were clear of the trap, Starbuck said:

"Thanks, Greenbean."

"Figured I owed you one. Heck, I owe *everybody* at least one."

"You're paying back just fine. On your tail!"

Greenbean looped and knocked off another Cylon. All in a centon's work.

Smoke was now seeping into the command chamber. Lucifer and Baltar had been frantically giving orders, testing strategies futilely. Without even communication equipment on which to call up a visual, it was impossible to conduct a battle properly. This was the most devious attack Lucifer had ever seen from the humans. It very much resembled the kind of battle Cylons usually originated.

"Imperious Leader's base-star has successfully cleared our ship and escaped the human onslaught," a centurion reported.

"He could have stayed and helped," Baltar muttered.

Lucifer replied to Baltar's criticism matter of factly:

"It is the Imperious Leader's first duty in a position of danger, especially threat to his person, to remove himself from the battle in order to preserve his leadership for—"

"I know all that, Lucifer. All I'm saying is that his honor should have allowed him to—"

"Honor? Honor is a human concept. It does not apply to Imperious Leader."

"Or Cylons in general."

"Baltar, Cylons have an alternate set of ethics that you would not understand."

"No, I'm sure I wouldn't. Well, at least Spectre got out of here intact."

That remark caught Lucifer short.

"I do not understand. Why is Spectre's welfare important to you?"

"I don't know, Lucifer. I honestly don't know. I just like the little guy's moves. Even when he's double-crossing me."

Lucifer might have commented on Baltar's myopic view, but another hit on the base-star sent him gliding awkwardly across the floor. Baltar fell against him, sending both of them sprawling. Baltar's head hit the wall painfully. He sat up, holding it between his hands.

"I think, Lucifer," Baltar said, "it is time to cut our losses. Order a retreat."

Lucifer turned to the nearest messenger-centurion and said:

"Order the raiders to return to the ship and—"

"NO!" Baltar interrupted. "There's no time for that. Too many vipers have broken through. We're going to light-speed immediately."

"And leave our fighters behind?"

"Fortunes of war, Lucifer. A tactical necessity. Their sacrifices in battle will cover our retreat. But before we leave you can send out a message ordering the stragglers to rendezvous with us at a specific point. A few hectares down the road, say."

"But most of them will be killed. It would deplete—"

"Accelerate to light speed, Lucifer!"

Lucifer did not approve but his programming forced him to accede.

"Yes, commander."

As he sent the code for acceleration through his backup system, Lucifer dispassionately examined the remains of his guilt machine. For all its failure, and the havoc it had been responsible for, the invention had left Lucifer with one pleasurable memory, that of the Imperious Leader chewing out Baltar for creating the device in the first place. There was in that a kind of pleasing revenge on the human commander for taking credit for what was not his. Was not that what the humans termed poetic justice?

Some day he might try the machine again. Perhaps, if he defected to the humans, a plan now taking form as he thought of the futility of serving Baltar and perhaps even the Cylons, they might be able to discover some less catastrophic use for the device. That was an interesting idea, Lucifer thought, the one about the humans. He wondered how they might treat an ambulatory cybernetic sentience.

"I think we've got them on the run now!" Adama observed as he viewed the furious Vailean battle on the various screens.

"Sir," Tigh said, "the Vailean prime minister is in contact. He says their capital city is under direct attack."

"Communicate that to Athena."

Athena received the message and called to several of her best pilots over her commline.

"Dietra! Brie! Carrie! Melika!"

They all responded quickly.

"The Vailean capital's being shelled," Athena informed them. "It's up to us."

The five vipers peeled away from the main battle and

flew to the capital. A phalanx of Cylon raiders was trying to level the city, and the Vaileans apparently were improperly defended by ground artillery. Bombs were exploding and the civilians were running for cover from diving Cylon ships.

"Carrie and Melika," Athena ordered, "you guys go in low, get the strafers. Dietra, Brie! You stay with me. We're going into triad formation."

"But Athena," Brie said, "we only *practiced* that one. We never—"

"Time to show the hotshot pilots what we can do, Brie."

Their triad formation turned out to be skillful, drawing admiration from the viewers of the battle aboard the *Galactica*. The three vipers headed for their rendezvous with several Cylon raiders.

"All right now," Athena said. "Split formation and fire at will!"

Dietra and Brie's vipers moved away from Athena's viper in a smooth arc, while Athena kept her craft on a straight course. The three-way firing from the vipers blasted a half-dozen of the enemy into fragments that fell like rain upon the city. Then they chased the rest of the Cylon ships and, with the help of Carrie and Melika, who had taken care of the strafing craft, the quintet of pilots finished off the phalanx.

"I believe the Vaile battle is over, sir," Tigh announced. "Thanks to Athena and her squadron."

"Yes," Adama said, "it was quite impressive."

"The news from Vaile is minimal losses, with some destruction of the capital city."

"Good for now, but we're going to have to leave them some protection against future attacks, Tigh."

"How about Sire Uri, to be used as a decoy?"

"I'll consider that. Any news from the strike wings?"

"Nothing yet. They might not even have located Baltar's base-star."

Adama nodded and settled himself for the long wait for Apollo and his colonial warriors to return.

• • •

Apollo, in the midst of the fray, at first didn't detect the movement of the base-star. Then he saw it edge away from the battle, and then gradually accelerate, so that it quickly became a distant point, and then nothing.

"Base-star has retreated," Apollo reported to his squadrons.

"Yahoo," yelled Starbuck, impairing the hearing of several pilots along the commline.

"They're leaving their pilots behind?" Boomer said.

"As hanging targets evidently," Apollo noted sardonically.

The Cylon pilots became aware of their base-star's sudden absence. Many of them looped their ships away from the battle, as if to pursue the unpursuable. Others followed.

"They're leaving," Jolly said. "Should we go after them?"

"No," Apollo said, "let them go."

"But Apollo—" Starbuck said.

"There's no time to chase them all over creation! We got work to do back at the *Galactica.*"

"Well, all right then. But, as sure as God wears the Kobol pyramids for triad shoes, you have an obsession about duty, Captain."

Apollo laughed.

"You better believe it, bucko!"

There was a lot of laughter and rough jokes along the commline as the *Galactica*'s pilots eased their vipers around and started back for their mother ship.

CHAPTER FIFTEEN

The party in flight crew lounge was vastly different from the last celebration held there, the one for Greenbean's return. This time the partygoers frolicked and danced cheerfully, with a considerable sense of relief that they were able to.

One similarity to the earlier party was that Ensign Greenbean was again the center of attention. But the glum Greenbean of the first party had been transformed into a happy smiling warrior for this one.

Jolly stood on a table and led the revelers in a toast:

"Everybody, let's hear three cheers for Ensign Greenbean, our new ace of aces!"

The cheers were raucous but jovial.

Starbuck climbed on a chair for another toast:

"To Greenbean." He smiled a sly starbuckian smile. "Well, old buddy, you are guilty again. Guilty as charged." Greenbean, befuddled, stared up at Starbuck. "Guilty of heroism beyond the call of duty."

The revelers laughed jovially.

"Hey, Greeny, you just been starbucked!" Giles said. To be starbucked was a fate that regularly befell anyone who associated with the brash young lieutenant.

"He saved your bacon, Starbuck," Boomer said.

"Saved it, cured it, and served it sizzling on a plate. Thanks again, Greeny."

Greenbean, as was his habit when given compliments, blushed. His red face could be discerned clearly by Commander Adama and Tigh, who had placed themselves at a remote side table so as not to dampen their subordinates' spirit.

"I believe we can dispense with the company punishment for Ensign Greenbean, Colonel," Adama commented.

"Agreed. He's paid his debt."

Apollo came to their table.

"Vaile operation is completed, sir," he reported.

"Very good, Captain," Adama said. "Have the Vaileans that intend to join our quest completed their farewells and shuttled up?"

"Yes. They look like good potential warriors to me."

"Good."

"And, commander—"

"Apollo, you don't have to be so formal, not here in the lounge."

"Father, the Vailean representatives asked me to inform you that they are extremely grateful for the long-range telemetry equipment."

"Well, I'm happy we were able to spare some."

Adama had requisitioned the telemetry devices from a support ship that didn't really need them. Now the Vaileans, if attacked by the Cylons, would be able to detect their presence beforehand, which would allow them plenty of time to prepare for defense or to flee to hiding places in their vast forests.

"Well, Tigh," Adama said, turning to his aide, "I think we should continue on our journey at the earliest possible opportunity."

"Yes, sir."

"After the celebration, of course."

In the middle of the room, Bojay had now taken over the toasting ritual.

"And how about a toast to our other heroes? To Athena, Brie and Dietra, for showing those Cylon creeps some real fancy flying—before reducing them to atoms."

The three women waved proudly as they were honored with the crowd's enthusiasm.

"And here's to us all," Sheba toasted. "May we live to fight, fight to live, and always touch wings in triumph."

After they'd taken their sip of ambrosa, many of the people in the room touched fingers, a part of the ritual.

Apollo found Starbuck with Cassiopeia.

"What say, Cass?" Starbuck was saying in a sexily suggestive voice. "It's hard on the muscles, those long trips in a viper. I'm in pain. Let's go someplace and you can massage the agony right out of me."

Cassiopeia smiled indulgently and said:

"God, Starbuck, that line's no better than your old stale ones."

"Up to your old tricks?" Apollo said as he joined them.

"What tricks, Apollo?" Starbuck said. "I'm the exemplar of sincerity."

"More the distemplar of sincerity, you ask me."

"Hey guys," Starbuck said genially, "Apollo made a funny. But you got to work on wordplay, pal. Make it precise. You know, a little precision wording, as the commander likes to say."

"I give up," Apollo said. He smiled amiably and walked off.

Starbuck returned his attention to Cassiopeia. He grimaced.

"What's wrong?" Cassiopeia said, her nurse's instincts aroused. "You all right?"

"Just a little muscle spasm. If you'd only rub—"

"Starbuck, stop it!" Cassiopeia interrupted angrily. "Don't you feel just a little guilty?"

"About what?"

"About the way you treat women, the way you treat me!"

"Well, I guess I do, a little."

"That's a relief."

"Why don't we go somewhere quiet and discuss my guilt? I got a little bottle of wine just waiting—"

"Starbuck, you're absolutely degenerate."

"God, I hope so."

Cassiopeia groaned in mock disgust, then kissed him. Starbuck, startled, almost forgot to kiss back.

"I thought you were angry," he said.

"I am. But I'd like a little wine just now."